Daisies, Deadly Force, and Disastrous Divorce Disputes

by

J L Wilson

Daisies, Deadly Force, and Disastrous Divorce Disputes

COPYRIGHT © 2011 by J L Wilson

Cover Art by *Kim Mendoza*

The Wild Rose Press
PO Box 708
Adams Basin, NY 14410-0706
Visit us at www.thewildrosepress.com

Publishing History
First Crimson Rose Edition, 2011
Print ISBN 1-60154-944-X

Published in the United States of America

Charlie straightened,
his deep green eyes perplexed.

"I said as much. John said something weird, something like 'the knowledge of a thing is worth money in the bank.' I didn't know what he meant. I was more concerned about his allegations against Janelle. He made it sound like she was sleeping with me—that she got pregnant—in order to force me to get you to change your mind about Grandy's inheritance and share with John." He stopped, his mouth thinning into an angry line. "I almost hit him then."

"I probably would have hit him," Livvie said. "Long before that." She regarded Charlie with exasperated affection. "You didn't answer my question about marriage. Are you and Janelle getting married?"

"I asked her and she said no."

I exchanged a look with Livvie. "Well, duh," she said cheerfully. "Obviously she doesn't want to marry you just because she's pregnant."

"I don't know how to convince her I want to marry her anyway."

"Do you?" I asked. "Or do you just feel obligated?"

He didn't answer for a long minute then he looked me straight in the eye. "How do you feel about marrying Sam? Don't you feel obligated to marry him after that accident last year? How will he get along without you?"

We stared at each other and I saw all my guilt, worry, and insecurity mirrored in his eyes. I loved Charlie and I loved Sam.

What was I going to do?

Dedication

To my grandmothers,
who taught me
a love of learning and a love of gardening.

Chapter 1

I was minutes away from my first orgasm in five months when my ex-husband called. "Cassie, pick up the phone. I know you're there." Charlie's impatient tenor voice echoed from the answering machine on the nightstand in the bedroom where Sam Barlow, my lover, and I were entwined in an awkward, passionate embrace on the bed.

It was awkward because Sam was only recently strong enough to undertake anything physical and that included sex. His injury the previous October resulted in extensive surgery to his right leg and it still hurt him to rest his weight on it. I was on top, leaned over Sam and trying to avoid putting weight on his recently healed leg. When I heard Charlie's voice, I jerked upright in surprise.

"Don't you dare," Sam warned, his hips bucking upward. He winced, his darker-than-dark brown eyes narrowing with pain.

"Cassie, John called and wanted us to meet him. I just got the message. I was in meetings most of the afternoon. Are you available tonight? If you're there, please pick up." Charlie's voice was subdued, not his usual joking, teasing tone. I could imagine him standing with his Blackberry pressed to his ear, his handsome face perplexed and his dark green eyes

1

beseeching.

"Cassie, damn it." Sam's urgent whisper jerked me back to the here and now. His hands moved up to my shoulders and he pulled me to him, his hips moving in a rhythm that sent heat racing through me. It had been a long, long time since I felt such excitement and it momentarily drowned out Charlie's anxious voice. A familiar rush of adrenaline pulsed in me. I stared down into Sam's eyes, my hands on his pillow framing his head and his thick white-gray hair, now tangled with sweat from our activity.

For an instant, it was as though the accidents—mine and Sam's—hadn't happened. I felt whole, healthy, and sexy again, ignoring the spasm of pain in my ribs where they were broken and not quite set right. I dismissed the pain mixed with pleasure I saw in Sam's face. He was so much thinner than six months ago. Then he was solid, muscular, and sexy in an aggressive, macho way. Now he was lean and sometimes, in the wrong light, he looked almost frail.

"Yes," he whispered, his voice raw. "Just a little more. Just a little…"

"…me when you can," Charlie's voice said from a distance.

Sam pulled me hard against him, his hands on my waist to jam me down onto his erect penis. The frenzied lust of a moment before was fast leaving me, my mind clearing. What was wrong with Charlie? Why did he sound so upset? I automatically played my part with Sam, falling into habits we formed in the year we'd been lovers, but my thoughts were flittering and flying away even as my body responded to his touch and my orgasm began.

Heat, love, excitement flooded me as Sam cried out, his frenzied pumping intensifying my experience. For an instant we were once again in tune with each other, once again two bodies sharing one soul. I stared into his eyes as pleasure filled me, marveling at the love, lust, and happiness I saw there.

Then I was lying against his sweaty chest, his crinkly hairs tickling against my breasts. It was too hot for cuddling, though, and I soon slid away to lie next to him, my left leg draped over his thighs and my left arm curved around his upper chest. "Are you okay?" I asked softly.

Sam stared up at the ceiling. "Why do you ask? Aren't you okay?"

I heard the tension in his voice but I just spent six months helping him through physical therapy. I wasn't going to blow all that hard work on a few minutes of fun. "I'm fine."

"So glad you could join me," Sam said softly.

I sat up partially to look at him. "What's that supposed to mean?"

He stared at me, his dark eyes accusing. "You were distracted."

"Charlie doesn't call me unless it's important," I said weakly.

"He's called a lot lately."

"He's called about the estate and the lawsuit." I lay back on the bed, not anxious to rehash this fight.

Sam turned and swung his legs over the side of the bed. I caught a glimpse of the scars on his right leg, starkly white against his tanned skin. We had recently spent two weeks in Florida at the home I inherited there, enjoying the April warmth. We returned to Minnesota yesterday so we could prepare for my ex-sister-in-law's wedding on May Day, this Friday.

"I thought that was being settled," Sam said, his back to me as he stared across the room.

"Four million dollars is a lot to settle."

Sam looked at me over one shoulder. "I thought

you said it was fifteen million."

"I set up a trust fund with five million, John is contesting five million, and I sold the house on Lake Minnetonka for two million. The lake part is the part that's getting settled."

"And the Florida house, of course." Sam looked around the bedroom in my townhome in Pickaway, a southern suburb of Minneapolis. The furnishings didn't compare to the ones in the house in Naples, Florida. "Don't forget the Florida house."

How could I forget? I inherited a house in Minnesota, a house in Florida, a house on Lake Vermillion in northern Minnesota as well as millions in assorted bonds and other investments. I sold the house in Minnetonka, I was keeping the house in Florida for use in the wintertime, and the house in Northern Minnesota was really a family place so I wouldn't sell it. Sam and I were going there in a few days to open the house for the summer, something I had done on the first weekend in May every year since I was a child and I accompanied the family for the Whittingtons's spring tradition.

Even with the lousy economy I was still filthy rich. Or I *would* be rich once the inheritance lawsuit was settled. Charlie's brother John was suing me to block my inheritance. I had just spoken to him, though, and the end might be in sight.

I stood up, using movement as distraction. "Charlie would never call when he knew you were here." As soon as the words escaped, I longed to retract them.

Sam dragged on his blue T-shirt. "So what you're saying is you and your ex have regular conversations behind my back?"

"Oh, for heaven's sake. You just weren't around when he called." I glanced at the bedside clock. It was almost five on a Monday afternoon, which meant Charlie was calling from his law office. On

4

most days, Sam left after lunch, going to one of the two landscape centers he owned with his sister, Mary Hannon, coming home at six or so for supper. He came home early today, though, which led to our unplanned fun in the sheets.

"You said he called when I wasn't here." Sam pulled on his boxers and balanced on one leg to drag on his blue jeans.

I resisted the urge to tell him *Be careful.* I'd been telling him that for months. "He called when you weren't here because he knew you would act this way."

"What way?" Sam tottered on his right leg, grimacing as he tried to stuff his left leg into his pants. I held my breath, waiting for him to tumble back on the bed. Instead he staggered against the dresser, knocking over a bottle of hand lotion, which in turn made a fragile porcelain statue of a woman holding a child totter precariously.

"Like a jealous fool," I snapped. The house in Florida was chock full of antiques and precious objet d'art. It was part of my inheritance from Theodora Penningford, my ex-husband's grandmother, the woman who helped raise me. I had brought back a few of the smaller objects with me when we returned, one of which was the statue that now was in jeopardy.

"What's to be jealous about?" Sam jammed his leg into the jeans and jerked them upward. "Charlie Whittington is a dead ringer for George Clooney, he saved my life, he's rich, he's single, he's a nice guy, he's in love with you, and he's rich."

"You said 'rich' twice."

"He's really rich." Sam's brown eyes twinkled with a touch of humor. "Richie Rich rich."

I took that as a sign he wasn't truly angry. Of course, with Sam it was hard to tell. A clam showed more emotion than Sam did. "Charlie's also in

Minnetonka and you're here," I pointed out, keeping my voice light as I tapped the rumpled sheets. "You're right here."

Sam picked up his glasses from the nightstand and put them on, their silver frames highlighting his angry brown eyes. He opened the bedroom door. "Yeah. How about that?" He left, closing the door gently behind him.

I glared at the white door, wishing I dared go after him and confront him. It seemed like every chance he got, Sam brought up the fact that Charlie was wealthy, handsome, and my ex-lover. It still rankled with him that Charlie was on hand last fall to save our lives when Sam and I were attacked. Why couldn't he count his blessings instead of complain?

I took my bathrobe from the hook and went into the hall then into the bathroom, shared between my bedroom and the guest room across the hall. The room was cool in the late April afternoon, feeling like air conditioning after the warmth of the bed. I peered at myself in the mirror over the sink. My sweatshirt-gray hair, cut short around my face, was a tousled mess. As always, my resemblance to Sally Fields was even more pronounced when I was angry. Now I saw an older Norma Rae glaring back at me—tense, defiant, and pissed off.

I took my time showering as I tried to puzzle out how I was going to convince Sam that he couldn't return to active duty at Barlow's Nursery and Landscaping, the family business. I had hatched a scheme to find him a new job but he was resisting all hints that I dropped. I wasn't sure how to broach the subject without being blunt. *Sorry, Sam. You can't manhandle plants any more. If you want to just be the manager, that's fine, but you know and I know you're really not needed in that capacity. They don't need a desk guy, they need a working manager, and you aren't that guy anymore.*

How was I going to tell Sam that I was purchasing shares in a botanical research company in hopes he would 'retire' from active work at Barlow's? Sam was prickly about accepting help from anyone. I had insisted that he move in with me after our accident last October so I could help him with his physical therapy and he equally insisted that he pay his way, even though I was now Rich with a capital R.

As I showered I thought about the house in Florida, the big one on Lake Minnetonka and the elaborate 'cabin' up north. I didn't belong on Millionaire's Row in Florida or in Minnesota. I was raised with the Whittingtons and married one, but that didn't change the fact of who I was: Cassie Wheelock Whittington, fifty-one year old ex-software programmer and now a horticultural assistant at Barlow's Landscape and Nursery.

I gave up on thinking and got out, drying my hair then going into the bedroom to dress in clean jeans and my *I try to lose weight but it keeps finding me* T-shirt. I straightened the bed before going into the living room. Sam was nowhere in sight, so I went into the kitchen where my two cats, Truffles and Houdini, were lounging on kitchen chairs, peering out the big bay window at the setting sun.

Sam was outside, spreading mulch in a flower bed that surrounded a life-size concrete statue of St. Francis, hands upraised and holding a platter for bird seed. It was too early to put out flowers, of course, but the gardening bug always hit Minnesotans as soon as the snow melted. This was the busy time of year at the landscape company. Fresh plants were arriving daily and it was hectic as they prepared for the rush of sales in May and June.

He's too thin, I thought. *I'm glad he's lifting weights again, but he needs to gain some weight to support it.*

My Blackberry in the charging stand on the counter chimed *The Boys of Summer*, my ringtone for Charlie. I turned away from the sight of Sam, struggling to bend his leg so he could kneel next to the statue. I clicked the 'Connect' button. "Hello?"

There was silence on the line.

"Hello?" I prompted.

"Hold on, Cassie." It was Charlie, sounding breathless.

"Charlie's what's up? I'm sorry I couldn't talk earlier. I was busy. What's wrong?"

"Did John call you? He left me a message and insisted he wanted to see us both."

I remembered John's smug face when he and I last talked. A familiar clench of anger made me strangle the gadget in my hand. I took a calming breath before speaking. "Why does the world's biggest asshole want to see me?"

"He called earlier and asked me to have you meet him. He needed to talk to you about Sheila Peavey and the lawsuit."

I glanced at the clock over the sink. It was almost six. "Why would John be at a construction site? He designs houses. He doesn't build them, not personally, at least."

"He said…because of Sam's involvement…and I wanted…"

"Charlie?"

"Sorry. There's a bad signal here. Can you and Sam come out? I'm on my way to that new subdivision of John's in Lakeville. You know the one? It's off the 166th Street exit."

I thought of Sam and his earlier anger. Sheila Peavey was Sam's ex-wife and a murderer, or so I suspected. A meeting about her wouldn't cool his temper. "I doubt if I can talk Sam into meeting Sheila."

"Can you come? Maybe he wants to talk about the lawsuit." Charlie's voice faded again.

I turned as Sam came into the kitchen through the door leading to the mud room, which subsequently led to the garage and the outside world. "I don't know if we can. Why would John want to talk to us about Sheila?" I shrugged both shoulders when I saw Sam's quizzical look.

"I don't know, but you know John—if he can mess up your life, he will. I think you should talk to him."

I held the phone away from my face. "John wants to meet with me. Charlie said it has to do with Sheila."

Sam clenched his jaw. "What's she up to? Why is she buddying up with that creep?"

"I don't know. There's only one way to find out, I guess."

Sam thought about it then nodded. "Where?"

"We'll meet you there, Charlie. We'll leave now."

"Good. I'll see you in a few minutes."

I clicked 'Disconnect' and headed for the mud room door, tucking my phone into my purse as I grabbed it from its hook near the entryway. "I can drive," I said, snatching my car keys from an adjacent hook.

Sam put a hand on my arm, bringing me to a halt. His dark blue shirt and his pale blue jeans were a beautiful contrast to his golden tan and his salt-and-pepper hair. Except for his thinness, he looked healthy and happy. "Hey."

I smiled tentatively. "Hey."

"I was a jerk."

I tilted my head. "Yeah, you were. You know how it is with Charlie."

He nodded ruefully. "You're friends, he saved your life, you saved his, you were raised with his family, you've known each other all your life."

I pursed my lips in exasperation at this succinct summary. "We have a past together," I said patiently. "Something beyond being married."

"We have a past together, too," he whispered as he took me in his arms. "And we have a future together."

I smoothed his thick hair back from his forehead. "I know." I rested my head on his shoulder. It was so familiar to be there with him. His warm, earthy, faintly sweaty aroma was so uniquely Sam. It was sexy, familiar, masculine, and safe.

"I was thinking…" He kissed the tip of my nose. "We're going to be busy this week. We won't have much time to relax. Let's get this thing done with Charlie then come back and have a glass of wine and put our feet up." He smiled, his warm brown eyes darkening. "It's been nice these last few weeks to be away from everyone."

I nodded agreement. "I know. The Whittingtons can be a bit much. Between the inheritance, the lawsuit, and Livvie's wedding, we've been in their back pocket since last year."

His expression shifted, his face stilling and his eyes taking on a guarded look. "Livvie was talking to me about her wedding. She mentioned that there's room for two in it, if you'd like." The words were said overly casually, telling me how important they were to him.

"What do you mean, room for two in it?" I had an inkling what he was saying but I didn't want to deal with it. I gently disentangled myself from his embrace and led the way to Bilbo, my plum-colored Lexus SUV that sat in my garage next to Sam's ancient maroon SUV.

"You know. Like a double ceremony thing." He got into his side of Bilbo, giving me a precious few seconds to gather my scattered wits.

"Are you proposing?" I forced myself to meet his

eyes as I slid into the driver's seat. What I saw there didn't reassure me. He looked alternately hopeful, worried, and uncertain.

"Yeah, I guess I am. Well, you know, we weren't sure about me and we didn't know if I could, you know...." He smiled slyly. "Now that we know I'm not incapacitated in the bed department, well, yeah, I guess I am proposing."

I started the car and got us out of the garage before answering. "I wasn't really worried about the bed department."

"I was."

His flat tone told me just *how* much he worried. I filed that little nugget away for later reassessment. "It's a big step, Sam. To be honest, I've never considered another marriage." I glanced at him, surprising a look of bewildered hurt quickly masked by an attentive gaze. "I need to consider it."

"Why don't you just sleep on it?" he suggested. Then his mouth quirked with humor. "Or better yet, let's *not* sleep on it."

"I don't want to undo months of physical therapy." We were at a traffic light so I leaned over and kissed him quickly. "It's good to have you back, Sam."

"Good to be back. Think about it, okay?"

I nodded, focusing on my driving. "I will, believe me." I was pretty sure it was one of the main things I would think about for the next few days. I turned my focus back to driving. Our exit was just a mile down the road, but it was bumper-to-bumper, all of us going seventy miles an hour. I needed all my attention on the road.

Sam shifted in his seat. "I suppose I should start looking for an apartment soon."

I resisted turning in my seat to stare at him. "Why?"

"I moved in with you temporarily, when my leg

was all busted up. I'm mobile again." His voice was straightforward and logical, but I heard the question in it nonetheless.

"No need to move out," I said as I eyed a semi-truck driving hell bent for leather just a foot or two from my driver's side door.

"Yeah, but it's not right." He stared out his window. "Think about how it looks. You inherit a bunch of money and I move in."

I hazarded a quick glance at him. "Who said that?"

"Nobody. I was just thinking about it, that's all."

He wasn't a good liar, but I didn't want to pursue it, not right on the heels of a marriage proposal. Someone had said something to him that bugged him, but he would tell me in his own good time. Or maybe he wouldn't. It was always hard to say what Sam might do.

Sam drummed his fingers on the leather armrest. "I was thinking I would accept Sheila's offer to settle the patent dispute."

I veered onto the exit, anger pushing our speed a tad high. "You're crazy. You deserve the money, Sam. You and Mike Peavey developed that azalea hybrid together. He had no right to patent it under his name alone." I waited for traffic to pass then took a left off the exit onto a county two-lane blacktop. Stands of woods on each side of the road almost hid houses set far back among them. Traffic moved at a brisk pace but not the breakneck speed of the nearby freeway, thank God.

I resumed my argument. "You can't take her up on that offer. You deserve to get a cut of the profits. Who knows how well that plant will do over time? There might be others like it that you can develop." I stared over the steering wheel, flipping down my visor to block out the setting sun. "It's along here..." I eyed a sign on the right side of the road.

"Elysian Woods?" Sam peered at it as we passed.

"That's not it." I slowed as we drove by another large sign on the right near a road leading back into a heavily forested site, alternately glancing at traffic behind me and the paved road in front of me.

"Penningford," Sam said, staring at the sign.

"That's it. Penningford is Charlie's mother's maiden name." I swerved onto the road. I drove slowly into what would be a thriving neighborhood...some day. The wide boulevard wound sinuously past empty lots with signs advertising them for sale. A few mansions, obviously under construction, dotted the landscape. None were occupied although one nearer the road sported a *Model Home* sign.

We came to a fork in the road and I stopped Bilbo. "Which way now?" I muttered. Both sides of the road led into heavily treed areas. I drove forward down the left fork until we came around a curve. I spotted Charlie's navy blue Jaguar in front of a McMansion on the far side of a cul-de-sac straight ahead. A gray Benz sedan was parked in front of Charlie's car. "This must be it." I drove forward and parked Bilbo behind the Jag.

Sam and I walked up the driveway, each of us eyeing the house. "It's as big as some hotels," I said. "The..." I counted, "...four-car garage is bigger than my townhouse."

Sam paused near the front door. "Probably five or six bedrooms. What do you bet it's got at least four bathrooms? It's open." He touched the oversized oak front door and it swung inward. "Charlie? John?" he called out.

I walked behind him into a foyer the size of my kitchen. The house was almost finished, with dry wall delineating the space and long stretches of indoor/outdoor carpeting covering the light colored hardwood floors. A winding staircase in front of us led to an open landing above and big rooms opened off either side of the entry. "Charlie?" I yelled.

"Cassie! Back here!"

Sam and I exchanged an anxious look. It was Charlie's voice, but he sounded upset, almost frantic. Sam strode down the hallway straight ahead and I followed, pausing briefly to peer into an enormous kitchen as we passed. It appeared to run almost the length of the house and had two islands, huge windows overlooking a stream, and a fireplace at one side. I gawked at the pricy cabinets while I walked, running smack into Sam when he stopped on the threshold of a room.

I peered around him. The room was curved, floor-to-ceiling windows showing us a view of the woods behind the house. A corner fireplace was to my right and kitty-corner to the left was a bar with built-in cabinetry. *Family room*, I thought. *Or entertainment center*. The place was big enough to serve as a small movie theater.

Charlie stood in the center of the empty space, a big, clunky-looking power tool in his hand. At his feet lay John, his brother. It took a second for what I was seeing to register and when it did, I said, "Holy shit."

John lay on the hardwood floor in a pool of blood, his sightless eyes staring up at the skylight overhead.

Chapter 2

"Holy crap, Charlie. What happened?" I started forward but before I got far, Sam pulled me back. "Let go." I wiggled my arm in his grip.

"Stay here." Sam's voice told me he meant serious business.

"But—"

"It might be a crime scene. Don't mess it up." Sam took two long steps forward to stand a couple of feet from Charlie. "What happened?" he asked, his voice calm.

"A crime..." I gulped and turned my attention to my ex-husband. Whenever I saw Charlie after an absence, I was startled by his amazing good looks and this time was no exception. His thick black hair was trimmed short and tousled, the touches of white at his temples like highlights for his dark green eyes. Charlie was classically tall, dark, and handsome, like a throwback to an old-time movie star or a lost twin to George Clooney but today he looked like a worried, tired fifty-three year old man with the weight of the world on his shoulders. Of course, those shoulders were clothed in a casual dark denim Armani jacket over a white Brooks Brother oxford cloth shirt tucked into crisp, ironed Calvin Klein denims that fit Charlie to a T. "Weren't

15

you at the office?" I blurted. "You're wearing jeans."

Charlie blinked at me in surprise. "I went home and changed before coming." He looked down at his younger brother. "I found him like this." He started to gesture towards another doorway with his right hand, the one holding the power tool. He held it up. "I almost fell over this when I came in."

"What is it?" I leaned forward.

"It's a nail gun," Sam said, staring down at John. "Is he dead?"

Charlie nodded dumbly.

"Dad? Where are you?"

I whirled when I heard voices behind me. Two people walked down the hall and as they passed the doorway of the cavernous kitchen, their faces were illuminated.

"Shit. What's she doing here?" I glared at Sheila Peavey, Sam's ex-wife and my nemesis. She was in front of Matthew Whittington, John's oldest son. I moved out into the hallway to meet them and prevent them from coming further.

"Good, I'm glad you're here," Sheila said in that annoying businesslike voice she always affected. Her dark blonde hair with artful highlights framed her oval face and her skin still had a porcelain smoothness that I envied. Her navy slacks and blue-trimmed white sweater set looked expensive and fit her slender figure like a glove. She hadn't changed much in the six months since I last saw her. She still looked like a sly and somewhat mean Katie Couric.

Matthew peered past her at me. He looked like his father, who in turn had looked like a pale imitation of Charlie: *almost* handsome, *almost* charming, *almost* sexy. Matthew was in his mid-twenties with a clean-cut, Republican, all-American look that would help him fade into any accounting department in corporate America. He went into business with his father after attending Brown or

16

Emory or some other East Coast school. "Is my father here?" He looked past me as though I didn't exist, which was typical for Matthew. After my divorce from Charlie, I became *persona non gratis* to John, and Matthew was carrying on the tradition.

Sam stepped out of the room to stand next to me, blocking the wide doorway. Sheila stopped dead in her tracks. "What are you doing here?" she demanded, her voice dripping acid. "I told John I wanted to talk to her, not you."

"There's been a..." I swallowed, not sure what it was. "Something's happened."

Sheila stalked forward, stopping a foot or so in front of me. She was almost Sam's height and she met his gaze, glare for glare. Then she turned her face to me, obviously dismissing Sam as beneath her notice. "John and I wanted to talk to you about our lawsuits. We're willing to come to an understanding."

I saw Matthew shift behind her, starting to edge past us. His hazel eyes widened. "What is that? What's going on?" For an instant his face stilled then a succession of emotions seemed to flit through his eyes: anger, surprise, anger again then finally suspicion.

Sam put a hand on his chest. "We need to call the police."

Shelia took advantage of Sam's distraction to muscle her way forward. I made a grab for her but she slipped past me, stumbling forward into the room, her navy pumps echoing on the wood floor. "What did you do? You killed him?" Her voice rose in a crescendo like nails scraping on a blackboard. I shivered.

"Killed—?" Matthew looked over my head, his face draining of color.

I put a hand on his arm. "Matthew, I'm sorry. It's John. Your father."

I don't think he saw me. His eyes were so wide his irises were edged in white. With one hard shove he pushed me to the side, strode into the room, and swung at Charlie.

I went down, tumbling into a pile of cardboard boxes. As I tried to right myself, I saw Sam jerking Charlie to one side, Matthew on the floor near his father's body, and Sheila bending to pick up the power tool.

"So much for taking care of the crime scene," I muttered. Then my feet went out from underneath me as I slipped on the boxes. I thought, *I'm damn close to that fireplace, aren't I?*

My face hit something unyielding and lights ignited all around me.

****

I was checked by a paramedic after my run-in with the hearth and pronounced fit, although I was warned that if a bad headache flared up to get to the hospital ASAP. I nodded agreement, happy it wasn't worse. Lucky for me the fireplace was composed of polished rocks and not flagstones. The med-tech pointed that out, too. "Otherwise you probably would've torn a hole in your face and required stitches," he said cheerfully as he packed up his bags. I counted a bruise on my right temple a small price to pay.

After I was declared mentally competent, we were interrogated at the Lakeville Police Station. Charlie, Sheila, and Matthew were also 'interviewed' then we were all told to go home—except for Charlie. I wanted to stay but Charlie's girlfriend, Janelle Rime, showed up and convinced me to leave, promising to send me email updates via Blackberry. She was an attorney in the same legal firm as Charlie and had already called for a criminal attorney to join them at the police station.

I went reluctantly home where I fell asleep on

the couch, waiting for the phone to ring. I was vaguely aware of Sam checking on me periodically, but I was pinned down by two cats pressed against me and random nightmares that made me sweat.

My Blackberry chimed *All She Wants To Do Is Dance* at seven-thirty the next morning as Sam and I were drinking a cup of coffee in the kitchen. I put it to my ear to talk to my ex-sister-in-law, Charlie's younger sister, Olivia Carlyle.

"Family conference," she said. "Come on over."

"Where?"

"The house. Father called in everybody. Get on over here." Livvie usually wasn't snappish so I dared a question.

"What happened with Charlie?"

"They're going to charge him with murder or manslaughter or something like that. Get over here, Cassie, as soon as you can. As though that isn't bad enough, it's all over Facebook."

"Huh?"

"Somehow it got onto Cory's wall on Facebook and now the whole world is tweeting about it. Get over here. Please."

"Will do." I hung up, my hand trembling.

Sam regarded me over the top of his coffee mug. "Is it bad?"

"Charlie's going to be charged with murder," I said, strangling the words as I said them. It was like saying *Charlie is broke and living on the streets* or *It never snows in Minnesota.* The words did not compute. "There's a family confab at the house in Minnetonka. I have to go."

He finished off his coffee. "Want some company?"

I was surprised. "Do you mind?"

"Mind what?" He took my mug and his and put them in the sink.

"Going with me?"

Sam got the kibble container from the cupboard and topped up the cat food dishes. "Do you want me there?"

"Of course."

"Then I'll go." He smiled briefly. "It'll be a chance to see the Whittington family in action—minus the jerk, of course."

The jerk. I stood, trying to erase the image of John lying on the hardwood floor. Memories crowded me, images of John as a child, a teenager at school events, at the beach, at house parties. I grew up with the Whittington family in a life of luxury and wealth, watching from the sidelines until I married Charlie. For seven years I was fully a part of the family then Charlie and I divorced and I was once again on the periphery. John was an integral part of all of those memories. "John's dead," I whispered.

Sam put the kibble canister back in place. "Yeah. The asshole's dead."

His cavalier tone shook me out of the gloomy thoughts. "Is the world insane? Why would anybody think Charlie killed John?"

"Because he was standing next to the body?" Sam held up a hand when I glared at him. "Hey, I'm just stating the obvious."

"You don't know Charlie like I do. He's like a brother."

Sam shot me a disbelieving look.

"Okay," I amended. "He's like a really good friend with whom I used to have sex." I went to the hook where my purse hung and slung it over my shoulder, checking the icons on my Blackberry as I walked. "Whoa. Updates." I reached for my car keys but Sam beat me to it.

"I'll drive, you read email. Just give me directions."

"Directions? You've been..." Then I realized that no, Sam had never been to the family home. "Sure.

Head toward Grandy's house—I mean, Livvie's house—and I'll give you directions from there." We got into Bilbo and buckled up. "You remember the place? We were there last fall before we went to that costume party."

"I think I remember enough to get us in the neighborhood." He piloted Bilbo out of my subdivision onto the county highway that would eventually take us northwest. I turned my attention to my Blackberry and let Sam deal with the flow of early morning rush hour traffic.

I looked at the still-unfamiliar icons on my new phone. I recognized email, Messenger, and the media app, but the others were still relative strangers to me. Cory and Nathan Stuyvesant, my ex-sister-in-law Becky's teenaged boys from her second marriage, had Facebook pages and showed me how to set up a page and a Twitter account on my computer and on my phone. I posted a random update now and again and forgot all about it until I got an email reminding me someone wanted to befriend me. I considered using the Facebook app now, but discarded the idea. Email was a known program I could easily handle.

I quickly skimmed through the seven emails Janelle sent the night before as I silently applauded her quick thinking. By using email to update everyone in the family, we all knew what was happening. I don't know if I could have been so clear-headed if the man I loved had his life on the line. I breathed out a shocked sigh. Charlie, in jail? His life on the line?

The man she loved? The thought still gave me pause. For so many years Charlie and I had been more than friends, less than lovers. It was still...odd to be replaced in his affections.

"Bad?" Sam asked.

"Hmm?" I looked up from my email, fear making

my stomach roil. "Charlie was in jail for a few hours before they could get him out."

Sam jerked the wheel and almost put us in a ditch. "Is he okay?"

I nodded. "I think so. Janelle didn't go into a lot of details."

"That was probably a real character-building experience for him."

I forced myself to smile. "At least it was in Lakeville and not the Minneapolis lockup." I shuddered to think of Charlie among rapists, murderers, and drug dealers in the metro jail. Lakeville was a middle class suburb. Hopefully their criminal population was a bit more genteel. "Apparently they got some judge who wasn't impressed with Billy Armstrong as Charlie's defense attorney. He dithered around on the bail and finally set it at two million. His dithering meant Charlie had to sit in jail for a bit."

Sam blinked. "Two million? Dollars?"

I nodded, tucking the phone back in my purse. "The Second is good for it, of course."

"Of course. I remember last year when he posted bail for T.J." Sam smiled wryly. "The old man must be getting tired of bailing out his kids."

I had forgotten about that part of last fall's drama when Livvie's fiancé, T.J. Watson, was accused of murder. C.R. Whittington the Second posted T.J.'s bail, too. "Janelle said the D.A. is going to press charges. They think they have enough evidence to proceed." I grimaced as I thought of what I read. "Death by nail gun."

"Nail gun?" Sam nodded slowly. "I know those things seem lethal, but I didn't think they were that bad." He thought for a minute as we drove through traffic-jammed streets. "I suppose it depends on the size of the nail. The ones I've seen would probably cause a wound, but I doubt they could kill someone."

"In the throat," I said, repeating what I read. "There were several wounds in his throat and upper chest. Apparently one nicked the carotid artery. John bled to death."

"Oh." Sam blew out a long breath. "I can't say I'm sorry the asshole is dead, but that's rough. And messy."

We were silent for several minutes. As we left Pickaway and entered the pricier enclaves of Minnetonka, the houses changed. Bigger lots, glimpses of lakefront, and expanses of lawn took the place of my more prosaic suburb with its two-and-three bedroom homes and views of softball fields and highways.

"Why was Sheila there?" Sam asked suddenly.

I revisited the scene in my head. "She said something about the lawsuit."

"Lawsuits," he corrected. He glanced at me then returned his study to the road. "John was involved in a lawsuit with you and Sheila is involved in a lawsuit with me about the patents for the plant I developed with Mike. She said lawsuits—plural."

I struggled to keep my face looking puzzled. I knew why Sheila wanted to talk to me about the lawsuit against Sam, but I wasn't quite ready to reveal that knowledge yet. Sam was fussy enough as it was about accepting any help from me. "Go straight ahead instead of making the left for Grandy's house," I directed. "Then take a left on Manitou Road and a right at 9th Avenue."

I stared out my window at the expensive homes then at the lake as it came into sight. Minnetonka was one of the biggest lakes in the Twin Cities environs and I grew up on its shores alongside the Whittington children. Lakefront properties, expensive and secluded, were handed down through family generations. The Whittingtons, who had lived on the lake for a mere fifty years, were considered newcomers.

When Sam made the turn onto 9th I glanced at him, seeing how he eyed the large homes with the exclusive lakefront property. "High rollers," he commented.

"Yeah. They are." I could imagine how it looked to him with his solid, middle-class background. "The house is over there, on the left." I gestured to the three-story white rectangular house barely visible behind the stone wall. "Take a right inside the gate. We'll park in the side driveway."

Sam turned at the entry then followed along the curved drive around the house to the five-car 'carriage house' on the right. He parked Bilbo next to another Lexus, Charlie's Jag, a Porsche, and two Benzes. I barely glanced at the house and the immaculately landscaped grounds, already green and verdant despite the cool spring weather. Lots of money and a good landscaping service could work wonders.

I started for the back porch door, which led to the family room where I suspected everyone would be gathered. As always, there was a cool breeze off the lake that morning sunlight couldn't combat. I shivered, not yet accustomed to Minnesota's April chillness after the warm Florida sun.

Sam got out of his side of the car but instead of following me, he walked out onto the expanse of lawn that led to the shores of Lake Minnetonka. "Is this where it happened?" he asked, his eyes on the white sand beach in the distance and the gray waves beyond it.

I walked back to join him. I knew what he meant. Sam knew all about the tragedy in my past. The so-called Charity Murder was a newspaper sensation in the Twin Cities decades earlier and I had been an integral part of it. "I forgot you've never been here." I looked across the lawn, memories sharp in my mind. "Charlie's mother gave my mother and me a home when Mom ran away from my father after he got abusive. My father came through the trees over there." I gestured to the windbreak on the right side of the property. "Charlie saw him first and tried to stop him, but my father kicked him into the lake. Then my father shot Gloria, Charlie's mother, right there." I pointed to the bright blue Adirondack chair at the fringe of the lawn, facing out toward the lake. A chair was always left in that exact spot for the past forty-three years, denoting where Gloria Whittington was murdered. "My mother struggled with my father for the gun while I went into the lake after Charlie, to try to save him from drowning."

Sam turned to look behind us and I followed his gaze. The house was draped in shadows in the morning because it faced west, but on that awful afternoon it was bathed in light, the massive windows open to the world outside. I remembered like it was four days ago, not forty years.

"Charlie's dad was in the study." I pointed to the far end of the house and the three floor-to-ceiling windows there. "He grabbed his gun and came running. He shot my father." I stared at the lakeshore, memory, smells of blood and fear mingling with the scent of emerging lilacs and daffodils. "He killed him."

"And the old man let you and your mother stay and she became the family nanny. And you stayed with the family all those years, finally marrying Charlie." Sam put an arm around my shoulder and gave me a squeeze. "What a tangled web."

"Cassie? Thank God you're here!"

We turned to see Livvie standing in the door to the porch. She was tall and willowy, her ash-blonde hair framing an aristocratic, Audrey Hepburn-like face. Then a man stepped out of the shadows behind her. T.J. Watson, Livvie's soon-to-be husband, was a lanky man only slightly taller than Livvie with short brown and gray hair above a narrow, triangular face. His right arm ended in a hook, his forearm amputated at the elbow due to an injury sustained during his stint in Viet Nam.

I waved in return and walked to the house, Sam beside me. "I'm glad I saw it," he said, glancing back at the beach then upward at the three-story, eight-bedroom mansion ahead of us. "I always knew they were rich, but I never realized just how rich they were." He sounded subdued and I suppose it was a bit intimidating. I grew up here, though, so to me it was just a house—not quite a home, but not a showplace, either.

"You both look tanned and healthy," Livvie said as we approached them. "Vacation time in Florida agrees with you."

"You look good, too. I'm glad the wedding plans aren't making you too crazy." I hugged her, as always feeling like a pansy next to a rose when I was with Livvie. "Is everybody here?"

Livvie sighed heavily. "Becky's in Europe. They're flying back tonight." Becky was John's twin, a matronly woman with three children and a husband fifteen years her senior.

I pulled back to examine Livvie more closely. "Are you okay?"

"Yes. I hate to admit it, but I'm so busy getting ready for the wedding, John's death hasn't really soaked in." She wrinkled her nose. "And besides, he was such a pain to be around lately. All he did was gripe and complain. I avoided him as much as I could. I'm glad the wedding is Friday, though. I can't take much more." She shot Sam a questioning look. He shook his head negatively.

"I'm thinking about it, Livvie," I said as I walked past her into the big screened porch.

"Thinking about what?" T.J. asked.

"I'll explain later." Livvie fell into step beside me. "I suppose you heard the other news," she said in a low, confiding voice.

I stopped short of the French doors leading in to the family/game room. "What other news? What could top Charlie being charged with murder?"

Livvie stopped, too, and stared at me. "He didn't tell you?"

The family room door opened before I could answer. Charlie looked out. "Coming in?"

I felt Sam tense, his habitual reaction whenever Charlie was in the vicinity. "Family conference?" I stepped past Charlie, catching a whiff of his aftershave, a unique fragrance created just for him at an Aveda salon in town. It reminded me of wind on waves, summer golf, and lazy afternoons in a hammock.

"You could say that," Charlie said softly. "Or a war council."

I spied Claire, the Second's fourth wife, across the room sitting on a sofa near the mammoth fireplace. As always she blended in perfectly with her environment, today looking like the calm, competent companion to the man standing near the wet bar. And as always, C.R. the Second looked the part of 'concerned family patriarch,' with his silver hair, a craggy face, and calm, assessing green eyes. He was a construction foreman before marrying Gloria Penningford and entering a life of high society almost sixty years earlier. He still looked tough, fit, and ready to do battle—very polite battle, but battle nonetheless.

"Come in, Cassie," he said, his voice carrying easily across the vast space. "I'm glad you and Sam could join us."

I doubted if he was happy to have Sam there, but he hid it well. The Second, Charlie, and John all

27

suspected Sam of being a gold digger and all had told me so in blunt terms. I had told them what I thought in equally blunt terms and thereafter we pretended the topic didn't exist and didn't purse the conversation any further.

Janelle Rimes, Charlie's lover and fellow lawyer in his law firm, smiled at us from the right where she stood near the pool table. Her long black hair was in a tidy braid hanging to the middle of her back. Like Charlie, she was dressed impeccably but casually in jeans, and a loose, lightweight sweater that seemed two sizes too big for her. Her faintly Asian eyes, up-tilted at the corners, examined both Sam and me. She looked pale and tired, dark circles under her dark blue eyes and hectic spots of color on her cheeks.

"You look rested," she said. "You're not as thin as you were when you left."

"I wouldn't miss spring in Minnesota," I said.

"You're going to the cabin on Saturday?" Livvie asked as she settled on the couch next to T.J. "To open the place?"

The 'cabin' was a six-bedroom home on Lake Vermillion in Northern Minnesota with a guest house nearby that slept six. The family always had a grand 'Opening Day' in spring to start off the summer season. "It will be ready for Mother's Day, the way it always is."

"I'm glad you're maintaining that tradition," the Second said. "Grandmother Theo would happy to know that her home is still being used by the family." His glance went to Sam, who smiled blandly. "You look tan, Sam. Spend some time on the beach in Florida?"

"A bit," Sam said. "I needed to rest up so I can get back to work. It's our busy time at the nursery."

Janelle blinked in surprise. "Nursery?" She looked wildly at Charlie. "Nursery?" Then she shook her head angrily. "I'm sorry. I have to—" She put a hand to her mouth and bolted toward the door near the pool table, moving so fast she almost ran.

"Are you okay?" I called after her. "Janelle, what—" I automatically followed her.

Janelle brushed by Charlie, who put out a hand, whether to stop her or support her, I wasn't sure.

"I'll come with you," I said when I saw her totter.

"I'm okay." Janelle paused at the door and looked back at us. "I'm just pregnant." She jerked open the door and vanished into the hall outside.

Chapter 3

I gasped. "What? How?" My gaze swung to Charlie, who stared at me with a flat, angry look that made his face look carved from stone.

"The old-fashioned way, I guess," Sam said. He looked at Charlie. "Congratulations." The word ended on an inquiring inflection.

Charlie shoved the cue ball on the table, scattering the other balls. "Thanks."

Oh, oh. I recognized that pissed-off look on Charlie's face. I edged past him to the door. "I'll go see if I can help," I muttered. "Congrats."

Charlie glared at me as I escaped the room. I glimpsed Janelle disappearing into the pale blue powder room off the front entry foyer. I hurried after her, almost slipping on the marble floor in the wide hallway that bisected the house. I tapped cautiously on the carved oak door. "Janelle? Are you okay?"

I heard the toilet flush then water running. I tentatively opened the door. Janelle leaned on the granite sink, patting her pale face with a dampened towel. She smiled shakily. "Morning sickness," she said with a grimace.

A million thoughts raced through my brain and I settled on, "How far along are you?"

"Four-and-half months." She peered at herself in

the mirror. "I look like shit."

"Nonsense. You're beautiful." I was only half-lying. She looked pale and drawn, but otherwise she was her usual porcelain-pretty self. Janelle always reminded me of a slender, non-puffy-lipped Angelina Jolie and today was no exception. Imagine Lara Croft dressed in Grace Kelly-style Liz Claiborne clothes and you have Janelle. I eyed her figure. Now that I knew what she was hiding, I could see the telltale bulge of her belly under the loose sweater and the puffiness around her wrists and ankles. I wasn't an expert on pregnancy, but she looked bigger than four-and-a-half months would warrant.

I wondered how to pick my way through the minefield of questions I had. "I didn't realize you and Charlie were—"

"We've been together for a while now. I—we—didn't decide to have—I mean, Charlie and I didn't really decide—" She stopped, her face flaming red with color.

I opened my eyes wide in shock. "What?" Then I realized how demanding that sounded. "I'm sorry. You don't have to explain anything to me or to any of us," I said softly. "Not unless you want to." I impulsively put my arms around her. "You know if I can help you, I will."

"Thank you," she whispered. She pulled away to look down at me, her dark eyes luminous with tears. "It was an accident. I've always been irregular and I just started taking medication for allergies. It interfered with my birth control. By the time I found out I was pregnant..." She dabbed her face again with the blue plaid towel. "I want Charlie's baby. I really do. I'm not trying to force him into anything."

I held my tongue, a rare feat for me. No matter what she said, a pregnancy would inevitably force Charlie into marriage. There was no way a Whittington was going to have an illegitimate baby out on the fringes of the family. "You and Charlie can work that out later," I said, wondering how the hell they would manage it.

"I know." Her smile was brave but strained. "We have to make sure Charlie..." She suddenly gripped my hands. "He can't go to prison, Cassie. He just can't. Even if he did kill John, he can't go to prison. Prison would destroy Charlie."

Holy buckets. Did she really think Charlie did it? I was saved from voicing this shocking idea by a voice echoing in the long hallway. "Cassandra? Is everything all right?"

I peeked out the door. The Second was peering around the door that led to the family room, light from the two-story window at the end of the hall giving him a halo effect. "We're coming back right now," I said. "Everything's fine." I gently pulled my hand free from Janelle's painful grip. "Come on. Let's get it over with."

Janelle took in a deep breath then nodded. She peered at herself in the mirror, smoothing a strand of her hair back and dabbing one last time at her face before dropping the towel on the toilet tank. "I didn't mean to blurt it like that," she whispered as we walked down the hall. "I just told Charlie on Saturday night and I guess I'm still so excited about it. He told the family about it on Sunday. He said later that he and John argued afterwards." Her cheeks flushed a becoming shade of pink. "John gave him some advice. He said to drop me like a hot potato and make sure a paternity test is done, to make sure it's Charlie's baby."

"That sounds like John," I said, forcing my voice to sound light and dismissive instead of cursing the stupid bastard the way I wanted to do. "He made Diane do the same thing when she got pregnant." I smiled mirthlessly. "Matthew is such a prig I'm sure he has to be John's kid. I don't know why John bothered checking." A sudden thought struck me. "I wonder if John did the same thing with the other kids." The idea vanished as Janelle spoke.

"I think Charlie planned to tell you yesterday but then the thing with John..." Her steps slowed as we neared the Second, who regarded us with calm impassivity from the doorway ahead. "What do you think he's thinking?" she whispered.

I suddenly grinned. "If I know the Second, he's pleased as punch there's going to be a Fourth." I smiled up at the old man as we neared. "Am I right, C.R.?"

A ghost of a smile made his lips twitch. Charlie often looked the same when he was trying to be stern but was secretly pleased. "It might be a girl."

"Or it might be twins." Janelle nodded at our surprised looks. "Twins run in my family and Charlie's family." She put a hand on her gently curved abdomen. "I go in on Thursday for an ultrasound to find out." She looked at the doorway. "I hope Charlie will go with me."

I gave her an encouraging pat on the arm. "Don't worry. Sam and I will help even if Charlie acts like an asshole. I'll go with you if he doesn't. Maybe you'll have a boy and a girl. That would be something, wouldn't it?"

The Second stepped aside as we passed him to re-enter the room. "My son is very good at being an asshole," he said. "Don't hesitate to call me in to give him a piece of my mind."

Janelle shot him a surprised and grateful look then came to a halt one step inside the room. All eyes turned toward us. Her face once again reddened then she lifted her chin and walked into the room, skirting the pool table where Charlie stood, glaring out the window at the lake. Janelle hesitated but didn't speak as she took a seat on the sofa across from Claire.

I followed more slowly to sit next to her. Sam was watching Charlie as though he expected he might need to intervene. The Second returned to the wet bar and poured himself a mug of coffee from the pot there as Charlie spoke to the room at large.

"Janelle and I have a lot of decisions to make. Our personal problems have nothing to do with the issue at hand, which is John's death and who killed him."

The Second started to speak then subsided. I thought I saw a glint of humor in his eyes as he poured cream into his coffee and returned to his seat. "I hope you'll keep us informed. We are family, after all." He emphasized the word 'family' before lowering his head to sip his coffee. When he looked up again, I saw sadness reflected there. No matter what I thought about John, he was the Second's child. I felt a rush of sympathy for his loss.

Charlie flinched. I could imagine what was going through his mind: *me, a father? With a family of my own? No way. Not me. I'm too old for that.* Then Charlie glanced at Janelle and I saw the conflict clearly in his green eyes. *A family? A child? A child with Janelle?* He smiled briefly before looking away, his eyes narrowed in confusion.

Gut-twisting jealousy pulsed through me. When Charlie and I were married we talked about having children...someday. That day never came and somehow, in the intervening years, I never met anyone I wanted to be a parent with. I always thought Charlie felt the same way. But now he was seeing a future that was alien to me. Charlie and I had shared almost everything in our lives, including violent death. But this was something I would never experience. We were parting ways. Panic—or maybe a hot flash—made me break out in a cold sweat.

Sam crossed the room to Janelle and me to brush a kiss against Janelle's cheek. "You'll be a great mom," he said gently. "I know you will." He straightened and smiled at Charlie. "And she'll probably teach you how to be a great dad, too."

Charlie looked startled then he almost smiled. Sam's words seemed to release the rest of the family from their shock. Livvie and T.J. beamed at Janelle and I could tell Livvie was already plotting a baby shower and I would be roped into helping.

"Despite Janelle's surprising news, I think we need to return to the topic at hand," the Second said, putting his coffee mug on the oak table next to him. "The police believe they have means, motive, and opportunity, Charlie." His words were calm but I heard flinty hardness underneath the civility and ... did I hear a question there?

"I never would have harmed John, no matter what he did." Charlie strode across the room to stand next to Janelle.

"The police said you had motive." The Second regarded Charlie steadily. "Was it something to do with Cassie?"

I looked from Charlie to the Second in surprise. "Me? Why would Charlie have a beef with John because of me?"

"It didn't have to do with Cassie," Charlie interrupted. "It was..."

"Was what?" Claire demanded.

"Janelle."

"Me?" Janelle looked up at him, her black braid brushing against his thigh. Her oval face looked pale in the chill morning light. "What do you mean?"

Charlie put his hand on the back of her neck, a possessive, sensual gesture that made goose bumps rise on my arms. "He threatened you."

"What the hell could John do that would possibly hurt Janelle?" I demanded. Sam looked at me from his spot near the pool table, opening his eyes wide to show his surprise at my exasperated tone. I modulated my voice slightly. "How could she be hurt?"

"He told me he was going to bring action to have her disbarred for her work regarding Grandy's estate."

"Can we back up a second?" T.J. asked mildly. "I'm not sure I understand the intricacies of all this."

"John was suing to prevent me from inheriting the estate," I said with all the patience I could muster. My head was spinning like the Wheel of Fortune with the marker landing first on 'death penalty' then 'pregnancy' then 'lawsuit.' There were too many important issues being tossed around for me to focus on just one. "Janelle was Grandy Theo's lawyer and now she's my lawyer. We negotiated the sale of Grandy's Minnesota home to you and Livvie then John conceded the other homes to me. I don't think he cared about them. But the bulk of the estate is stalled in probate court. John took exception to the fact that his grandmother left me her estate. I planned to set up a charitable trust with a third of the money, but that was put on hold as long as everything is tied up."

"Can the lawsuit go forward now that John is dead? Would that be legal?" Sam looked at Janelle then at Charlie. "Or does it take on a life of its own regardless of who started the proceedings?"

Silence was his answer. Then Claire asked, "Do you have an interest in the outcome of the lawsuit? Besides its effect on Cassie, that is?" Her tone was polite but I saw a supercilious tilt to her chin as her gaze went from Sam to me.

"Now wait a minute," I started to protest.

"That's a good question," Sam said smoothly. "I'm not really involved because I assume there'll be a pre-nup." He smiled blandly at the shocked looks that greeted this statement.

"You're getting married?" Charlie asked in a low

voice.

I peered up at him. Janelle was between us and when I looked at Charlie, I saw her expression in the periphery of my vision. She appeared surprised and pleased. Charlie frowned at me, his green eyes accusing and hurt.

I had the brief thought that Sam's bombshell might cancel out Janelle's, then I banished it. Pregnancy trumped potential marriage any time. "You might say that's under discussion." I decided to get back to the subject at hand.

Before I could, though, the door near the pool table opened and Diane Whittington, John's widow, entered. Her son Matthew was close behind her, his face pale and set. Diane was the picture of the grieving widow with her black skirt, black-and-white sweater set, and her short dark hair immaculately coiffed. Her face was composed but she was pale and her eyes seemed sunken in her face. Diane was always thin but she had a brittle quality now that made me think of fragile porcelain.

"We felt we should be here." Diane's gaze settled on Charlie. "We felt it was important to represent John to the family."

Claire stood. "Of course. I should have called you."

That old expression, 'Butter wouldn't melt in her mouth,' popped into my mind. Claire was a cool one for sure. I watched with reluctant admiration as she gestured to the seat next to her. Diane crossed the room and sat, Matthew taking up position behind her, his hands on the back of the couch.

"We were discussing motive," the Second said. "Trying to determine who might want to hurt John."

I could think of several people who might kill John in the heat of the moment but I refrained from saying so. Why rub salt in their wounds? I wondered if the family would be okay financially then I pooh-

poohed the thought. The Whittingtons were among the wealthiest people in the Twin Cities and John was one of the most prestigious purveyors of McMansions to the Hoi Polloi. Diane was probably rolling in dough.

"Did he have business rivals?" Sam asked.

"Of course he did," Matthew said. "But that's hardly a reason to kill someone." His tone of voice clearly said that Sam knew nothing about Real Business.

I saw Sam's face still and knew he was inches away from superciliousness of his own. "What did he say to you, Charlie?" I asked. "About Janelle and the disbarring?"

"John implied on the phone that he would ask that Janelle be removed as executor of the estate on the grounds that she mishandled the financials. He implied she's being unduly influenced by me." Charlie snapped out the words like missiles.

"Well, duh." I longed to take the words back as soon as they slipped out of my mouth. "It stands to reason you two would discuss the lawsuit and the inheritance." Then the rest of his words soaked in. "Wait a minute—mishandled? In what way? Grandy wouldn't name her as the executor unless she trusted Janelle." I looked at Janelle, whose cheeks were pink with embarrassment.

"Unduly influenced," Charlie reiterated. "He said that I was in collusion with her in order to get the inheritance settled on you. Once that was done, I'd be able to get my hands on it because you and I have…history."

I almost laughed out loud. "Anyone who knows us knows that's stupid," I said with a grin. "I mean, we're divorced, for cryin' out loud. Why would a judge think our so-called history has any weight?" I looked around the room, surprised to intercept several skeptical looks. I looked at Sam last, relieved to see he looked as amused as I felt. Had I encountered skepticism there, I wasn't sure what I would do.

"Father felt strongly that it was unfair that he and his children were not granted any proceeds from Grandmother Theo's estate," Matthew said.

I regarded him warily. Since Matthew was one of the 'children' I wondered what his feelings were on the matter. John had always treated his children like incidental appendages in his life. They were stock pieces necessary to round out John's idea of himself and the persona he presented to the world. Unlike Becky and her kids, who were the life of the party at any family gathering, John's family always acted like we were the black sheep and they were solid gold. Hell, they even pitched a fit about the family Facebook pages, making comments about how distasteful it was to share details of their lives with total strangers. Becky pointed out they didn't *have* to share with strangers, but they still acted like it was something only trailer-trash would do. The rest of the family ignored them and cheerfully updated their Facebook statuses on a regular basis, giving us all a chance to stay in touch even though separated.

Why would Matthew be worried about the estate? Surely the family wasn't worried about the money. Grandy's estate was worth several million dollars, even with the lousy economy and stock market, but that was probably chump change to John's family. They lived in a huge house and Pauline, the youngest daughter, went to Vassar, or Wellesley, one of those East coast bastions of correctness. Matthew attended a private boarding school during his teen years then went to a private college. Jon was in his last year at Harvard. Everybody in the family had a BMW, Porsche, or Benz. Nope, they didn't need the money.

It was probably all just a pissy attitude on their

parts. "It's irrelevant how John felt about Grandy's will," I said. "She made her decision and it was up to Janelle to implement it. The fact that she ignored your father is no reason to imply that Janelle is a crook."

"It's out of our hands, of course," Matthew said, as always ignoring me and focusing on the Second, who sat like a lion waiting to pounce on someone, his green eyes sharp and cautious. "When Father filed his objection, the case was referred to a probate judge. We should have his ruling any day now."

"And it's about time," I grumbled. "It's been a year since she died."

"That's not unusual," the Second said. "It often takes six months to a year for a will to go through probate. Since her estate was so large and since her bequests were unusual it's not surprising."

I sat back, quelled by his logic but still complaining inside. I didn't care about the money, really, although I was starting to get a sense for what capital-M Money could do to my life. When I sold Grandy's house to Livvie the previous year for two million dollars, I was suddenly wealthy even after all taxes and fees were processed. I wasn't Richie Rich rich, like Charlie was, but I was now Well Off. It was a heady feeling to not worry about debt any more. "Did the police talk to you, Matthew?"

He turned his gaze on me for the first time since coming into the room. He smiled briefly, looking so much like John for an instant that I blinked in surprise. His oval face, like a younger and softer version of Charlie's, seemed to freeze and his hazel eyes deadened as he flicked a glance from me to Sam. For an instant I saw unabashed hatred there. Then it smoothed and he was simply a polite young man talking to his elders. "Why would they talk to me?"

"You were at the scene," Charlie said. "Why were you there?"

Matthew pursed his lips as though contemplating a refusal to answer. "Father asked me to come out and confer with him," he said reluctantly. "When I got there he and Mrs. Peavey were talking. I left to get a cup of coffee and when I came back, Father had gone and she was awaiting his return."

"What the hell was she doing there?" I muttered. "I didn't think they knew each other."

"She invested in my business and perhaps she invested in John's, too." The Second looked at Matthew. "We need a complete accounting of the business. We need a list of creditors, debts, and so on...a balance sheet. The police will want it and it will be needed to settle John's estate, of course."

Matthew's shoulders drew up as though protecting him from a blow. "I will need to check with our investors first."

Diane twisted, craning her neck to peer up at him. "It's your father's death." She turned back to face the Second. "Of course we'll do anything to help."

I checked Matthew to see how he was taking this maternal fiat and was surprised to see him shoot her an exasperated frown before smoothing his expression to bland attention. I used to see a similar look on John's face when he was being asked to do something he found distasteful but necessary.

The door once again opened and Consuela, the housekeeper, peeked in. "I'm sorry, but there are some people here to see..." She looked around the room, her eyes settling on me. "They're here to talk to Cassie." Her dark face creased into a worried frown as she said it and her eyes flickered from me to Charlie then back to me. I had known Consuela since I was a child and I recognized that look.

Something that would annoy Charlie was on the horizon.

The door opened wider and two men edged past her and came into the room. They looked like comical contrasts to each other. One was tall, black, and bulky. The other was short, round, and white. Consuela glared at them and muttered something then retreated, closing the door behind her. I grinned, wondering what Hispanic deprecation was being leveled at the two men for their rudeness.

All thoughts of humor vanished from my brain when they paused near the threshold and examined the room, eyes sweeping around us and finally settling on me.

"Cassandra Whittington?" the black man asked.

I nodded, my stomach starting a little tap dance against my spine.

He held up something and I gaped. It was a badge of some kind. "My name is Seth Callahan. This is Paul Sanders." The white guy nodded briefly. "We're with the Lakeville P.D. We have some questions for you about the murder of John Whittington."

"You already talked to her," Sam said, moving to stand to the right of the couch where I sat like a bump on the sofa.

The white guy—Sanders—looked at Sam, the tight line of his eyebrows drawing together when he frowned. "That was before we knew the time of death. We have some more questions now that we know the victim died three hours before he was found."

"Three hours?" Charlie looked down at Janelle. His face relaxed as relief flooded through him. "I was in a meeting three hours before I found him. I was in a meeting with four other people. I've got an ironclad alibi."

"I don't." I had to clear my throat before I could

speak more. "I don't have an alibi. In fact, four hours before you found him, I was arguing with John out at that subdivision." I looked at the stunned face staring at me.

Damn. I was in deep shit now.

Chapter 4

"What the hell do you mean?" Charlie looked past Janelle at me.

I huddled on the couch, wishing I could sink between the cushions. "I was out at that subdivision in the afternoon. John called and—"

"Don't say anything," Janelle interrupted. She got to her feet and crossed the room to the two officers. "Can I see your identification?"

I blinked in surprise. Gone was the quaking, frightened pregnant girl. A businesslike lawyer took her place. Janelle took the badge wallets handed to her and examined them, then handed them back to the officers. "Wait here, please."

She came back and I stood to meet her, my knees wobbly. Charlie moved in closer, as did Sam. We looked like a football huddle. Janelle said in a low voice, "As your lawyer, I advise you not to speak any more."

"You're not a criminal lawyer," I pointed out. "You practice estate law."

"I'll do until we get another lawyer in."

"I'll represent her," Charlie said.

Oh, wrong thing to say and wrong way to say it, I thought. I know he meant well, but I winced at the proprietary, almost paternal, way he said it.

Janelle's blue eyes were frosty. "No, you won't. You're under suspicion."

They stared at each other, blue eyes meeting green eyes, both sets of eyes narrowed. I started to speak when Callahan, the black cop, cleared his throat. "I believe the charges are going to be dropped, ma'am. The time of death changes things." He took a step back when Janelle leveled a *don't fuck with me* gaze at him.

"I appreciate hearing that, but until I get word from Mr. Whittington's lawyer that the charges are dropped, I'm Ms. Whittington's lawyer." Janelle plucked up her handbag from the floor near the couch. "Any questions?"

Charlie opened his mouth then closed it when she leveled that cool gaze at him again. "I'll call Billy Armstrong," he said, pulling out his Blackberry.

"Good." Janelle looked at me, her face softening with sympathy. "Come on, Cassie."

I gulped in a breath to steady my ragged breathing, praying I didn't get hiccups from fright. I snagged my purse from the chair where I dropped it and started walking toward the cops, my feet dragging like lead weights were attached. "You'll come with me, won't you?" I could barely get the words out around the dry lump that choked my windpipe.

Janelle kept pace beside me, her black braid snaking over her shoulder when she shook her head. "I can't come in the car with you." I shot her a stunned gaze and she smiled reassuringly. "Don't worry. They'll take you to the station in their car but I'll be following right behind. Don't say anything until I get there."

"I'll meet you there," Sam said.

Oh, crap. I had forgotten all about him. I stopped in my tracks and turned to him gratefully. "You've got the keys and you can drive and..." I looked up at him, trying to will incipient tears from falling.

He correctly interpreted my emotion as mindless fear. "Don't worry," he said. "Janelle won't let anything happen to you, and if she falters, I'll sic Charlie on 'em." Sam looked past me where Janelle and Charlie were talking in low voices just a few feet away. "It'll be okay." He pulled me to him and kissed me quickly then kept an arm around my shoulders as we walked to the door.

I leaned into the comforting warmth of his body until we got to the two officers. "This way, ma'am." Sanders appeared at my side, gesturing toward the door.

Janelle joined me. I paused to look back. The Second stood near Claire, his gaze fixed on me. He nodded once when he met my eyes and relief flooded me at his tacit support. My glance swept over Claire, who maintained her calm, slightly disapproving façade. As I turned I glimpsed Diane and Matthew. I hesitated, trying to interpret what I saw. Smugness? Pleasure? Relief? None of that really made sense but then I wasn't really thinking clearly.

"This way, ma'am." Callahan touched my arm.

Janelle and I fell into step behind them as they led the way out of the room. "Don't say anything," she repeated as we walked down the marble hallway. "Charlie and I will meet you there. Is Sam coming?" She looked over her shoulder and nodded. "Good. You'll need a car as soon as they release you."

"They will release me, won't they?" I was pleased my voice didn't tremble as much as my hands and legs did.

"Don't worry," Charlie said. "It's going to be okay, Cassie."

I gave him and Sam one last longing look before I was bustled outside where a black non-descript sedan was parked in the curving drive in front of the house. I headed for the front passenger side but I was intercepted by the chubby detective, who steered me to the back door. I clambered into the back, twisting to stare out the back window at Janelle, who was hurrying around the side of the house, Charlie and Sam by her side.

Then the car door closed behind me. I turned to face the grillwork that separated me from the two cops. "It's sort of claustrophobic," I said.

The black detective looked at me in the rear view mirror. "We'll be fast."

Oh, joy. I sat on my hands as we drove, half afraid they'd handcuff me and half afraid to touch anything. It looked clean but there was a suspicious odor, as though old pee had permeated the thick vinyl seats. I stared out the window barely noticing first the houses then the highway as it flitted past my vision. One thought kept pounding through my brain.

John was alive when I left him at two-thirty in the afternoon. Somehow I had to prove that. Somehow I had to convince them that when I left him, he was alive and well and pissed off at me. I stared down at the floor, trying to order my thoughts, and when I looked up again, I saw Callahan watching me, his face thoughtful. I lowered my face again, not anxious to inadvertently give him fodder for his suspicions.

I breathed a sigh of relief when we got to the Lakeville Police Station. I had barely noticed the place the previous day since I was still a bit groggy from my close encounter with a fireplace. Now I saw that it was an impressive glass-and-concrete structure, attached to an older brick building by a glass-enclosed walkway. As we neared I saw "City Hall" on a sign in front of the older structure. Apparently it was an original building, looking like the staid older sibling next to the younger rock-and-roll brother.

The car pulled into a garage-like space where I was escorted from the car through a series of doors into a large room. "We're just going to get your fingerprints," Sanders said. "Why don't you have a seat?"

"I don't know if you should." I sat down on the hard wooden chair and watched as he pulled a black briefcase from a metal cabinet on the wall. "My lawyer should be here."

"We're getting prints from everyone in the room that day," Callahan said, taking a seat opposite me. "That way we can make sure to catalog who was in there and who might have touched the murder weapon."

I considered it. I remembered Charlie holding it and Sheila grabbing it. "I suppose that makes sense," I agreed. "Several people touched it."

Sanders looked sharply at me. "They did?"

I nodded, eyeing the various tools he took out of the case. "Is that ink?" I asked.

"It's a special dye," he said. "It washes off easily." He took my hand and had my fingertips inked, pressed, and annotated so fast I barely knew it was happening. Then he handed me some handy-wipe damp towels. "Sign here, please." He smiled but it didn't quite reach his gray eyes. "Just to show you did this of your own free will."

I carefully read the fine print on the back of the fingerprint card, but it seemed straightforward. I signed it then stood when Callahan did. "I need to see my lawyer," I said as we left the room and walked into a corridor lined with doors on each side.

"We'll get you settled in the interview room then check and see if she's here," Sanders said from behind me. "Can I get you anything? Some pop? Coffee?"

I remembered the TV shows I had seen where

cops plied innocent schmucks with drinks only to withhold bathroom privileges later. I swallowed in a dry throat. "No, I'm fine."

"In here." He opened a door at the junction of two halls and gestured me into a room with pale yellow walls, green carpeted floors and a round table with four chairs. I took a seat facing the door and Callahan sat across from me. Sanders left, leaving the door open.

I leaned back in the chair, reminded of my days as a software programmer and endless design meetings I sat in on. The room was like a conference room at Lerner Software. The only thing missing was the plastic bowl full of ice and cans of Mountain Dew, the programmer's drug of choice. I looked at the bland landscape paintings, the faux wood end tables, and the faux wood grain in the table top—anywhere but at Callahan.

"...right here," I heard Sanders say.

I looked up as Janelle and Charlie came into the room. Janelle carried a burgundy leather briefcase, slender and very feminine. "Two lawyers?" Callahan asked, his mild voice at odds with the sharp look in his dark brown eyes.

"You can be my lawyer now?" I asked Charlie. "It's true? You're off the hook? Where's Sam? Is he here?"

"He's in the waiting room," Janelle said as she took the seat on my left and removed a leather maroon portfolio with gold embossed initials from an inner sleeve of her briefcase.

"Can't he...?" I subsided when Janelle shook her head.

Sanders sidled into the room, taking a seat away from the table, against the wall. He and Callahan exchanged a look then Callahan said, "What did you mean, off the hook? Were you concerned about your ex-husband being accused of murder?"

Janelle started to speak but I beat her to it. "Look, I've got nothing to hide. John was an asshole and the world is probably better because he's dead, but if every asshole in the world was killed we'd be neck deep in bodies and probably have world peace and an end to greenhouse gas emissions. So while that's a laudable goal, it doesn't mean I killed him."

Charlie paused in the act of pulling out a chair on my right and glared at me with exasperation evident in his bright green eyes. "Cassie, just for once would you not express your opinion?"

Callahan's lips twitched. He had an oval, babyish face but I saw sharp intelligence in his eyes. He wasn't about to be fooled by my flippant attitude. "So he was an asshole?"

"Yes, John was an idiot. He—"

"John Whittington sued Cassie to prevent her inheritance from John's grandmother. He was very bitter that he didn't receive what he felt was his fair share of the estate." Janelle pulled a pen out of a side pocket in her leather briefcase and arranged it next to her leather bound portfolio. "It was a bone of contention with him."

Callahan jotted something on a notepad. "How much was the estate?"

I sat back in my chair. "I'll bet you know."

His lips twitched again. "Why do you say that?"

I leaned forward and clasped my hands on the table and looked him in the eye. "Just because this is a small suburb it doesn't mean you guys are stupid. You've probably researched everybody at the job site, everybody in the family, and anybody who does business with John. So you know it was several million dollars. And you probably also know that it's in the hands of a probate judge and John and I agreed to abide by the decision of the judge."

"What about his children?" Sanders asked from his corner.

I looked over my shoulder at him. "I beg your pardon?"

This time it was Charlie who put a restraining hand on my wrist as he spoke. "John's children weren't named in my grandmother's will."

Sanders eyed Charlie. "It's your brother who was killed. I take it there was no love lost between you?"

"That's irrelevant," Janelle snapped. "Mr. Whittington has been cleared as a suspect in his brother's murder.

I barely heard her. "Why did you ask about John's kids?"

"Why don't you let us ask some questions?" Callahan phrased it as a question but it came out as a command.

I lounged back in the chair again. "Okay. Ask."

"Why did you meet John Whittington at two in the afternoon on April twenty-sixth?"

I glanced at Charlie, sitting on my left side then turned my attention to Callahan. "John called me on Sunday night when I got back from Florida."

"Why?" Callahan made a quick note in his own portfolio. Unlike Janelle's, his was vinyl with *Lakeville PD* stamped on the front in flaking gold letters.

"Because of Sam."

Charlie jerked. "Sam?"

I ignored his sharp tone. "John also wanted to talk about the inheritance, but I didn't find out about that until I got there. He told me his lawyer said that the judge would be handing down a decision soon, a decision in my favor."

"Really?" Janelle jotted a note on cream-colored lined paper in her leather clad notepad. "I wonder why he thinks that."

"What did he say that made you want to meet him?" Callahan asked. "You said it was about your friend, Sam Barlow?"

Friend. I snorted softly. At my age, it sounded stupid to call Sam a boyfriend, but *lover* sounded odd, too. "John told me it had to do with the patent lawsuit. Sheila was willing to negotiate."

Charlie sat up straighter. "What about the lawsuit?"

"Another lawsuit?" Sanders asked. "Your family is prone to them, aren't they?"

"It's not the family's, it's Sam's," I explained. "Sheila Peavey and Sam were married and they got divorced. She married Mike Peavey, who was Sam's best friend in college. He went to college late in life," I added, just to give them a sense of the timing involved. "This wasn't decades ago it was..." I thought, "Well, ten years ago. Anyway, Shelia divorced Sam and ran off with Mike and with a plant that Mike and Sam developed together. An azalea." I sat back, anxious to see how the police would take this revelation of skullduggery.

Callahan stared at me, obviously waiting for me. "And..." he prompted.

"Charlie is Sam's lawyer in the lawsuit about the patent."

Sanders ran a hand over his balding pate. "A plant?"

I ignored his doubtful tone of voice. "John said that Sheila Peavey, Sam's ex-wife, contacted him. She wanted to make a deal. I'm in negotiations to buy her late husband's share of a botanical research company. If I would pay her five hundred thousand dollars, she'd drop her objections to the sale."

"That's a lot of cash," Sanders commented.

"Cash I don't have yet. I pointed that out to John. He said that he would drop his lawsuit about my inheritance if I gave him one million dollars." I glanced sideways at Charlie. "They were in cahoots. He said that if I paid her, she would consider dropping her objections to the patent dispute. She would negotiate with Sam to split the profits."

"That's a total turnaround from what she was saying a few months ago," Charlie muttered, pulling out his Blackberry and thumbing a quick note.

"Why didn't she just call you herself?" Callahan asked, scribbling another line on his already crowded pad.

"Because she and I hate each other and I would never talk to her." I tapped a nail on the tabletop, remembering my acrimonious conversation with John. "You see, her husband was a partner in a biological research company. I want to buy into that company to..." I stopped, not sure I wanted to explain that I was trying to provide Sam with a viable lifestyle after his devastating accident. "I'm interested in biological research. But Sheila refused to sell her share of the company to me, the share she inherited from her husband... whom I think she killed," I added for good measure.

Sanders stared me, his mouth sagging open. "You think she killed her husband?"

I nodded as Charlie shook his head, interrupting me when I would have elaborated. "It's a suspicion, nothing more. I've told you not to say that. Sheila Peavey can sue you for libel."

I started to stick my tongue out at him but remembered I was in the hands of the law. I settled for a glare instead. "Sam and I have a memorial service to go to next week."

"Memorial service?" Janelle asked me.

"For the boy who died last year at school." I felt a pang at the memory. Although the events of the previous year introduced me to Sam, they were also tragic. Springtime would always be a reminder to me of the loss of a young life and a horrible death. "The service is next week at the school."

"Peavey...She was also at the scene when you

and your ex-husband found the body," Callahan murmured. He looked down at his notes and scribbled something. It looked wrong to me, like an excuse to look away from us. I shifted my gaze to Sanders, just moving my eyes so I caught his expression in the periphery of my vision. He frowned, looking perplexed.

"Your phrasing suggests that you're not concerned about Cassie's possible involvement. Is that true?" Janelle asked quickly.

"We need to gather more evidence before we come to any conclusions." Callahan tilted his head, eyeing me politely then switched his attention to Charlie. "Can you think of anyone who would want to kill your brother? I'm sure all of us could incite murder given the right motivations." He shifted his gaze to look directly at me as he said it.

Janelle straightened. "You're questioning Ms. Whittington, not Mr. Whittington."

"Wow," I muttered. "I think I'm flattered. I can't think of anyone who wants to kill me."

"Sheila Peavey," Janelle said without a pause. "Trust me. She'd kill you if she could."

A knock on the door made Sanders get to his feet. He consulted briefly with someone outside then said to Callahan, "The witness is here."

"Witness? Witness to what?" Janelle demanded.

"A witness to your client's argument with John Whittington."

"Oh, for heaven's sake. John and I argued all the time. We had…" I considered a polite way to say he was a snob, a jerk, and a creep. "We had philosophical differences."

Charlie made a strangled noise. "Way to restrain your opinions, Cassie," he murmured.

"If you're done with us, can we go now?" Janelle asked, closing her leather portfolio.

Callahan regarded us all thoughtfully. "Where

did you meet Mr. Whittington?" he asked me. "Was it in the same house where you found the body?"

"Nope. It was that model home place. I'll bet if you dust it for prints, you'll find mine." I smiled. "You can match them to the ones you took earlier."

"They did what?" Janelle stiffened, leveling a frosty glare at Callahan.

"They did my fingerprints." I wiggled one hand for her inspection. "I didn't handle the nail gun, Janelle." I frowned, an errant thought bouncing around in my brain. "I think Matthew did, and Sheila, and Charlie, of course. There're a million fingerprints on that gun. But mine aren't on it."

"You should have told them to wait until we arrived."

I shrugged. "It's not a big deal."

"It's a big deal." She ran a hand up her forehead, touching her tidy, pulled-back hair. I saw the small beads of sweat that she wiped away. I remembered her earlier bout of nausea and felt a stab of guilt.

"I'm sorry." I looked at Callahan, who also regarded Janelle with alert curiosity in his dark eyes. "Can we go now? You know where to find me if you have more questions." I didn't wait for an answer but got to my feet.

Callahan rose, too, and waited for us by the door where Sanders stood. "I'd like you to make a formal statement and sign it, describing what you and Mr. Whittington discussed." He walked down the hallway and we fell into step behind him, Sanders bringing up the rear.

"Sure." Then I remembered Janelle and asked, "Can my lawyer be there when I depose?"

"Of course." We came to a doorway and Callahan opened it. "If you'll just take a seat in the waiting room, I'll have someone meet with you." He stopped, staring ahead of him.

I peered around his body. "Oh, shit," I muttered.

Sam and Sheila Peavey were standing in the waiting room, fists clenched and glaring at each other. A receptionist sitting in a nearby glass-walled enclosure watched them, her gaze swiveling to us as we entered.

Sam turned. "Is it true?" he demanded, his eyes intent on me. "Did you agree to buy her share in Mike's company so she'd drop the lawsuit for my patent rights? What are you doing, Cassie? I can manage my life without your help." His dark eyes were accusing as he looked first at me then at Sheila.

When his gaze shifted, his posture changed, relaxing slightly. I had a brief, harried impression of Sheila in her fitted denim jacket, pale jeans, and oh-so-fitted pink sweater. She eyed me, her sweeping glance taking in my old blue jeans, navy blue *my weight is perfect for my height—which varies* T-shirt, and faded purple windbreaker. Then she looked back at Sam, her eyes narrowing.

I remembered what he told me about her, how she could make a man feel like the most special person in the world. She smiled in triumph as Sam took a step toward her.

That's when I darted around Callahan and made a grab for that lying bitch.

Chapter 5

"Hey!" Callahan made a grab for me but I eluded him, using moves that would make a football star proud. Unfortunately I tripped on the area rug in the middle of the room, which flung me against a row of chairs bolted to the floor. The jarring impact to my right thigh made me stop, which gave Charlie a chance to get his hands on me.

"Hold on." He jerked me upright and back at the same time.

"You bitch," I snarled, straining in Charlie's grip to get at Sheila, who regarded me with startled wariness. "John said our talk was private."

Janelle put a hand on my other arm and I subsided when I saw Callahan loom up next to her, ready to intervene.

"Well, Cassie? What about it?" Sam demanded.

"It would be in your best interests to wrap up that lawsuit," Charlie said. "It's been dragging on for almost a year now."

Sam's jaw tightened. "Are you worried about your fees?"

Charlie's hand tightened on my arm. "Not at all," he said levelly. "As we discussed when I took the case, my fee is predicated on the outcome, so it's irrelevant to me how long it takes. But it's harder for us to retrieve lost revenue if it continues on like this. A settlement might be to your benefit." Charlie looked down at me. "Can I let go of you now?" I saw the humor in his green eyes, but I was still so pissed off I just glared back at him. "Cassie?"

I jerked my arm and he let go. Janelle squeezed my forearm reassuringly. "That's why I went to meet John," I said, my eyes focused on Sam. I willed him to hear the sincerity in my voice, praying he would understand I had his best interests at heart. "He called me and said that Sheila was considering settling with Sam over the patent dispute. I went to talk about it." Then I remembered my earlier conversation with Sam. "Wait a minute. You told me you were thinking of settling out of court with her anyway. So why are you pissed off at me?"

Sam's cheeks reddened. "You don't have any right to talk about this stuff behind my back with her."

"No right?" Slow anger started to bubble up in my gut. "I'm trying to find a way to help you, Sam. You know as well as I do that—" I bit my lip, glimpsing the amused twist in Sheila's smile. "We can talk about it later." I turned my ire on Callahan. "What's she doing here?"

"I'm doing my civic duty," Sheila said, edging her way around Sam and approaching me. She settled her tooled leather purse on her shoulder as she smiled at Callahan. "The detective asked me to come in and make a statement about what I heard." Her warm brown eyes turned flat and cold when she looked at me. "About what you and John were arguing about yesterday when I went to talk to him."

"You?" I quivered with anger. "You? What were you doing there? Were you eavesdropping on me?"

"Don't flatter yourself." She glanced sideways at Sam. "You aren't my concern."

Ooh, I was so close to hitting her. So close.

Janelle sensed it because she stepped slightly in front of me. "Detective, Callahan, I'd like a copy of Mrs. Peavey's deposition when it's available," she said in a brisk, businesslike voice. "And if you're done with your questions, we're leaving now."

"Don't you think we should…?" Charlie's voice trailed away when Janelle leveled a scathing look in his direction.

Callahan was up to the challenge of a pissed-off Janelle. "You can leave as soon as your client makes a deposition about her actions on the day of the murder." He gestured to Sanders, who went to the receptionist's desk. He spoke to the woman sitting there who watched us all with a curious, amused expression. I suppose she had seen odder things in her waiting room than a succession of ex-husbands and ex-wives, all pissed off at each other.

Janelle pulled me to one side, Charlie following her. "They brought you here so they could observe you and Sheila," she murmured.

"What?" I jerked in surprise, twisting to look at Sheila who now spoke with Callahan, Sam several feet away and watching them.

"Keep your voice down." Janelle's face remained calm and unconcerned. Only her blue eyes reflected her smoldering anger. "They're fishing for suspects and they don't care who they hook. So stick to the facts and only the facts when you give your statement."

I nodded. "Do you think Sheila really overheard John and me when we argued?"

Janelle considered it. "You didn't see her?"

"No. John told me on the phone to go straight to that house when I got there. He was in the kitchen." I sniffed disdainfully. "The damn kitchen was the size of my kitchen and living room combined. You could feed an army in that place."

"Was the door unlocked?" Charlie asked, jerking

me back to 'just the facts.'

"Yep. I walked right in. John came out of a doorway at the back and called to me."

Charlie and Janelle exchanged a look. "That means Sheila might have been there the entire time before you came in," Janelle said. "Was there somewhere nearby where she could stand and not be seen?"

I squinched my eyes in thought, remembering the McMansion I visited the day before. "When I came in, John was walking around the kitchen, fussing with stuff—you know, moving the toaster, straightening the dishtowels. He said something about making sure the house showed at its best." I rolled my eyes. "There was even a bowl of fruit on the counter. It was real. I picked up an apple and looked at it. I wonder if somebody changes it every week." I noted Charlie's peeved expression and got back on task. "There was a door at the end of the kitchen, near a French door leading to a patio. John closed that door partway when I got there. He said something about the laundry room not being done yet."

"Was Sheila's car there?" Charlie asked.

"Three or four cars were in the same cul-de-sac as the model home. She drives..." I tilted my head, struggling for memory. "A Mustang or something, I think. I don't know if one of those was hers or not." I hazarded a glance at Sam, who stood near the outside door, glaring into the parking lot. "I don't understand it. He was talking about giving up his patent rights. I figured if I could buy into the company, it would be the best of both worlds. Sheila would be happy and willing to negotiate, Sam would have a job he could love, and Sam could reap the rewards of his work years ago."

"Mrs. Whittington?" Sanders gestured to me from the receptionist's window. "We're ready for your statement."

"Ms. Whittington," I corrected automatically. Sheila was walking away with Callahan. She flashed me a smirky smile as she disappeared into the doorway leading to the rooms we used earlier. I wondered briefly if she had a Facebook page. Man, if she did, I was going to plaster her 'wall' with words. I caught a glimpse of Sam's disgruntled look before he resumed staring at the parking lot. I walked over to where he stood. "Wait for me, okay?" I asked.

He nodded then smiled briefly, but it didn't thaw the ice in his dark brown eyes. "It's your car. So yeah, I'll wait."

I considered snapping off a reply but restrained myself. "Thanks," I said with only a touch of sarcasm. I walked back to Callahan, Janelle meeting me but Charlie staying behind. "He's going to talk to Sam," Janelle said in a low voice as we paused to let Callahan open a door near the receptionist's desk. She looked back at Sam. "Give him some time to get used to it all."

"He's had six months." I modified my angry tone of voice. "It's time he faced it, Janelle. He can't return to his old life."

"It's hard to face change." Her eyes went to Charlie, who was speaking to Sam. Neither man looked happy about their conversation.

No shit, I thought. I looked at the two men who were so influential in my life. "Sometimes there is no choice."

****

My stomach was grumbling by the time we finished. I snuck a look at my Timex and saw it was almost noon. No wonder I had the rumbles. When we emerged from an interview room at the police station, Sam was nowhere in sight. I felt a momentary panic, replaced by concern when I saw him and Charlie outside, sitting on a bench and

61

watching someone working in the flower bed surrounding the flagpole. Both men were staring intently at the worker, the flower bed, the cars—anything but look at each other.

"Why can't they get along?" I muttered as Janelle and I walked through the waiting room to the outside door.

"They both love you. And they're both afraid of losing you."

I stopped in the vestibule between the outer door and the inner door. "Charlie's already lost me. There's nothing between us anymore."

"So I have a clear field, is that what you're saying?" Janelle looked at Charlie who sat with his back to us, his face partially lit by the sun. "I love him, Cassie, but I'm still not sure what he feels for me. The baby—or babies—complicates things so much."

"And it simplifies things." I smiled when she looked startled. "Charlie isn't clinging to the past. He's just afraid of the future. You've catapulted him right into a brave new world." I pushed open the outer door.

Both men stood when they saw us coming. "How did it go?" Charlie asked.

I wasn't sure if he was asking me or Janelle. She answered for both of us. "Fine. They don't have any evidence against her. I told you, this is a fishing expedition."

"All I had to do was give them details about my meeting with John." I avoided looking at Sam since those details included a discussion of my plans for his future. His tight jaw and narrowed eyes told me we weren't done discussing that topic yet.

"So we're free to go?" Sam looked toward Bilbo then to the flower bed. "I'd like to get to the store. I didn't spend much time there yesterday." He quirked an eyebrow at me. "We were busy in the afternoon."

Yesterday afternoon? Oh. I smiled when I remembered our afternoon activity. Sam had gone to Barlow's after lunch and I went to meet John. Then Sam came home early from Barlow's and that's when we ended up in bed.

"We can go. I'm going to talk to Billy Armstrong," Janelle said, walking toward Charlie's Jag parked next to Bilbo. "I want to make sure everything is handled properly. He handles criminal proceedings more than I do."

"Sounds good." I remembered Armstrong. He was a retired linebacker with the Minnesota Vikings and a shrewd defense attorney in Charlie's law firm. "If he needs to talk to me, just give me a call. I plan to be at home for the most of the rest of the day. I still haven't unpacked."

We all paused at the cars. Mine automatically unlocked when it sensed the car keys Sam handed me as he walked around to the passenger side and pulled open the door. Charlie moved closer to me. "I'm sorry, Cassie. I let it slip. Sam's really pissed off."

"What?" I stopped with my hand on the door handle.

Sam jerked open his door then stood on the runner to peer over the top at us. "Cassie? Ready to go?"

"Sure." I opened my door. "What's the problem, Charlie?"

He looked at Sam then at me. "Nothing. You'll find out. I'm sorry."

"That sounds ominous." I tried to keep my voice light but it was a struggle. All I could think was, *Now what?*

"Charlie? I need to get to the office." Janelle waited patiently by the door of the Jag. She looked tired, her face pinched and her shoulders sagging.

"Take care of her, Charlie. She's one in a

million."

He smiled wryly. "Yeah. Aren't we all? See you later." He bent down and brushed a kiss on my cheek then went to the Jag.

I slid into the driver's seat of Bilbo and pressed the ignition button. "I'll be glad to see this police station in my rear view mirror," I said, putting the car into gear. I glanced at Sam, but he was staring at Charlie in the Jag, pulling out beside us.

We drove in silence for a few minutes then Sam said, "Did you know I talked to Whittington Two before we left for Florida?"

Whittington Two was Sam's nickname for Charlie's father. "No, I didn't. What did the Second have to say?"

"I think you know." Sam continued staring out his window. "He said he wanted to buy shares in my company."

"*Your* company? The one you own with your sister?" I couldn't keep the tart rebuke out of my voice. His sister Mary had kept the company going the entire time Sam was hospitalized and was on vacation in Florida.

"Yeah," he snapped. "Our company. The old man also said something that tells me he thinks I'm after you for your money."

"The Second said you were freeloading on me?" I didn't believe it. My ex-father-in-law was a lot of things but he was seldom out-and-out rude.

"Not in so many words. But he said he thought you would win the lawsuit and the inheritance would go through. He said something like, 'that will probably change your relationship with Cassie, won't it?'"

"He's just playing father," I said in dismissal. "He's nosy."

"Hmm." Sam continued staring out his window, answering noncommittally as I described my deposition-giving. I finally subsided, letting him stew in his own funk. Sam was the kind of guy who would snap out of it in his own time and nothing I said could speed up the process.

Or maybe he wouldn't snap out of it. That thought made my stomach hurt. I decided to do a Scarlett and think about it some other day.

We pulled into the parking lot at Barlow's Nursery and Landscape Center. Noontime shoppers crowded the front lot of the landscape center where the annuals were on display. Sam hopped out but I paused before following him, taking a quick look around to see what had changed since I was there the previous fall. The retail building, long and rectangular, faced north with customer parking next to the fence separating the property from County Road 35, which ran east and west through Pickaway. Behind the retail building were the grow-houses: one for forcing spring bulbs, the middle one for annuals, and the third one, the "Hard-off House," used to help plants get acclimated to Minnesota's variable spring temperatures.

The tree lot was on the east with a gate nearby, locked at night on the Barlow Boulevard side of the grounds. The southwest corner was the truck entrance where we received bulk orders of top soil, mulch, fertilizers and other commercial deliveries.

The buildings all had a fresh coat of white paint with green trim around the doors and windows. Tidy tables full of pansies, petunias, marigolds, and other annuals were outside the double doors leading into the retail center, a riot of color against the gray parking lot. As I walked through their fragrant, leafy aisles to the front door where Sam vanished, I inhaled a deep breath of Minnesota springtime. This was the perfect time of year with low humidity, no bugs, bright sunlight, and cool, crisp evenings. Even the occasional bout of cold weather and a late spring snowstorm couldn't dampen enthusiasm for the upcoming season. The frenzy of planting usually started on Mother's Day as Minnesotans took advantage of their brief summer. This Tuesday in late April was the calm before the storm.

I entered the retail building bustling with seed racks, gardening equipment, planting guides, and garden statuary. On the opposite side of the building I saw the tables outside on the south side full of vegetables waiting to be snapped up by eager amateur gardeners. My spirits lifted despite my worries. Spring in Minnesota was a time of hope, eager anticipation, and energy. It was hard not to be affected by it.

I spied Sam deep in conversation with his sister Mary, a tall, plain woman with short brown hair and a round face already tanned by sun. For a minute I forgot the past and smiled to see Sam in his element, surrounded by the tools of his trade with tables full of tomatoes and green peppers in the distance behind him. Sam belonged in the outdoors, among plants and growing things as surely as Charlie belonged in a board room with his business suits.

Then Sam turned, twisting awkwardly on his bad leg. He grimaced, grabbing the edge of a display bench full of hand tools to catch his balance. Mary put a hand under his arm to steady him, saying something in a low voice. He shook his head angrily, his silver-rimmed eyeglasses catching the light and giving him a blind-eyed look like Little Orphan Annie. Although he was getting his strength back, he didn't look like the fit and muscular ex-Marine I met a year earlier.

Mary turned to smile at me, her blue *Barlow's Nursery and Landscaping* T-shirt straining across her ample chest. "Sam was telling me what happened. Is everything okay with you and with Charlie? He's okay, right? No one's being charged with anything?"

"It's fine," I assured her. Charlie was in the process of helping Sam and Mary with a contract dispute and Mary developed a mild crush on him, a not-unusual occurrence where Charlie and women were concerned.

"Why didn't you tell me your ex-father-in-law already invested in my company?" Sam demanded. "Mary just told me."

I took a step back, legal niceties forgotten as I tried to get out of the range of his temper. "I wasn't sure if he did it or not," I blurted then I winced, realizing how that sounded. "He talked to me about doing it but I wasn't sure—I didn't want to—" Didn't want to what? Intrude on Sam's financial arrangements? Didn't want to let him know that I knew how tight money was for him? Landscape companies had to invest heavily in their stock and a bad year could hurt. Last year was a terrible year for Sam, with vandalism at his greenhouses in southern Minnesota and more vandalism at the two Barlow retail centers in town.

"Let's go into the office." Mary didn't wait for our reply but led the way to the cramped little office tucked into the northeast corner of the building.

It was unchanged from the year before. The battered steel desk took up most of the space, its surface littered with dog-eared catalogs, stacks of paperwork, garden gloves, and seed packets. Two tottery wooden chairs were positioned in front of it and a desktop computer on a metal stand was wedged into the corner. I took one of the 'guest' chairs and watched as Mary took the seat behind the desk—the seat Sam usually used. He hesitated then settled for leaning against a dented file cabinet near the doorway, crossing his arms on his chest and shooting angry looks first at me, then at Mary.

"What's the problem?" I asked, knowing that we

were finally facing down the issues we had avoided for the last few months.

"You know damn well what the problem is. It's you and Charlie, that's what the problem is. The problem is you and him and all that money."

Okay. The gloves were off and it was time to deal with it.

Chapter 6

"It's got nothing to do with Charlie." Mary's voice was loud in the small office. "C.R. Whittington the Second invested two-hundred-and-fifty thousand dollars in the company in January. He plans to invest another quarter-million in the fall." She clasped her hands on the desktop and regarded Sam with a calm, impassive demeanor. I wasn't fooled. I had worked with Mary for a year and knew that inwardly she was quavering. Like me, she hated confrontations and, like me, she avoided them whenever she could.

"You had no right to accept the money," Sam said, his voice low. "We're business partners and I should have been consulted about something that affects the business."

"Isn't Mary the financial manager? I thought you were the Operations Manager?" I struggled to keep my face innocent. "I mean, you were the ops manager before your accident."

"My accident won't affect that," Sam snapped. "I can still manage day-to-day operations at the retail centers and at the growing facilities."

"Can you?" Mary asked, her quiet voice slicing through the tension in the room like a knife homing in on a target.

Sam straightened. He still couldn't put his full weight on his right leg so he stood crookedly, tilted slightly to one side. "I'll be fully recovered in a month or two. I'll be able to—" He stopped when I turned in my chair to stare at him. "What?"

"You know what the doctors said, Sam. You can't go back to being a hands-on manager. You can't do the heavy lifting and manual labor you used to do. "

"So?" He shrugged. "I'll delegate."

Both Mary and I simultaneously said, "Yeah, right," in the same skeptical tone.

"You know as well as I do you can't resist getting in there and helping out," Mary said.

Sam shifted his glare to Mary. "That's not what we're talking about here. We're talking about the Whittington family investing in our company."

"Don't let your problems with Cassie's ex-husband affect your judgment," Mary said. "We need the money, Sam. Our insurance premiums are sky-high after your accident last year and we have to be one-hundred-percent compliant with OSHA regulations this year after that vandalism in the stores. If we aren't, we'll be shut down. Compliance means a lot of remodeling and changes in the way we're doing things. We can't afford to..." She stopped, took a deep breath then said, "We can't afford to have anybody on board who can't pull their weight and more." Her gaze went to me and I saw no sympathy in her light brown eyes. "That means you, too, Cassie. Your accident last year knocked you out of commission as well. You won't be able to do a full range of work in the greenhouse or the store."

I was surprised at the disappointment I felt. I wasn't planning to return to my seasonal job at Barlow's. I had my inheritance to deal with and after I sold the house in Minnetonka, I didn't need the money. Still, it felt odd to be 'let go' like this. I nodded reluctantly. "I understand," I said. "I suppose even with that cash from Charlie's father, you have to be careful."

"No kidding." Mary glanced at the computer. "Whittington's investment means we can afford to upgrade some equipment here and in the greenhouses. We need to replace the sprinkler system and those aren't cheap. Plus..." She looked at Sam. "We need to hire a replacement manager for day-to-day operations. I still want you to help with long-term planning, but you can't be in here all the time, Sam. I need to get someone in and trained. I can't have you butting heads with whoever I get."

Sam's lips tightened. "I suppose you have someone in mind," he said acidly.

Mary met his glare evenly. "I asked Polly Dawson if she would be interested. She's been with us for almost ten years and she has a degree from the University in business and in landscape management. She could be overall general manager, the way you were. We'll keep Tim Jorgenson here as the Pickaway manager and Betty Dunlap at the Roseville store, just like we've done in the past. I'd like you to focus on planning." She gave Sam a conciliatory smile. "We always said we wished we had more time for planning. Well, now you do."

Sam's glare shifted to me. "Sheila said you want to buy out her share in Joe Swenson's botanical research company. I don't suppose that has anything to do with this?"

"Joe needs a partner to replace Mike Peavey so I thought I could buy out that share in Min-Gen Technologies." I glanced nervously at Mary who was doing a credible job of looking surprised. She knew all about my attempts to make the purchase, of course. We had discussed how to get Sam into a research job before Sam and I left for Florida. "Mike was the lead scientist and Joe needs to replace him."

"Lead scientist is just a fancy name for a glad-hander who raises money. Joe was the real brains in the place. I'm not surprised he's looking for someone else to help out." Sam looked suspiciously at Mary. "Did you know about this?"

She shrugged. "Cassie and I kicked the idea around."

"They're working on some exciting stuff," I said hurriedly. "I read all the brochures and talked to Joe. He said he went through Peavey's papers and found some dead ends that look promising now. It's research, Sam. You love doing that kind of stuff. You could—"

Sam broke in. "Sheila told me she'd give me five-hundred-thousand dollars to drop the suit and cede all rights to the azalea to her." I started to protest then he said, "She said that if I would agree to that, she would drop the land dispute."

I sat back, surprised. Sheila inherited the land where Barlow's Nursery was located from her father. She wanted to sell the land, but couldn't as long as Barlow's was in business.

Sam shifted his attention to Mary. "It could all drag on for months. Between the patent lawsuit and our land dispute, we'll be swimming in legal fees. Can the business handle that?"

Mary met his stare steadily. "With the investment capital, we'll be okay. And I'm not too worried about the legal fees."

"That's right." Sam's flat-eyed gaze returned to me. "Charlie's helping us out as a favor to you. So we don't have to worry about legal fees."

"Would you rather he charged full price?" I demanded. Then what he said soaked in. "Wait a minute. Where's she getting that kind of money to buy you off? Just yesterday she wanted me to buy her share in the business. She said she'd negotiate with you, to share the profits from that plant. John made it sound like she needed the money." I remembered John's smug expression when he said, *it will help you support Sam in a way that won't offend him. It's a win-win situation.* The son of a bitch was right, but it pissed me off to hear him say it out loud in that smirky voice of his. "There was a business clause that if one of the partners died, the share could be sold but the partner had the final say on who could purchase it. I've already talked to Joe and he's fine with me buying it."

"You did this for me, didn't you?" Sam crossed his arms on his chest but I saw that they trembled. Was it rage or exhaustion? He raised his voice in a crude mimicry of Sheila's throaty contralto. "If he can't make his own way in the world, you'll buy it for him, won't you? What is it, pity because of the accident? She was driving and now you're crippled so now she'll support you for life?"

There was just enough truth in his words to make me jump to my feet, so angry I could barely see straight. "Pity has nothing to do with it," I spat.

"Cassie didn't cause the accident," Mary said, standing up and leaning on the desk. "The car was sabotaged." She looked from Sam to me. "Why is she so anxious to get that patent lawsuit settled? Does she know how well the plant is doing?"

"Maybe she knows how hard it is to prove who developed it in the first place," Sam said bitterly. "Mike and I worked on the genetics of that plant almost a decade ago. It's going to be hard to prove in court that he used my research for the development of a new azalea strain." Sam went to the doorway and paused. "This isn't over, Cassie. Just because you bought a botanical research company, it doesn't mean I'm going to work there."

"I know how you love research." I went to him, putting a hand on his arm. "It's a match made in heaven. Look, I've inherited some money. Why shouldn't I invest it how I see fit?'

He shook my hand off. "This isn't an investment. It's a bribe." His eyes narrowed and he examined my face intently. "Is it guilt? Is that why you're doing it?"

I glared at him. "Yes, I feel guilty, but not about you." I was surprised how easy it was to lie. "I'm guilty about Joe Swenson and what happened to him last year."

Sam looked momentarily ashamed. "You're right. It's been a hard year for him."

"Exactly. He's got enough going on in his life. He shouldn't have to worry about his business." I started to reach for Sam but stopped, not anxious to be rebuffed again. "It's the same with you, Sam. I know you love research and with your injury...This seemed like a great way for me to help two people at the same time."

Sam stared at the floor, obviously considering my words. Then he raised his head and looked at me, his eyes cold. "Do you expect me to quit my life and what I love to do just to change and do what you want me to do?"

Anger started to bubble up inside me. "I expect you to be an adult and accept the fact that your life might have changed."

He stared at me for a long, considering minute. "Yeah. Maybe it has. It just makes me wonder what other secrets you're keeping from me."

I considered and discarded several replies. None were totally truthful. I changed tactics. "You're too stubborn to take help when it's offered."

"If I need help, I'll ask."

We stared at each other for a long minute then I said, "I think I'll leave now. You obviously don't want to talk rationally about this."

He shrugged. "Fine. I'll walk home when I'm done."

"Fine."

Mary started to speak but I held up a hand. "I'll talk to you later." I left before either she or Sam could see the tears that were starting.

I drove the short distance to my townhouse, hands trembling on the steering wheel. What was it Janelle said? Something about facing change. I looked back at the landscape center receding into the distance behind me. Everything was on the table now between me and Sam. Time to face the future.

I just wasn't sure what I'd find there.

****

Livvie looked at me sympathetically. "He's being childish," she agreed.

We were sipping a cup of coffee, sitting in my kitchen on Wednesday morning. Livvie showed up at ten, sweeping into my home with her tousled ash-blonde hair and her bright yellow sweater and stone-washed jeans, making me feel as though a ray of sunlight had decided to visit me and disperse the gloomy atmosphere that permeated my modest little townhome.

"Did you check the updates I put on my Facebook page?" She glanced at my Blackberry, sitting in its charging cradle. "I added some photos of my dress and the flowers."

"Sorry. I haven't been online today." I sipped my coffee, my mind in a whirl. Sam didn't come home the night before. He called me in the late afternoon to inform me that he and Polly were going out to dinner, to 'discuss the transition.' I went out to get groceries and when I came home his ancient Jeep was gone and he had left a note saying he would be late and might just sleep on the couch at the Roseville store, where he and Polly were going to 'go over the inventory and talk about future planning.'

Polly was pert, pretty, and petite, a thirty-six year old dynamo of energy and competence. She had worked at Barlow's since graduating with a Master's in Botany from the University of Minnesota, a degree I know that Sam coveted. Research botany was his first love and one I hoped he would return to.

At this point, though, I was just hoping he would return to me. I spent a sleepless night, tossing around in the bed then finally got up at dawn and went for a long walk. When I came home Sam still wasn't there, so I did what I always did when I was upset: I baked. The fruits of my labor now sat on the kitchen table.

I watched Houdini and Truffles lounge in the morning sunlight. The two cats appeared none the worse for my absence in Florida. Livvie had stopped by daily to feed them and they now regarded her with benign appreciation, probably expecting a treat or two before she left. I wished I could have such a savoir faire attitude.

I heard a car in the driveway and looked out to see Charlie's navy blue Jaguar. "Just what I need," I grumbled. "With my luck Sam will come home and Charlie will be here. Why the hell isn't he at work?"

"I suppose the senior partners in the firm want him to remain out of sight until John's murder is solved. The story in today's newspaper wasn't good publicity." Livvie twisted in her seat to peer out the window.

I answered as I walked to the front door, just a few steps from where we sat. "Will the paper do a follow-up story to report that Charlie's no longer under suspicion?"

"They probably won't. Let's face it—a rich guy implicated in murder is big news."

I jerked open the front door before Charlie could knock. "What brings you out here on this beautiful Wednesday morning?" Like the previous day he wore jeans but today he wore a navy golf shirt with

Pinehurst CC embroidered on the breast.

Charlie came inside, looking around warily. "Where're the escape artists?"

I led the way into the kitchen and gestured to the resident felines, who barely flicked their tails in greeting. "They no longer try to escape, not since someone tossed a cherry bomb in my house last Halloween and scared the poop out of them. Have a seat." I went to get him a mug of coffee, skirting the two critters under discussion.

"A cherry bomb that almost hurt Janelle," Charlie said darkly. He jerked out one of my faux oak chairs from under the faux oak table and plopped down. "Hey, Livvie. I should have known you'd be here. Are you going over wedding stuff?" He tugged at his shirt. "I'm going out to the club later on to meet Dan Fairchild for a quick round of golf."

"I'm just getting caught up with Cassie." Livvie sipped her coffee and regarded her older brother with curiosity. "While it's nice to use Twitter and Facebook to stay in touch with the younger members of our clan, I'm still old-fashioned enough to enjoy a face-to-face talk now and again." She smiled innocently at him. "Speaking of bombs—that was quite the bomb you dropped on Cassie yesterday."

"That's why I stopped by. She and I need to talk," Charlie said, taking the mug from me. "In private."

"Bullshit." Livvie took another cookie from the tray in the middle of the table. "There's nothing private in our family. You're going to be a father, Charlie. How do you feel about that?"

He watched me as I resumed my seat across the table from him. "Surprised as hell," he admitted. "I'm fifty-three years old. I don't know a damn thing about raising a kid."

"I suppose Janelle will have to quit work," I said. "She'll probably get a nanny."

Charlie leaned back. "I never thought of that."

"I wonder how she feels about all this," Livvie said. "I mean, there she is with an up-and-coming legal career and all of a sudden she's pregnant. And she's not that young. I wonder how it feels to be starting a family at—what is she—thirty-five?"

"Thirty-six," Charlie said. "I never thought about that."

"Of course you didn't," I said. "I'm sure it never crossed your mind."

"Raising kids can't be that hard," Livvie said. "Becky's done it. Even John's done it and his kids appear to have turned out okay." She frowned. "Although I have to admit, Matthew sometimes gives me the creeps."

"Did you ever want kids, Livvie?" I asked curiously.

She picked up her spoon and bounced it against the placemat. "I didn't want to have children with Kenneth. It was bad enough that he abused me. I couldn't expose a child to that."

It was the first time she spoke openly about her asshole husband who died almost ten years earlier. I briefly put my hand over hers, her simple engagement ring from T.J. a small lump against my palm. "You and T.J. are going to have a great life together." After all, I reasoned, they had so much in common. Both were recovering alcoholics and both had faced down marital tragedy in their lives. They now jointly owned La Suzette du Paris, an exclusive restaurant on the shores of Lake Minnetonka where T.J. presided as *chef de cuisine*. Livvie had assumed the role of restaurant manager and she seemed to be thriving in it.

"How do you feel, Charlie?" I asked softly. "Not just about Janelle, but about John?"

I watched as he analyzed my question. His face, so rugged and handsome, relaxed and I saw a gleam of excitement in his eyes. "Scared and nervous about the baby." He smiled wryly. "And about John, too. I know I should feel grief, but all I keep thinking is, 'isn't this like John, to screw us up even in his death.'"

Livvie nodded. "I know. I avoided him as much as I could. He and Diane were acting so oddly lately." Her eyes took on a faraway look. "I keep trying to remember John when we were young, but even then I didn't much care for him. I suppose if I feel any grief, I feel sorry that I didn't care for him. Does that make sense?"

I nodded. "I know. I feel the same way." I thought about her words. "What do you mean, he and Diane were acting oddly?"Monday was the first time I had spoken with John face-to-face in months and I was so mad at him, I didn't notice any differences.

"He was even more high-strung than usual. I think he was having financial problems." Livvie's face, usually so placid and happy, took on a grim look. "And I think he was cheating on Diane. Believe me, I recognize the symptoms. Kenneth did it to me all the time. Diane looked like she knew, too. Or at least she suspected."

I tried to imagine dull, narrow-minded, critical John in a passionate, clandestine affair, and failed. "Who would have him?"

Charlie snorted with laughter. "There are all kinds of gold-diggers in the world."

"Now just a minute," I snapped. "I wish you'd get past that nonsense. You're in my house and you're not going to criticize Sam while you're sitting there drinking my coffee." I glared at my ex-husband, my face getting hot with anger.

He held up a hand. "Sorry. I didn't mean Sam. I meant Sheila Peavey."

I almost dropped my coffee mug. "Sheila? And

John?" I looked from Charlie to Livvie, who nodded agreement. "That's not possible. She's—and he—and—But why?"

"Maybe the usual? Sex?" Charlie suggested.

"Oh, please. Sheila Peavey doesn't do anything unless it benefits her. How was she using John? She offered to buy Sam off last year with half-a-million dollars. I wondered where she got that money. Was it from John?"

"Nope. Her dead husband's estate," Charlie said with authority. "She inherited three million dollars from him. I checked when she started pursuing the contract dispute with Sam and his sister. She invested with Father, too, remember? His holdings have remained solid, although they've taken a beating in this economy."

"If John was having financial worries, why didn't he just borrow from her?" I still couldn't wrap my head around the idea of John and Sheila Peavey in an affair. I could easily imagine Sheila sneaking around to meet John, but I couldn't imagine John indulging in shady behavior. He was so damn prim and proper. John, in the throes of passion? Not imaginable.

"If John had financial problems, a few million wouldn't help him," Charlie pointed out. "One of his homes sells for a million or more. I happen to know that he had several that probably won't be finished because buyers have backed out of their contracts."

We all silently considered it then Livvie pointed her spoon at Charlie. "Enough about them. When will you and Janelle get married?" She glanced quickly at me. "There's room in my wedding for more. I'm not one of those diva brides who want to hog the spotlight. The more the merrier."

Charlie missed her inquiring look in my direction, which was just as well. He had definite ideas about Sam and me, most of them negative. I long ago quit arguing with him about it. "Thanks, but Janelle might have other ideas. It's an accident, you know. The pregnancy. We didn't plan it. It just...happened. She wants to have the baby and I...well, I used to think abortion was an option but now that it's my baby..." He smiled wryly. "My thoughts changed."

"Janelle told me it was an accident," I said. "When she was puking in the bathroom."

He winced. "Morning sickness. It's been really bad. I know that sounds like bullshit, but it was an accident."

"Bullshit?" I sipped my coffee. "Who said it was bullshit?"

"John did." Charlie looked around my kitchen, so plebian compared to the elaborate kitchen in the family home in Minnetonka or the gleaming masterpiece in his condo. "That's one of the things he and I argued about on Sunday, when I told the family."

"Why should he be accusing you of bullshit?" I tried to puzzle it all out. "I mean, what does it matter to John if Janelle is pregnant or not?"

"Inheritance," Livvie said immediately.

"Inherit...Oh." I stared at Charlie. "Was that it? Was there some kind of inheritance thing going on with your father?"

Charlie avoided my look by bending over to rub Houdini's belly, an action that elicited rumbling purrs from my portly yellow feline. "John has always felt our father favored me and the girls over him. He was afraid that if I had a child, then Father would favor us in his will."

I snorted derisively. "The old man will outlive everyone. Why worry about it?"

Charlie straightened, his deep green eyes perplexed. "I said as much. John said something weird, something like 'the knowledge of a thing is worth money in the bank.' I didn't know what he meant. I was more concerned about his allegations against Janelle. He made it sound like she was sleeping with me—that she got pregnant—in order to force me to get you to change your mind about Grandy's inheritance and share with John." He stopped, his mouth thinning into an angry line. "I almost hit him then."

"I probably would have hit him," Livvie said. "Long before that." She regarded Charlie with exasperated affection. "You didn't answer my question about marriage. Are you and Janelle getting married?"

"I asked her and she said no."

I exchanged a look with Livvie. "Well, duh," she said cheerfully. "Obviously she doesn't want to marry you just because she's pregnant."

"I don't know how to convince her I want to marry her anyway."

"Do you?" I asked. "Or do you just feel obligated?"

He didn't answer for a long minute then he looked me straight in the eye. "How do you feel about marrying Sam? Don't you feel obligated to marry him after that accident last year? How will he get along without you?"

We stared at each other and I saw all my guilt, worry, and insecurity mirrored in his eyes. I loved Charlie and I loved Sam.

What was I going to do?

Chapter 7

A soft tone chimed from Charlie's shirt pocket. "Excuse me." He pulled out his Blackberry and checked the display. "I need to take this, it's Billy Armstrong."

Saved by the bell. My knotted stomach relaxed. I joined Livvie at my kitchen counter, giving Charlie some privacy. "I still can't believe John and Sheila had an affair."

"Diane said something to me when you and Sam were hurt last year. Remember how she came out to the hospital and sat with you? And how she helped me get this place all organized so you and Sam could come home?"

I nodded, remembering my surprise at seeing my ex-sister-in-law sitting by my bedside as I recovered from a nightmarish car accident. She also helped retrofit my townhome to accommodate a man in a wheelchair and a woman with fractured ribs and a broken arm. It was as surprising as the truce between Livvie and her sister Becky. They had been at odds for years but my accident seemed to bring all of the family back together.

"Diane commented how nice it was that you had found such a great guy in Sam." When Livvie saw my shocked look, she smiled wryly. "I know, I thought the same thing, but she was sincere. She said something like, 'just think, if Cassie and Charlie had stayed married, they probably would have been at each others' throats by now. They would have been married almost as long as John and me and look at us' or something to that effect."

I considered it. She was right. Charlie and I married almost thirty years earlier, when I was only twenty. What would it be like, to be married to him all these years? We stayed friends after our divorce, but to have one man as my lover, one man as my social companion? I couldn't imagine it.

"That brings me to another topic," Livvie said, glancing from me to Charlie, who was now standing at my dining room window, staring at the bright spring morning outside. "About my wedding. I want you and Charlie to sing."

"Sure," I said immediately. "But he's out on bail for murder. He might not be available for the wedding." I tried to sound facetious but it fell flat.

Livvie put a hand on my arm as though to jerk the words back into my body. "Don't even think it. The wedding is on Friday and you and Charlie will be there." She spoke as if saying it would make it so. Perhaps in her mind it would.

"Of course." I patted her hand then turned, tripping over Truffles who had silently padded over to watch as I neared the Magical Cabinet of Kitty Kibble and the counter where the Catnip Cat Cookies were 'hidden' in a canister.

"You know why I chose Friday?" she asked. "It's the anniversary of when I entered rehab last year. That's when I met T.J."

"An auspicious day." This time I wasn't being facetious. The day she met T.J., Livvie's healing truly began.

"So here are the songs," Livvie said, reaching across the kitchen island to grab her purse, which she had plunked on the countertop when she entered. "I'm sure you know them. They're staples at a lot of weddings. Of course, this one isn't, really, but I know you guys can do it. Didn't you sing it at Charlene Martin's wedding?" Livvie forced a chuckle as she slid a folded piece of paper across the counter to me. "I guess it didn't help her, she got divorced then married then divorced again. I heard she's dating a man ten years younger than her. Maybe she'll want you to sing it again. I remember how great it was when you and Charlie sang it. I always swore that if I married someone I really loved, not an asshole like Kenneth, then I'd have you and Charlie sing that song at my wedding."

Charlie and I sang at a lot of weddings through the years, but I didn't remember Charlene Martin's. I vaguely remembered that she was a sorority sister of Livvie's, which meant the wedding took place somewhere in my antediluvian past. "As long as we remember the words, I'm sure we can sing it."

She thrust the paper at me as Charlie turned to look at us. He smiled and my tense shoulders started to relax. He was so handsome, with his black hair tipped with white, his deep dimples, and his warm, laughing green eyes. Charlie *always* made me smile and if he could smile like that, so open and honest, then I knew whatever Armstrong was telling him couldn't be bad. I opened the paper, glanced down at the words on the page then dropped the paper on the counter in order to deal with Houdini, who had joined his foster sister in pressing on my feet, their eyes imploring me for the yummy treats in the kitty cookie jar.

"Here you go," I said, scooping out the little nuggets then bending over to deposit the fish-shaped crunchies on the floor. "Not too many because—" Suddenly the import of what I had just read hit me. I straightened so fast several treats went flying out of the canister in my hand. "No way, Livvie," I said, dropping the ceramic fish jar on the counter with a rattling thud. "No way." I snatched up the piece of paper. "I can't sing this song at your wedding." I pushed the sheet away from me and leaned back, crossing my arms against my T-shirted chest. "No."

"But you and Charlie sang it before."

I ran a hand through my untidy hair, exasperated. I loved Livvie dearly but there were times when she could piss off the Pope. This was one of them. "Charlie and I were married when we sang that duet. We're not married now."

"So?" She smiled, trying to look innocent. I knew Livvie, though. This was part of her Master Plan to force me to finally choose between Sam and Charlie—in public, at her wedding.

"No." I shook my head. "People will get the wrong idea."

"People? Or Charlie?" She leaned over to rub Truffles' inky black head. The petite little female kitty replied in kind, rubbing against Livvie's legs. "You know how Charlie is. He's never been able to move on since you two got divorced."

"That's not my fault," I pointed out. "Now that Janelle is pregnant, he'd better damn well start moving on. He has other obligations. I won't sing that song in a duet."

"Then how about as a solo?" She stared at me imploringly. "Please, Cassie. I love that song and I want it at my wedding. I'm so happy. It's such a perfect song for T.J. and me. Please."

"That's a relief," Charlie said, tucking his phone back into his shirt pocket and joining us at the kitchen counter.

"What is?" He looked so gleeful I knew something momentous must have happened. I momentarily shelved the worry about singing Stevie Nicks' *Beauty and the Beast* in public with my ex-husband and focused on Charlie, who smiled happily.

"Sheila Peavey is in the hot seat now. Her fingerprints were found on the nail gun, too."

"Well, duh. I knew that. I saw her pick it up."

"I didn't." Charlie frowned. "Matthew picked it up but I didn't see Sheila."

I tried to remember but my memories were jumbled up with the pain I felt when I hit the fireplace. "You can't just pick up one of those things and aim it, can you? I mean, it's not like a real gun, right? She couldn't have stood on the other side of the room, aimed, and fired. The thing isn't that accurate, is it?"

We all contemplated the idea. "I don't know," Charlie finally said. "I know it weighs a lot. I was surprised when I picked it up. I almost dropped it. I was lucky the safety switch was on or I would have shot myself in the foot." He nudged the folded paper I dropped on the counter. "I'm just glad the cops have someone else to focus on for now. What's this?"

"It's the set list for Livvie's wedding," I said, keeping my voice neutral.

"It's about time," he said, unfolding it. "I've been bugging her to give it to me so we can practice, but she kept saying she wanted to wait and ask you personally..." His voice trailed away when he saw the songs listed. "Well, look at that. We sang that song at Charlene Martin's wedding. It was our second wedding anniversary."

I rolled my eyes. Trust Charlie to have 20-20 memory for the times we sang together as well as anniversaries, birthdays, and other events. He was good that way.

He looked up at me, his green eyes fringed by dark lashes laughing at the memory. "We lived in that apartment over on Grand, remember? The one with the gold striped wallpaper in the bathroom and that claw-foot tub?" He waggled his eyebrows, looking like a mischievous boy. "We had some good times in that tub."

"I'm not singing that song in a duet with you," I snapped, making a grab for the paper.

He relinquished the paper, his eyes narrowing slightly, the only sign of his evaporating humor. "Of course not. I mean, heaven forbid. Someone might get the wrong idea."

I blew out an exasperated sigh. "Yeah," I said evenly, glaring at him. "They might."

A frosty silence enfolded us until Livvie laughed nervously. "We'll figure out something. I have to admit, I can hardly wait to have it all done. I've been planning this for months. Have you got your costume yet, Cassie?" She looked at Charlie. "It's so not fair that all men have to do is rent the penguin suit but women have to try on clothes until they find the right outfit for the right occasion."

I nodded agreement. "It *is* like suiting up for a costume party, isn't it? I need to go shopping. I'm pretty sure I don't have anything that fits." In the past three years I had lost almost seventy pounds, taking me back to my college weight of one hundred-and-twenty. I hadn't replenished my wardrobe fully since I seldom needed dressy clothing anymore.

"Why does it become such a production?" Charlie grumbled.

"In theory, it's one of the biggest days in a woman's life. And in a man's, of course. But a lot of men don't see it that way, I guess." I vividly remembered my wedding. It was the social event of the season not just because the oldest Whittington boy was getting married but because we stood on the beach where Charlie's mother was murdered years before and exchanged our vows in front of the setting sun. Charlie and I left the party on a cabin cruiser sailing off into the sunset, trailing tin cans on strings bouncing on the waves behind us.

Charlie covered my hand with his. "I'm sorry, Cassie."

I looked at him in surprise. "For what?"

"For springing the news about Janelle's pregnancy like that."

"You didn't spring it," Livvie murmured. "She did."

Charlie frowned. "I wanted to tell Cassie about it, but Janelle beat me to it." He squeezed my fingers. "We need to talk."

I gently removed my hand from his. "There's nothing to talk about, Charlie. It concerns you and Janelle. It doesn't concern you and me." Neither he nor I had been serious about anyone since our divorce decades before, but I made the first steps by having Sam move in with me. Now Charlie faced a monumental change in his life. "Charlie, you need to think about what you really feel," I said, struggling to articulate what I'd been considering for months. "We're both so tied to our past, our childhood, as well as our adult past. We went through an experience few people ever face. No one can understand it. Livvie was just a baby and John and Becky were so young. You and I were the oldest ones and we knew what was going on."

"It's not just that, Cassie." He jammed his hands into his jeans pockets, hunching his shoulders as though to ward off blows, even metaphorical ones. "We know each other so well. We have so much in common." He looked at me, his eyes puzzled. "You're part of my life, Cassie. I can't walk away from that."

I glanced at Livvie, who stayed frozen in place, her eyes darting from Charlie to me. I decided it didn't matter if she heard. There really were no secrets in the Whittington family. I thought fleetingly of John in an affair and reconsidered that idea but shelved it for later mulling. "Moving on and loving someone else doesn't mean we let go of our past. We're putting it into a special place, behind us. We're making room for the future, with other people."

"Is that why you and Sam are getting married?" he asked, his voice low and husky.

This was a minefield I didn't want to negotiate. "We're talking about it," I said evasively. "But we haven't come to any conclusions yet. Like you and Janelle, I want to make sure I'm making decisions for the right reasons."

"I love her," he said softly. "But it's not the same as when I loved you. It's all different somehow. I'm not sure if I love her forever, like I do you."

I restrained an impatient sigh. "You can love me forever and you can love Janelle. There's no limit on love, Charlie."

"For heaven's sake," Livvie said impatiently. "Grow up, Charlie."

He shot her an angry glare. "Thanks for the understanding."

"I understand more than you know," she snapped. "Do you think it was easy for me to trust T.J.? Do you think it was easy to put my past behind me and face the future? I had a crappy first marriage and because of it I crawled into a bottle. I didn't come out for years and when I did, it was scary. I'm still scared that things might go wrong. You love Cassie because it's safe, it's a known thing. Love with Janelle is scary and unknown and let's face it, you're not a young man any more. It's tough for older people to take chances."

I turned away to hide a smile when I saw the stubborn look in Charlie's eyes. Livvie knew exactly which buttons to push and she did it so well. Would it work on him? Until I met Sam, I had no good reason to move on, to put Charlie in my past, behind me. He and I had a comfortable relationship and

Livvie was right—the future with a stranger was a scary thing. But I trusted Sam and I was ready to make that commitment…maybe.

I heard the distinctive rumble of an ancient car muffler. Sam was back. Charlie heard it, too. "I'd better be going." He started for the front door.

Livvie took her bag from the counter and followed him. "You'll consider it, won't you?" she asked, looking at the pages of song lyrics.

"I'll consider it," I conceded, anxiety about her wedding replaced by anxiety about Sam. I got to the door just as Charlie opened it.

Sam was reaching for the doorknob, hand extended. "Don't leave on my account," he said, his voice cool. He wore the same clothes as the previous day—faded jeans and a dark denim jacket but he had changed his white shirt for a black T-shirt. I wondered fleetingly where he got it. All of his clothing was at my house and the rest of the contents of his apartment was in storage or wedged into my spare bedroom.

"I need to get going," Charlie said, brushing past Sam. He was several inches taller than Sam and after months of relative inactivity, Charlie was now more muscular appearing than Sam, too. The sight made me realize, more than anything, how Sam had changed.

Sam turned to me. "Sorry. I didn't mean to scare him off." We both watched as Charlie strode to his Jag and jerked open the driver's door.

"I don't think it was you." I started to close my front door but paused when I saw Charlie stare at me.

"I'm sorry," he called out. "I'll talk to you later."

"Talk to Janelle," I called back. "Don't bother talking to me." I closed the door more firmly than I meant to.

Sam jerked theatrically. "Looks like I

interrupted something. Should I leave and come back?"

"Don't be an idiot," I snapped. "You live here. Or at least you used to. Where were you last night?" The words came out far more abruptly than I meant.

Sam paused in mid-step. "I told you. I slept at the store." He smiled at Livvie, who stood in the doorway that separated the foyer from the kitchen. "Hey, there's the blushing bride. Are you here to talk about the wedding? What does T.J. have planned for the wedding dinner?"

"He won't tell me. All he'll say is that it's fit for a queen." Livvie slung her purse over her shoulder. "Did you tell him yet?" she asked me. "About what Armstrong told Charlie?"

"Tell me what?" Sam shot me an inquisitive look.

"Your ex-wife is implicated in John's murder." Livvie smiled smugly when she saw Sam's shocked look. "Yep, her fingerprints are on the murder weapon."

A frown replaced his shocked expression. "She was there. Maybe she just picked it up." He moved to one side as Livvie took her place by the front door.

"I'll call you later," she murmured. "We'll talk about the songs. You'll sing them on Friday at the rehearsal, won't you?"

I opened my mouth to protest but didn't have a chance. "She hasn't sung a note all winter. She'll need all the practice she can get." Sam put an arm around me, smiling.

"Sure," I mumbled. "We'll talk."

"Please. Consider it." Livvie shot me an imploring look then sighed. "Okay. I'll talk to you later." Then she slipped outside, car keys in hand.

"What was that all about?" Sam asked, dropping his arm and walking toward the kitchen. I followed, curiosity warring with dread about his absence the previous night.

Houdini's ears perked up at the sight of his best buddy. "Hey, guys," Sam muttered, giving Houdini a fast back rub. "Livvie sure kept you well fed while we were gone." The big cat promptly flopped down and rolled over, doing his Superman-in-the-air imitation on the throw rug near the table.

I decided to take my cue from Sam's casual approach. "Did you get a lot done last night?" I asked, going to the sink to rinse out my mug. "Coffee?"

"We need to talk."

My stomach dropped. I hated it when men said *We need to talk*. It was always something unpleasant. I put my mug into the sink and turned to face Sam. He was sitting at the table, leaning forward to regard the cookies and avoiding looking at me.

"About what?" I asked, leaning back on the sink. I wasn't sure my legs would support me on a walk across the short space that separated us. First Charlie and now Sam.

A succession of emotions and thoughts rolled through me, one after the other, surprising me with their intensity. I was relieved to see him, pissed off he'd been gone all night, worried that he wanted to leave me, relieved that we were finally talking, and anxious to avoid the talk—all the conflicting feelings I experienced in the last twenty-four hours washed over me like a Florida tide.

"My future," Sam said. He nudged the cookie plate away from him then looked at me, his dark eyes serious, almost grim. "Our future." I started to speak but he continued, not giving me a chance. "I've known you for a year now, Cassie. We've been through a lot together, not the least of which was a car accident that almost killed us both." He looked at me, his head tilted to one side, his thick white-gray hair curling slightly around his ears and at the nape of his neck. "I love you. I don't tell you that enough." His eyes narrowed. "Neither of us says that enough."

My face got hot, but I knew he was right. I nodded mutely.

"This whole thing with Charlie and Janelle made me realize that we've been in a sort of holding pattern since the accident. Last year we focused on helping Livvie and T.J. with the mess they were in then we focused on getting well. We let everything else slip." Sam pushed back his chair and joined me, standing facing me with his back against the kitchen island and two feet of kitchen floor separating us. "We need to focus on us again. We need to think about the future."

"I've been doing that," I said softly. "I've been trying to, at least."

He nodded, his lips twisting in a wry smile. "I know. I've been too..." He looked away from me, toward the front door. "Charlie is hard to compete with."

I drew in a long breath. "You're not competing, Sam."

He ignored my disclaimer. "Thinking about Charlie made me think about my future. I talked to Joe Swenson. I'm not promising anything, but I'm willing to consider it. You might be right." Sam stared at the tile floor and my small black cat who sat so patiently, watching us both.

He looked so woebegone I felt no triumph at my little victory. "I'm glad," I managed to say around the flare of hope I felt. "I think it's a perfect fit for you."

"I want to make a change, Cassie. If we get married, I want to bring more to the table than a job as the owner/manager of a retail center." Sam's dark eyes met mine and I saw his insecurity in their depths.

"That doesn't matter and you know it."

"How did you feel when you and Charlie were married? It bugged you that you didn't have any money of your own, didn't it?" He smiled mirthlessly.

I silently cursed his astuteness. "It's not the same. Even if it was, it wouldn't matter."

He nodded. "And I'm sure Charlie said the same thing and how did that make you feel?"

He was right, damn it, so I changed the subject. "I think the research gig would be good to have an alternative in case you can't do your old job."

"I know I can't manage it. I've already talked with Polly. She'll take over as manager. I'll have to train her on some aspects of the job, but she'll be fine." He picked up the paper Livvie left behind. "What's this?"

I sighed with relief.

At least he was considering the idea of a desk job. If I could get him interested in the research job, then he might find a new niche.

He waggled the paper at me and I said, "It's the songs Livvie wants Charlie and me to sing at her wedding."

"*Beauty and the Beast*?" He looked at me, puzzled. "From the cartoon?"

"From Stevie Nicks."

He looked thoughtful then he nodded. "Yeah. I guess that's okay for a wedding."

He probably didn't know the lyrics well, and even if he did, he might not see how it could be awkward for me to sing it in a duet with Charlie. I decided not to pursue it further. I moved forward as Sam opened his arms to enfold me. He kissed me, his lips lingering on mine.

My phone on the kitchen counter rang. "Let the machine pick up," he suggested, his hands roving over my back to settle on my butt.

"Good idea," I concurred.

Charlie's voice echoed in the living room where my answering machine sat. "Cassie, it's me, it's Charlie. I just got a call. Janelle's in the hospital. She's had an accident. She's at Regions Hospital. Meet me there, will you?"

Chapter 8

By the time we got to the hospital, a million scenarios came and went in my brain. We spent a frantic few minutes trying to find Charlie in the emergency room then we were sent to another part of the hospital where someone pointed us in the right direction.

Charlie was pacing around a small empty waiting room outside a door labeled *Diagnostic Services*. A glass window framed a bored-looking receptionist where she sat behind a counter. The door next to her obviously led into the innards of the hospital.

Charlie stared at me blankly and I swear he didn't know who I was. Then he shook his head, his thoughts returning from whatever gloomy place they had visited and he gave me a tentative smile. "Thanks for coming. I didn't know what to do."

Sam gestured to a grouping of chairs around a table. "Tell us what happened." He sat down and I went with him. After a brief hesitation Charlie took a chair opposite us.

"Billy Armstrong called me again. A friend of his on the police force contacted him. Janelle was crossing the street and a car came out of nowhere and almost hit her."

Almost. I breathed a sigh of relief. "Where was she?"

"Around the corner from the office. She was on her way to lunch with friends. They saw everything that happened. One of the men with her pulled her to safety. He got hit and she ended up tripping then falling into a lamppost. The other people called the ambulance and the police and..." Charlie looked past me and jumped to his feet when the door next to the receptionist's window opened.

A young man in a white shirt, necktie, and slacks emerged, a suit coat slung over one shoulder. His shirt was stained and wrinkled and he limped. I glanced at his right leg and saw a tear in the fabric of his suit pants. When he saw Charlie, though, he hurried across the space to us. "I'm sorry, Charlie. I grabbed her but the damn car was going so fast. I tried to get her to the sidewalk but I hit the mailbox and—"

Charlie grabbed the man's hand, pumping it feverishly. "You saved her life, Carl. No apology necessary. Did you see her back there?" He looked to the doorway again. "They took her to ultrasound or something. I didn't really listen, the doctor said something about making sure—" He broke off when the door opened again.

Janelle emerged looking pale but composed, a large black purse over her left shoulder and a manila folder clutched in her right hand. Her black hair, normally in a tight, businesslike bun, was still in a bun but it was looser, with wisps of long hair fluttering around her face. She wore what I thought of as the BBB uniform—Basic Business Black— black skirt, a black jacket and white blouse and black pumps. Like her companion she was wrinkled and dirty and one jacket sleeve was torn.

When she saw us she stopped, her blue eyes wide. "You didn't have to come," she said, glancing from Sam, to me then finally to Charlie. "I'm okay. It's—" Her next words were lost as Charlie strode across the room and enfolded her in a hug. With a little cry she rested her head on his shoulder and I glimpsed tears rolling down her cheeks.

Sam and I approached them slowly, giving them some privacy. "Oh, God," I whispered. "Is she okay? What about..." I gulped, not sure if others in Janelle's office knew about the baby.

"I asked the doctor and they said she was fine," Carl said softly. "The baby's not hurt." He stuck out a hand. "Carl Madison. I work with Janelle."

I took his hand and gave it a brisk shake. "Cassie Whittington. Janelle's my lawyer."

"Whitting..." His voice trailed away when he looked at Charlie and I saw him make the connections in his head. "Oh. Yeah." He looked at Charlie and Janelle. "I'm just glad she wasn't hurt worse. And I'm glad the baby is, well, you know."

"Not baby," Janelle said, pulling away from Charlie and fumbling a handkerchief from her jacket pocket. "Babies." She suddenly smiled, looking radiant. "It's twins." She put a hand on her gently swollen abdomen. "They're twins."

Sam laughed softly. "When you go in for motherhood, you go all the way, don't you? Is everything okay? No problems from the accident?"

"It wasn't an accident." Carl shook his head adamantly. "That car was aiming for us."

"Who else was in the group?" Charlie asked. He kept his arm around Janelle and she leaned against him, the hand holding with the hankie trembling. I was surprised she could stay on her feet. Good heavens, she was almost hit by a car then she found she was going to have twins. That was a triple whammy.

"Why does it matter?" Sam asked.

"If there was a criminal lawyer in the group, it

might make sense for someone to try to hurt them. But..." Charlie's voice trailed off when he saw Carl shaking his head negatively.

"Just some folks from the Contract Division. I'm telling you, somebody was aiming for us. Someone was aiming for Janelle."

"Holy crap," I muttered. "If John was alive I'd suspect him, but he's dead."

"John was such an asshole, he'd wish ill of anybody Charlie loved." Sam put an arm around me and gave me a little shake. "Even my little woman, here."

Janelle laughed, the happy sound making us all relax. I looked at Sam gratefully.

Charlie's arm tightened around her. "Are you okay to go? Do the doctors need to talk to you some more?"

"The test results will be forwarded on to my doctor." She shyly held out the folder she held. "Look."

Charlie flipped open the folder and stared at the papers inside. I peered over his arm at the fuzzy gray images. "Is that..." He looked at her, his green eyes wide. "Is that them?"

She nodded, pointing to a paler gray spot. "That's an arm and that's a leg. The technician said they were in the perfect ying-yang position."

I tilted my head, trying to see what she was seeing but gave up when I saw Sam shake his head slightly. If Janelle thought she was seeing babies, then that was all that mattered.

Carl cleared his throat. "I hate to say this, but I should get back to the office."

"Do you need a ride?" I asked. "Charlie should take Janelle home. She needs to rest."

"I've got my car," he said, gesturing vaguely down the hall. "I followed behind when the ambulance brought Janelle." He looked at Charlie. "I wanted to make sure she was okay."

"Thanks, Carl." Janelle touched his arm. "I appreciate everything you did."

The younger man patted her hand awkwardly. "Not a problem. I'll let people at the office know you're okay and you're taking some time off."

"I'll call in when I get a chance." Janelle watched Charlie as he moved to one side to speak with him in a low voice. "I'm lucky Carl was there," she murmured, looking down once again at the pictures in her hands. "I don't know what would have happened if he hadn't pulled me aside." Her hands trembled along with her voice.

I put an arm around her. "You're okay now. What you need to do is go home, put up your feet, and let Charlie wait on you. Once those kids are born you won't have much chance to sit down and relax."

She smiled tremulously. "You're right." Her eyes followed Charlie as he and Carl talked. "I wonder what's going to happen."

Charlie turned to face us as Carl walked towards the exit. Charlie's eyes met mine. I saw confusion, love, and resignation when he smiled at me.

Sam saw it, too. He moved to block Janelle's view of Charlie, tapping the folder. "I can tell you what's going to happen. Chaos, craziness and fun."

"You're probably right." Janelle looked past him to Charlie and her smile widened. "I'll be able to manage it as long as..."

"Ready to go?" Charlie came to a stop next to me. "I need to talk to Cassie then we'll get lunch and I can take you home to get some rest. Sound good?"

"That sounds great." Janelle leaned forward and I hugged her briefly. "Thanks for coming, both of you." She looked past me to Sam. "I appreciate it."

"Not a problem." I looked expectantly at Charlie,

who tilted his head to one side. I followed him, casting one backward look at Sam as he looked down at the folder Janelle held, his face attentive. Then he glanced at me and I saw speculation in his dark brown eyes.

"I'm going to marry Janelle," Charlie said when we were out of earshot. "This accident and the other accident it's shown me how much I care for her. I don't know if it's love or obligation or a combination of the two, but I'm going to do everything I can to get her to marry me." I started to speak but he shook his head, his eyes intent on mine. "I love you Cassie, and I always will. Maybe that's wrong, but that's how it is. You've made it clear we don't have a future together and I have to accept that. You don't need me and she does. I have to let that guide me in what I do."

I didn't try to correct his interpretation of his feelings. For all I knew, that was as good a reason to marry someone as any. I said the only thing I could think of under the circumstances. "Good luck, Charlie," I said gently.

He looked briefly disappointed then he nodded brusquely before joining Janelle. They walked out together, her arm through his.

"That's interesting," Sam said from behind me.

I rounded on him. "What? That Charlie is going to marry Janelle? Of course he's going to marry her. Hell, for all I know, he loves her."

Sam leaned back slightly, getting out of range of my blast. "Actually, I meant the fact that someone tried to hurt her. I knew Charlie would marry her." He looked at the two people walking away from us down the hall. "The question is, will she marry him?"

****

Sam and I spoke little on the way back to my townhouse, each of us deep in thought. My feelings were all tumbled, wavering back and forth between concern about Janelle, worry about Charlie's motivations, and anxiety about the wedding, the murder, and my future. My brief clash with the police mixed in with my anxiety as well as speculation about a motive for murder, which had me totally stumped. John was an unpleasant, pompous asshole, but was that a motive for murder? I didn't think so.

As I pulled into the drive, Sam asked, "What's on your agenda for the rest of today?"

"I've got to buy a dress for Livvie's wedding," I grumbled. "That's probably going to take me most of the day."

He got out of the car and came around to the driver's side, leaning forward to kiss me quickly. "Are you upset about Charlie getting married?" he asked.

"Upset?" I thought about it. "No, not upset. Just…" I shook my head, unsure how to articulate what I was feeling—not even sure I *could* articulate it. "I hope it's the right thing for both him and Janelle. I'm just not sure it is."

"I am." Sam smiled at my surprised look. "I have the advantage of being an outsider looking in. Trust me. It's the right thing." He started toward his SUV, parked in the drive. "I'll be back for supper tonight. Why don't we toss something on the grill?"

"As long as you go out and buy the something we toss, that works for me." I waved to him and backed out, my jumbled thoughts once again popping into the forefront of my brain. I brutally thrust them aside and instead considered my shopping options. Livvie's wedding had to be my first priority this afternoon. I wasn't going to let her down.

The Mall of America, the Heart of Capitalism, was a shopping possibility because it was just a few miles away, but MoA always exhausted me with its endless options. I settled instead for the SMall, the

Eden Prairie Shopping Center just five miles from my house with several upscale stores where I could surely score an outfit.

When I got there I made a beeline for J C Penney, mentally keeping Sears and Macy as backup options. In ten minutes I was in the dressing room, stripped to my undies and tugging on a summer-weight black dress with white polka dots. I checked my look in the full-length mirror, pleased with what I saw. I had put on a few extra pounds after the accident but careful attention to my diet during the past month helped me shed them. I was back to my old size ten self.

I pulled off the dress and hung it haphazardly on the hook. What was the weather forecast for Friday? May First in Minnesota could have snow, a heat wave, or pouring rain, sometimes all on the same day. I tugged my Blackberry out of my purse and turned it on to check the weather app I had downloaded.

The little device thumped in my hand, my signal of choice for messages. I checked email and found one from Livvie, once again pleading with me to sing at her wedding. I also had an email from T.J., the nervous groom, adding his begging to hers. His was a little more to-the-point: "Cassie, she'll have a meltdown if you don't do it. PLEASE just sing the stupid song, please." I smiled at his blunt assessment of Livvie's state of mind as I checked my voice mail. If Charlie was truly committed to marrying Janelle, surely it wouldn't matter if I sang that damn romantic song?

I had three voice mail messages, a surprise because few people had this number. The first one was from Diane, John's widow. "I'd like a chance to talk to you if you have time. I have to plan John's funeral and..." Diane's voice trembled then she continued. "I'd like the family to sing at the funeral, the way you kids always sing at Whittington events. Would you consider it, Cassie? Please call me so we can discuss it." She recited a number then added, "It would mean so much to all of us—the children and me. Please."

Charlie, John, Becky, Livvie and I had sung at Whittington weddings, funerals, and graduations since we were children. I suppose it was only fitting that we sing at John's funeral, but I hated being put in the position of having to arrange it. "Why me?" I muttered as I considered the outfit on the clothes hook while accessing the next message.

"Ms. Whittington, this is Detective David Madison, with the Mounds Police Department. We talked last fall when you had your car accident. There's been a break in the case. I'd like to talk to you at your earliest convenience." He gave a phone number then added, "We think we know who caused your accident, but we need to verify a few facts with you. I look forward to talking to you soon."

The car accident? How could they catch a break on an accident that happened the previous October? I pulled on my next fashion choice, a black-and-white-and-red dress with swirly paint-like yellow and green swipes at random spots on the fabric. I eyed myself critically. The dress was long and I would need heels. I planned to dance at this wedding and I couldn't dance in heels. I shrugged out of the outfit and set it aside then pulled on my final choice, a black-and-white pantsuit with scoop-necked top and a red linen jacket.

I vaguely remembered Detective Madison, a plain, stoic man with an expressionless face and a brisk, no-nonsense manner. He had spoken to me in the hospital as I recovered from our car crash and later, at home, when he followed up with us weeks later. There were no leads on who might have caused the accident that made our car career into a ditch, pinning Sam against the doorframe and fracturing his leg in three places. I escaped with broken ribs and bad bruising, but poor Sam didn't get off so easily.

I surveyed myself in the mirror. "Good," I said to the gray-haired woman with tousled hair looking back at me. "Not bad at all." I scored two outfits in…I checked my Timex. "Twenty minutes. A record, even for me." I got out of the wedding duds and back into my jeans and knit top, scooping up my phone to check the final message.

"This is Sheila Peavey. We need to talk. Call me as soon as you can."

I blinked in surprise at the sharp, clipped words. Why the hell was Sheila calling me? And how did she get my phone number? I stuffed my phone back in my handbag and swept up an armful of dress clothes. I had more important things to do than call Sheila Peavey. I had shoes to buy, a handbag to purchase, and a funeral to help arrange.

****

I paused in the Food Court an hour later laden with shopping sacks and a wardrobe bag over one arm. I was tired but triumphant. I had three outfits, four pairs of shoes, two purses and assorted costume jewelry. I was ready for anything the weather might throw at me on Friday. I had made some purchases as a hedge against that future day when Janelle and Charlie got married. Unless they eloped—and I doubted that would happen—I anticipated another big Wedding Event in the future.

I bought a gynormous pretzel and sat down with a small tub of mustard and a diet soda. That would tide me over until supper that night. What to do next? I thought about the earlier phone calls and chose the least problematic one to answer. I pulled out my Blackberry and checked it. The Facebook icon had a red star on it, indicating updates, but I was befriended by so many strangers that wasn't unusual. I really had to sit down someday and figure out the whole 'friend' thing.

I decided to save friendship for another time and instead dialed David Madison's phone number. He answered on the first ring.

"Hi, this is Cassie Whittington." I tried rearranging the wardrobe bag slung over the next chair and narrowly avoided dribbling mustard on my red-white-and-blue top. As I juggled everything, I almost dropped the phone, thus missing his initial words.

"...responsible for your accident. He was in a bar and bragged to some friends about it."

"I'm sorry, who was in a bar?" A few tables away a baby started to wail, the sound echoing. I thought of Charlie dealing with a crying baby and started to grin. I could just imagine his perplexed look as he tried to cope.

"I said, a penny-ante criminal was talking to some friends about the death and said how he wasn't surprised. He said the guy got what he deserved."

I pulled the phone away from my ear and looked down at the icons on the tiny screen, wondering if the connection was bad. His words made no sense. I saw the bright green light indicating a good signal, so apparently the bad connection was in my head. "I'm sorry, Detective Madison. I'm not tracking what you're saying. Why would some, um, penny-ante criminal have it in for me or Sam?" I dunked the pretzel in the mustard and took a savory bite, turning away from the wailer and finally finding a small oasis of quiet.

"He said he was hired by Whittington to loosen the lug nuts on your tires. You told me you spoke to Whittington right before the accident, right?" Madison's voice was starting to sound a bit impatient as though he wondered about my veracity as a victim and/or witness.

Whittington? I spoke to…I almost choked on the chewy pretzel. "John? John hired somebody?" I said the first words that popped into my head. "How the hell could John find some low-life criminal to mess with my tires?"

"We're looking into that. The man—Alberto Munez—worked in the construction trades sometimes, whenever he was sober. We suspect that's where they met."

I chewed furiously, my mind as active as my mouth. "I still can't see John walking up to some guy and asking him to fix my tires. Why would John do that?"

"You and he were involved in litigation. Perhaps he wanted to eliminate you to clear the way for his case. It's a considerable sum of money."

"Well, yeah, but still…" Something didn't quite compute. John filed his lawsuit to prevent my inheritance more from anger at being excluded than for the money. Or did he? I was starting to form a new mental picture of my ex-brother-in-law but it was still incomplete. My phone vibrated in my hand but I didn't bother to check the display. It was probably just more email landing in my In Box. "Did you arrest the guy?"

"We did. He made a complete statement about how he did it. The D.A. will be pressing charges soon. We're also investigating Whittington's son. Munez said he was involved, as well as a woman."

This time I did choke on my pretzel. "His son? Are you kidding? What woman?"

"We're not sure." Now Madison sounded cautious, as though afraid he had spoken out of turn. "We hope to get all the facts in the next few hours. Until then, this is all confidential. As soon as it's official, we'll make a public announcement. I just wanted you to know that we've found the man responsible for what happened."

Not really, I thought. *Not if one of John's sons is involved.* I kept the thought to myself. The way Madison talked they would be on the Whittington kids faster than tornado in June. "That's going to make for an awkward funeral," I muttered.

"I beg your pardon?"

The phone thumped again then again. I had visions of my email queue filling up with pleadings from Livvie to sing at her wedding. "Thanks for letting me know," I said, dipping the pretzel once again. I maneuvered the tasty morsel toward my mouth. "Do I need to do anything? Testify or something?"

"You'll have to appear in court if we get a conviction. The judge will want to know about the effects of the accident."

I thought of Sam, so injured he could barely walk for months. "I'll be glad to tell anybody who will listen." The phone thumped again and this time Madison must have heard it because his next words were somewhat rushed.

"I'll be in touch and let you know how the case proceeds," he said. "I don't expect we'll have a court date for at least a month or two."

"I'll be available," I promised. "Thanks for calling."

He hung up and I set the phone down thoughtfully. John and his kids involved in our accident? I still didn't believe it. John was a lot of things, but I couldn't visualize him schmoozing with some low life and hiring a thug to hurt me. And Matthew or Jon? They were like little John Imitations, excelling at the right sports and attending the right schools. John's kids were the exact opposite of Becky's kids, who were free spirits and always getting into scrapes. The thought of Matthew or Jon being involved with a gangster was ludicrous.

The phone vibrated again, the little gadget rotating slightly as though angry at being ignored. I looked at the display. The voice mail icon had a flashing red star next to it, indicating a call was waiting for me. I clicked it, eyeing the number on the small screen. It had <*unknown*> next to it, which meant whoever called wasn't in my address book. I accessed the message and put the phone to my ear.

"It's Sheila Peavey. We have to talk, as soon as possible."

I rolled my eyes. "If I wanted to hear from an asshole, I'd fart," I muttered. What a bitch. Trust her to sound like the Queen demanding the presence of a peon. I heard a noise like a slamming door in the background. It sounded hollow, as though she was in an empty room or a large space.

"Wait," she whispered breathlessly.

A long silence ensued. I munched my pretzel, wondering whether or not to hang up. Then she spoke again. "I know who killed John. Meet me at Barlow's. We need to talk. You could be in danger. Oh. Wait." Muffled voices came through the speaker then I heard, "You can't! What are you—? Don't do that!"

She sounded pissed off, like somebody was taking her parking spot or something.

Then I just heard dead air.

Chapter 9

"Hello?" I chewed my pretzel slowly, straining to hear above the fussy baby nearby. "Hello?"

No answer. Had something happened to her? As soon as the thought came to me I dismissed it. Somebody probably saw her talking to me and she hung up rather than have to explain herself to whoever walked in. I clicked the Disconnect button and the phone immediately chimed *Friends in Low Places*, my ringtone of choice for all Whittingtons except Charlie and Livvie. I pressed the Connect button and put the phone to my ear, once again hunching to garner what privacy I could.

It was Diane and she sounded panicked. "Cassie, I need your help. We have to start planning the funeral. The police are releasing John's body today. I want the funeral tomorrow. You need to talk to Livvie about it."

"Livvie?" I almost choked on my pretzel. "Tomorrow's Thursday. The wedding rehearsal is tomorrow, Diane. Can't the funeral wait?"

"No." She bit off the word so fast I knew there was no use arguing. "We'd have to wait until Saturday, after her wedding. I don't want this—I don't want it hanging over us." She made a sound that might have been a forced laugh. "John wouldn't want Livvie's day to be ruined because of him."

Oh, yeah? I restrained myself from expressing such a sarcastic question. "Did you call the funeral home?" The Whittingtons had always been 'buried out of' the Tedesco Funeral Home in Minnetonka. There would be no church service because none of the family was particularly religious, unless you counted the Social Register and the New York Stock Exchange as deities.

"I called them. The service is scheduled for eleven o'clock. We'll have a light lunch afterward at the Club. John's father arranged it."

'The Club' was the Horse and Hunt Club, a bastion of snobbishness on the shores of Lake Minnetonka. The Second probably had to pull a few strings to get the restaurant reserved on such short notice. "You're cutting it close," I murmured. "The rehearsal starts at four."

She ignored my comment and barreled on. "I need to get in touch with Charlie but he's not at the office and he's not answering his phone. There are some legal papers that need to get processed in order for the insurance company to be satisfied."

"Did you try his apartment? Janelle was in an accident and I think they were going to his place. Or maybe to hers. I'm not sure."

"An accident? What happened? Is she okay?" Diane's voice rose and I heard someone ask in the background, "Who had an accident? Did Cassie have another accident?" It sounded like Pauline, Diane's youngest daughter, but I wasn't sure.

"She's okay," I said. "I think she was going to rest. They did an ultrasound and the baby's okay. The babies, I should say. They found out she's having twins."

"How do you know?"

"Charlie called me when she had the accident and I went to the hospital."

"I'm glad she's okay." This was said with such robotic coolness I suspected Diane didn't even know what she said. "The police want to talk to Matthew. Do you know why?"

I fumbled my cup of diet Pepsi, dribbling some on my jeans. Holy shit, Madison was moving fast if the cops were talking to Matthew already. "It's probably something to do with John's estate," I lied with what I thought was admirable coolness. "You know how it is when people die. The police always want to look into finances and stuff."

"Oh my God." She sounded stricken. "Oh no."

"Why, what's the problem?" I polished off one more bite and shoved the pretzel aside. I had just purchased size ten clothing and I wasn't going to endure the whole shopping thing again because I gained a pretzel pound or two. "What's going on, Diane?"

There was silence then another voice came on the line. "Cassie? This is Pauline. Can you come over here? Mom's really upset about something."

I mentally mapped out a drive to John and Diane's home. It was on the west side of Eden Prairie, nearly to Minnetonka, and I was at the mall on the east side. My home in Pickaway was southeast. It wasn't *that* far out of my way to drop by their house then hop on a different highway to get home. "Sure, I was just leaving the mall. I'll be there in a few minutes."

"Thanks."

I clicked Disconnect, holding my breath until I was sure the gadget wouldn't chime again. It was only three o'clock. I could stop by and see Diane and be home by five at the latest. No big deal. I swooped up my purchases and headed out.

Twenty minutes later I drove into a typical Minnesota exurb complete with lake in the distance, boats on trailers in the driveways or on docks, and big SUVs waiting to haul those boats. John's house was a typical two-story Snout House, with a three-car garage sticking out in front like the nose on a pig and a manicured back lawn sloping down to one of Minnesota's 10,000 lakes. A sporty red BMW sedan was parked in the three-wide drive. I parked at the curb and went to the front door.

Pauline opened it. Like Diane, she was tall and thin with thick dark hair pulled back from her face by a black and white scarf. The black slacks and pale yellow sweater set she wore emphasized the fine bones of her neck and shoulders. Her prettiest feature was her eyes, which were big and dark brown, almost black, fringed by heavy lashes. They gave her a wide-eyed, innocent look, like a child amazed at all she saw.

Now those eyes were red-rimmed with crying. I wasn't close to any of that generation of Whittingtons because I was on the periphery of the family after my divorce. But I impulsively gave her a quick hug now when I saw how haggard she looked. "How are you, Pauline?" I whispered as I felt her tremble in my touch.

She hugged me briefly then stepped back. "We're managing," she said with an obvious effort. "Mother is upset, of course. And the trouble with Matthew isn't helping." She began walking through a foyer the size of my kitchen, leading the way to a huge living room with clearstory ceilings, a ten-foot tall fireplace, and four conversational groupings of chairs and sofas at various points in the room. One grouping faced a huge wall of windows, which allowed a panoramic view of the lake in the distance.

Pauline went to the fireplace, looking at the arrangement of family pictures there. I followed, dropping my handbag on an end table near one chintz-covered couch. "Where's your mother? Is everything okay?"

"Of course it's not okay." Pauline touched one silver-framed picture of the family, aligning it with the one next to it of John and Diane, arm in arm. "Father is dead, his lover is accusing Matthew of murder, Father's company is almost bankrupt, and Mother is afraid she'll lose her home. Somehow it got onto Facebook and now the whole world is talking about it."

The whole world? Maybe the world according to Facebook, but I doubted that included people that she cared about. Or maybe it did. "How did that happen?"

She shrugged, thin shoulders rising and falling so fast I barely saw it. "Who knows? My stupid cousins probably did it. Cory is a brat and Nathan is just as bad. They're angry they didn't get into an Ivy League school."

I doubted it. An Ivy League school was not on the "Top Party College Lists," which Becky's boys always talked about. Then the import of her words soaked in. I sat down slowly, glad there was furniture nearby. "His...lover...? Sheila?" I tried to process all she said. Bankruptcy? Losing her home?

"You knew about it?" Pauline clenched her fists, her eyes narrowing.

I held up a hand. "I just found out about it yesterday," I protested. "Back up a minute. What's this about Sheila accusing your brother?"

"That woman called the police and said she was with Father the day he died. She and Father talked about Matthew and she *said* that Father said he was worried about Matthew." Pauline's pinched face narrowed even more as her lips pressed into a scowl. "I don't understand. All I know is Matthew is worried about the finances. He said that Father..." She sighed and suddenly sat down in a big armchair, looking like a Raggedy Ann doll someone tossed. Her entire body sagged and her face began to crumple.

"He said Father spent all the money and put it into offshore accounts. Matthew said that Father and that woman were going away." The rest of her words deteriorated into a sniffle-fest as she fumbled a handkerchief out of a pocket and held it to her mouth.

"That asshole," I muttered as I moved to take a seat perched on the arm of the overstuffed chair. I leaned over her, putting a comforting arm around her shoulders. "Pauline, surely it's not as bad as all that. John wouldn't have left his family in the lurch. He wouldn't—"

"He did."

I jerked upright, almost falling off the big chair. Diane was framed in the doorway, glaring at us like the wrath of God. Her short black hair looked brittle and electric, as though she had over-styled it and just sprayed it into place. The dark outfit she wore— black slacks, gray sweater-set, and black shoes— made her pale face even whiter as did the dark circles under her eyes. This was a woman in shock, a woman barely holding on to civility.

I knew I had to tread lightly. "I'm sorry, Diane," I said, straightening and standing next to the chair. "Pauline told me that there are some, um, complications. I'm surprised. I may not have had a good opinion of John, but I didn't think he would do anything like that."

Diane crossed her arms and hunched her shoulders, defending herself against…what? The truth? "We're all learning a lot about John, aren't we?" She took two jerky steps before sinking onto a hassock not far from where Pauline huddled, her hanky still at her face. "I found out about it all on Monday morning, before he died. Ironically enough, it started with an argument about Opening Day at the cabin."

"Opening Day? What's there to argue about?

The family always goes up to the lake house on Mother's Day to kick off summer." I looked from Pauline to Diane. "Was there a problem with that?"

"John didn't want to go. He was so angry that Grandmother Theo left the cabin to you. He refused to go."

John and his family didn't go to the cabin the previous year, either, but that had been a subdued Opening Day because Grandy Theo had died just weeks earlier. I didn't think anything about it at the time. "That's no reason to deny you and the kids the chance to go to the lake and have some fun."

"I pointed that out." Diane's voice was dry and brittle. "We argued." She glanced at Pauline as though assessing whether to speak.

Pauline must have sensed her mother's concern. "I overheard you," she said in a low voice strangled by tears. She shifted her gaze to me. "I was home for the weekend and didn't have to get back to school until Tuesday because my Monday classes were canceled. I think they forgot that I was in the house."

Diane tried to smile. "You're right. We've gotten so accustomed to being alone." Her eyes took on a distant look. "Always alone." Then she straightened and her voice was firmer. "John was staying out late often in the last year and he took several so-called business trips. But I knew. I sensed what was going on. Then I saw them together at the party last fall."

"You mean the costume party?" Holy crap. If Sheila and John were lovers in October that meant she took up with him just a few months after she was cleared of murdering her husband. John was either braver than I gave him credit for, or besotted. Or maybe both.

Diane tucked her hands under her thighs on the hassock, her shoulders still hunched. It was an uncomfortable pose, one that almost screamed *High*

Tension Line, Be Careful, Do Not Touch. "When I
saw them at the party, I suspected. But I was stupid.
I thought if I ignored it, the problem would go away.
It didn't. Monday morning John told me he wanted a
divorce. He and that woman were going to leave
town."

I resumed my seat, pieces of the jigsaw puzzle
that was John Whittington finally making sense.
"That's why he wanted to see me," I said, thinking
out loud. "If I agreed to his offer, he and Sheila
would get almost two million dollars—the money I
gave him to drop the suit plus the money she would
get from my purchase of the company."

"I told him repeatedly to drop that lawsuit,"
Diane said. "If his grandmother wanted to give you
her money, there was nothing he could do."

"He thought I was going to win the suit," I said.
"I asked him why I should pay him anything and he
told me he hadn't exhausted his legal options yet."

Diane blew out a long breath through her nose,
as close to an unladylike snort as she'd get. "Legal
options." Her voice dripped scorn. "He was bluffing.
He had no options."

"That jerk." I leaned back, controlling my anger
with an enormous effort of will. "I was going to do it.
I was willing to pay him and Sheila off, just to have
them both out of my life. Well, my life and Sam's." I
shook my head, catching a glimpse of Pauline's
appalled expression as I did so. The poor kid. She
was getting an earful about dear old Dad, that's for
sure.

Diane noticed, too. "I'm sorry, Pauline," she
murmured.

"It was terrible," the younger woman said, her
voice choked with tears. "It would have been better if
they yelled, but they didn't. Father was so cold and
angry." She looked at her mother. "How could you
stand it? I told Matthew later that I would have hit

him."

"You told your brother?" Diane tensed and I thought for a minute that she would jump up. Then she visibly relaxed, her shoulders sagging. "What did you tell him?"

"What I heard." Pauline dabbed at her eyes. "I talked to him."

"You did? When?" Diane looked intently at Pauline as though the answer was of dire importance.

Pauline sensed it. She slowly lowered her hanky, looking confused. "I called him. He was getting ready to go to work. I caught him as he was leaving his apartment." Her eyes opened wide as she looked past Diane. I followed her gaze and saw Matthew coming in the front door, his brother Jon behind him.

They were so damn preppy it was eerie. Both young men were handsome in a 1950s movie star sort of way, with groomed hair, pressed clothing, and a calm, impenetrable snobbishness that seemed to surround them like fine cologne. They were a Ralph Lauren ad come to life. Jon hesitated when he saw us but Matthew came into the room, his face set and hard.

"You're not needed here," he snapped.

I stiffened my backbone. "That's for your mother to say. She asked me to stop over."

Diane started to speak but Matthew didn't give her the chance. "You've stopped. Now you can leave."

I ignored his rudeness and turned to Diane. "Have you thought about the songs you'd like us to sing?"

"I don't think it would be appropriate for you to sing at our father's funeral." Matthew started toward the fireplace, brushing past me as though that ended the conversation.

"I'd like Cassie and your Uncle Charlie to sing."

Diane's voice was low, firm, and angry. "They'll sing…" She hesitated and I saw the desperation in her eyes.

"*Circle of Life?*" I suggested as I stood.

Diane nodded, her head jerking with the effort. "Yes. That would be fine."

"*Behind the Sun*," Pauline said suddenly. "He loved that album of Clapton's."

I struggled to remember the lyrics but failed. Who knew John was a Clapton fan? I'd figure it out. "How about—"

"I don't want her singing at my father's funeral." Matthew's voice cut through our quiet conversation as effectively as a gun.

Diane started to speak but I gestured her to quiet. "Why?"

"You're not part of this family."

I hate confrontation, but some of them just can't be avoided. "You're right. I'm a family friend, nothing more. But if your mother wants me to sing at your father's funeral, I will. This is about her, not you and what you want."

"No." He took a step toward me and I instinctively stepped back from six-foot-three of pissed-off young man.

"Why are you so angry at me?" I demanded. "Your father's death isn't my fault."

"Maybe not directly," he snapped with vast innuendo.

"What's that mean?"

"Matthew." Pauline jumped to her feet and put a restraining hand on his arm. "Don't get into it."

"Why not? Why should she be exempt?" He jerked his arm away from her and took another step toward me.

This time I stood my ground. "Exempt from what?"

"Exempt from the anguish we've all felt all these

months. Because of you my father obsessed about his inheritance. It was all he thought about, day or night. It consumed him."

I gaped up at him. "His inheritance? What inheritance?"

"Exactly." Matthew took a long, shuddering breath as though drawing in enough air to blow me into the next county like the Big Bad Wolf. "You wormed your way into Grandma Theo's life and looked what she did—she didn't have time for anyone else."

"That's bullshit," I sputtered.

"You spent every Saturday with her. She didn't bother with her real grandchildren—my father and his siblings."

"How would you know?" I met him glare for glare, my hands on my hips. "You were just a kid back then and by the time you were growing up, you didn't want to visit her."

"We weren't invited." He snapped off the words and tossed them at me. "Father told us all about it. You and Charlie were welcome, but Grandma Theo and Grandfather didn't care about us. You and Charlie were all they cared about."

Holy shit. What a distorted view of reality. I looked past him at Diane, hoping to glimpse some sanity there, but she was lost in thought, her eyes vacant and staring at something only she could see. "This isn't the time or the place to discuss this. If your mother wants us at the funeral, we'll be happy to sing. It's up to her." I snatched up my purse and slung it over my shoulder. "Diane, I'll see if I can track down Charlie and have him call you about those legal things."

She raised her head with an effort and nodded wearily. "Thank you. And thank you for singing. I'd like that." She fell into step beside me as I started out of the room, pausing to look back at Matthew as he began to follow. "I'd like a word with Cassie in private, please."

Her quiet dignity stopped the kids in their tracks although Matthew looked like he might ignore her. Jon murmured something to him and the two young men turned to one side. Pauline gave me one imploring look then she stood near her brothers, looking up as they talked.

"I'm sorry," Diane said as we walked to the front door. "Matthew is frightened. John embezzled a lot of money and with him gone..." She sighed so deeply I knew she was using it as a means to keep tears at bay. "Matthew will be implicated, too. It's such a mess, Cassie. I don't know what we'll do."

I was at a loss for words. No matter what opinion I had of Diane, it was terrible to see her world fall down around her like that.

She paused by the front door, hand on the doorknob. "Will you talk to Charlie and Livvie? I hate to spring it on her like this, but..." Diane looked past me to the living room where her children were all grouped together, talking. "I want this over with so we can try to make some sense out of our lives."

"Of course. I'll talk to Becky, too, to make sure she's available to sing for John. We'll do it. Don't worry, Diane. We'll figure out a song list."

What the hell were we going to sing at a funeral tomorrow morning where everybody was glad the asshole was dead?

Knocking on Heaven's Door?
Angel?
Ding Dong, The Witch is Dead?
So Long, Farewell?
See You Later, Alligator?

I shook my head as my mind delved into the ludicrous. "Don't worry," I said with confidence. "We'll figure it out."

Chapter 10

"What the hell are we going to sing?" Charlie asked three hours later as he munched on bratwursts and sauerkraut at my kitchen table.

I called him as soon as I got home. He and Janelle came over immediately then my phone started ringing. Soon Becky and her husband, Carlton Stark, joined us just as Livvie and T.J. came in. Sam threw a few more brats on the grill and people began to jam my kitchen, talking a mile a minute.

"Are you sure the funeral will wrap up by mid-afternoon?" Livvie asked for the third time as she sipped a cold beer. "Our rehearsal starts at four and I wanted everyone at the house by three-thirty so we could do some pictures ahead of time. T.J. has the rehearsal dinner scheduled for six at the restaurant." She smiled at T.J., who was on the couch in the attached family room, a plate of potato salad, bratwurst, and sauerkraut balanced on his knee. He was watching television with two cats sitting on the coffee table watching him. "There's a chance of rain on Friday."

"There's always a chance of rain," Sam said, leaning against the kitchen island so he could peer into the family room at the baseball game on the TV.

"It's spring in Minnesota. Just be glad there isn't snow predicted."

"I wanted to have the ceremony on the patio outside the porch but maybe I'll have the planners move it onto the porch instead."

"Makes sense," Becky said, her iPhone in hand. "That way you've got the best of both worlds, outdoors and indoors." She nudged her husband, a distinguished looking man with silver hair, fifteen years her senior. Carlton was her third husband and they had been married for almost six years, a record for Becky. "Don't forget to pick up the suits for the boys tomorrow morning at the tailor. My boys have grown like weeds this past year," she added as an aside. "They outgrow things as soon as we buy them."

"Where are the kids?" I asked.

"Marcy is with her boyfriend, and Cory and Nathan are with friends. Apparently they're a hot item since their uncle was murdered." Becky said this with her typical dry humor, her plump face reflecting her amused distaste. Her chin-length brown hair was pulled away from her face with a barrette shaped like a butterfly—an expensive, enameled butterfly. The deceptively simple hairstyle probably cost her a hundred bucks or more at her stylist's salon. Although she and John were twins, they were polar opposites in personality. "You should see the pings I'm getting on my Facebook page. It's amazing. People I haven't heard from in year are all of a sudden befriending me."

I thought of my own Facebook and Twitter accounts, probably gathering new 'friends' as I ignored it. "I wonder if I can hire your boys to manage my social networking."

Becky laughed. "They'd probably charge you and arm and a leg."

"They'd better not be planning anything

124

involving tin cans and my car," Livvie warned.

Carlton turned slightly, his lips twitching. When he saw me looking at him, he winked, looking like the mischievous banker from the Monopoly game.

"Don't worry, Livvie," Becky assured her. "They'll be on good behavior tomorrow. After all, my baby is seventeen now. It won't hurt Nathan to act his age." Her gaze swung to Charlie. "I can't believe you're going to be a first-time father and my youngest is almost leaving the nest." Her gaze shifted to Janelle. "And I can't believe someone tried to hurt you."

Charlie's hand holding the brat paused. "I hope the cops take it seriously." He looked so angry I was surprised steam didn't come out of his ears.

Janelle touched his wrist lightly and he set down the brat to briefly give her a hug. I smiled at the sight of him visibly relaxing when she leaned slightly against him. "It's a scary proposition," Janelle said. She wore a loose red-and-white striped top over jeans, looking like a preppy Asian schoolgirl with her long black hair pulled back from her pretty oval face. "I was the youngest in my family so I don't know anything about babies."

Becky laughed. "You'll need a nanny. Somebody hand me my bag. I'll put a note on Sylvie Jones-Stratton's Facebook wall. Her daughter had a nanny for the baby and that kid must be ready for kindergarten by now. I'm sure I can get the name from Sylvie."

I tuned out Becky's chatter and focused on the task at hand. "A song, people?" I tossed out. "We need two songs for the funeral."

"And don't forget the solo you're doing for me, too, at the wedding," Livvie said quickly.

"Solo?" I asked. "I thought it was a duet."

"T.J. said he asked Charlie to sing a solo, so I decided I don't mind it's not a duet."

Charlie took a swallow of his beer. "T.J. asked me to sing a special song for his lady love. And I agreed." He and T.J. exchanged a look and I wondered what song was chosen. I would find out soon enough at the rehearsal tomorrow.

"Well, you're safe with *Circle of Life*," Carlton said. "That's generic."

We all nodded then Sam said, "How about *All Things Must Pass*?" When Livvie and I both shot him a surprised look, he shrugged. "Diane must be hoping all things will pass and soon, if what you said is true. Embezzlement?"

"Poor Matthew," Becky said, peering down at the screen of her iPhone. "He worked so hard to make John proud of him. Of course, we all know that's a losing proposition. The only person John cared about was John."

"Tough words," Sam commented.

Becky looked up at him. "John was my younger brother by one minute so I've known him all my life. He was an asshole. If John really did fudge the books, Matthew will be liable, too. He was a senior partner." She glanced at Charlie. "Did Father have money in the company?"

"I don't think so."

"What might happen to Matthew?" I asked. "Jail?"

"It depends." Janelle pushed her plate away and picked up her diet Pepsi. "If the company's totally insolvent, they can declare bankruptcy and he'll get off without harm. But if they defrauded investors, he'll be liable. Remember what happened to Bernie Madoff and Tom Petters? It's the same kind of thing, but on a smaller scale." Her eyes widened. "At least, I think it's a smaller scale. I wonder what kind of money we're talking about."

"Several million, at least," Carlton said in his deep, sonorous voice. "John asked me to invest last year and I asked to have a look at the books."

"I didn't know that." Becky gestured to me. "I need some paper."

I passed her a notepad from Lerner Software, my former employer, and a pen. "So what did you see in the books?" I asked.

"Nothing much of interest," Carlton said. His gaze skittered past Charlie and I wondered what knowledge the two men shared.

"Claire said she wanted to have a shower for Janelle," Becky said as she copied a number from her iPhone to the pad. "I told her we would help plan it, Livvie."

"I can't plan a baby shower," Livvie said. "I'm just done planning a wedding."

"It doesn't have to be a big deal," Janelle said quickly.

Becky, Livvie, and I stared at her. "It's a Whittington event," I said. "Trust me. It has to be a big deal. Did Claire have a guest list ready?"

Becky grinned. "She's starting one. It's alphabetized."

Janelle turned wide eyes on me. "Alphabetized?"

"I believe it." Livvie put a hand to her mouth and belched softly. "Sorry. Claire is determined to uphold the Family Honor. I'll lay odds there'll be at least fifty people there."

"I think it's interesting that Father never had children with any of our stepmothers." Becky sipped her wine and regarded us all over its rim. "He married four times but only had children with Mom."

"What's the point?" Livvie demanded. "He still remarried."

"But he didn't have kids. I think that's significant."

"I think it's bullshit," Livvie snapped.

Becky pursed her lips and I intervened. The two

sisters had been bitter enemies for years and only recently forged a fragile truce. "I think Becky's right. He loved Gloria a lot. After all, he killed my father when he tried to protect her."

The words dropped into a sudden silence.

"That's a real succinct way to sum it up, Cassie," Sam said wryly.

"Well, he did." I remembered a conversation with the Second the previous fall, but that was private and I wasn't going to share it with his kids. "If it makes Claire happy to play Mrs. Thurston Howell the Third, let her. Let's get back to our problem. I need songs. I promised Diane."

"*Circle of Life, All Things Must Pass*," Becky said. "We can always toss in *Amazing Grace* if we need to." She filched a potato chip off Carlton's plate. "Or rather, *you* can toss in *Amazing Grace*. It's always better if you sing it solo *a capella*."

I had sung "Grace" so many times solo I could do it in my sleep, but the other songs weren't as well known. "I'll get some lyrics. We need to practice." I pushed away from the table and started toward the living room. "I could use another brat," I told Sam as I passed him.

"Your wish is my command." He smiled at me and turned to the pot of beer simmering on the stove where the grilled brats 'rested,' waiting to be consumed.

I went into my miniscule office positioned off the living room and fired up my new desktop computer, purchased just a month earlier. Truffles abandoned T.J. to follow me since I was going to play her favorite game of 'position things on screen to hit with paw.' A fast Google search gave me the lyrics I was looking for. I printed them as Truffles watched, black tail teasing the paper inching out of the machine. I dug out my Elton John and George Harrison CDs, popped them into the player on the bookcase and started to hum along with the songs as I skimmed the lyrics.

I was just finishing up my first run-through of *Circle of Life* when the Blackberry in the charging stand on my desk vibrated and chimed *Friends in Low Places*. I grabbed it, pressing the Connect button as I did so, but my finger must have slid over the tiny trackball because suddenly a voice blared out of the phone, startling Truffles into backing up, almost knocking my desk lamp over.

"This is Matthew Whittington. I need to talk with you."

"Oops." I picked up the phone, still unfamiliar with the icons and the controls. One of those little images or a side button probably controlled the private vs. conference capability, but I was damned if I knew which one.

"That woman just called me and demanded to know about the funeral."

I looked up at Sam came into the room, a plate in his hand. Truffles eyed him expectantly, her small black ears swiveling like food-tracking devices.

"She had the gall to call me," Matthew continued.

"What woman?" I asked, taking the plate from Sam.

"Sheila Peavey. She called me just a few minutes ago."

I broke off a piece of bratwurst and held it out to Truffles.

"I've already given her some," Sam said. "Don't give her too much, she'll get sick."

"Is that him?" Matthew demanded from my phone. "He needs to talk to her. He has to demand that she stay away. She won't listen to me."

"Who's that?" Sam asked, looking down at the phone in my hand.

I had to swallow my brat bite before I could

answer. "Matthew Whittington. He's having trouble with your ex-wife. He'd like you to talk to her." I held up the phone.

Sam gestured it away. I set it back on the desk as he barked out a laugh. "He thinks that having me talk to Sheila would do any good?"

"If she makes any trouble tomorrow, I'm holding you responsible," Matthew sputtered. "Both of you."

"Now just a minute," I said, leaning over to enunciate clearly into the device. I wasn't actually sure where the microphone was situated and I didn't want him to miss a word. "That's not fair and you know it, Matthew. I'm not responsible for what Shelia Peavey does."

"She wouldn't be involved in our family if it wasn't for you."

I took in a deep breath to blast this fallacy, but unfortunately I only managed to inhale a bit of brat bun. I coughed and by the time I could answer, Matthew was continuing with his rant. "She met my father because of that person you're sleeping with. If it wasn't for that, she would never have met him. She wouldn't be associated with the Whittingtons."

"Not just a damn minute," Sam said, reaching for the Blackberry.

I fended him off, succeeding in blocking him from getting the phone and dumping my brat on the desk, where Truffles pounced on it gleefully. The small cat grabbed the sausage—almost as big as her entire body—and was gone before I could do anything. "Stop her, Sam."

"Exactly," Matthew said triumphantly. "It's his fault she's causing problems."

"Grow up, Matthew. It's not Sam's fault your father wanted to have an affair. It's not my fault for introducing Sam and his ex-wife to our family."

"Our family?" His voice was vitriolic. I actually flinched, moving away from the phone on the desk.

"You're a member of our family on sufferance. Don't forget it."

He's under stress, I reminded myself. *He's young and he's stupid and he's under stress. Plus his father was an asshole and he probably inherited asshole tendencies.* "I appreciate that," I said through gritted teeth. "Your grandfather has always treated me fairly."

Oops. Wrong thing to say. "My grandfather? My grandfather has been a saint as far as you and that trailer trash mother of yours was concerned. You've caused nothing but trouble for this family since you were born, Cassie," he said acidly. "It would have been better for all of us if your father killed you and your mother that day instead of killing my grandmother."

I drew back at the venomous words, almost overbalancing in my chair. Sam scooped up the Blackberry and put it to his ear then he immediately lowered it again. "The asshole hung up."

I pushed away from my desk, stolen bratwurst forgotten. "I had no idea he felt that way," I said, my stomach churning from the confrontation—and from too much sauerkraut.

Sam put a hand on my shoulder. "Don't worry. Only the idiots in the family feel that way. The rest of them know the score."

"Sam, the cat has a bratwurst! Is that okay?"

He leaned over and kissed me quickly. "You're a part of the Whittington family, Cassie. It's got nothing to do with sufferance. If anything John was a member on sufferance. Don't let it bother you."

I smiled gratefully at him. "I won't. Thanks. Now go rescue my cat from bratwurst overdose." I turned back to my computer. "I need to print out some more copies of these lyrics. We have to practice tonight."

He left and I stared after him, lyrics forgotten.

Matthew was right. For years I had lurked on the periphery of the Whittington family, not quite one a member, not a stranger. With Janelle's pregnancy, my role had to change. Charlie and I would inevitably drift apart as his life took a different direction. Where would we be a year from now? I was always able to rely on having Charlie as my buddy, my confidante, my friend. Would that change?

Of course it would change. Charlie was...gone now. My stomach knotted as I considered a life without Charlie in it.

"Cassie? Where are those lyrics?"

I shook myself away from my fruitless musings and hit the Print button. I had a funeral to prepare for.

****

Fifteen hours later I relaxed back in my chair and crossed my legs, settling the linen jacket of my newly purchased J C Penney pants suit. I tuned out the last speaker, one of John's construction competitors. The funeral was finishing well. The large Memorial room in Tedesco Funeral Home was full with family and business associates and the event was being conducted with all the pomp and ceremony of a typical Whittington event.

The Whittington 'kids'—Livvie, Becky, Charlie, and me—kicked off things with our first song. Our scant practice session meant we were ragged, but *Circle of Life* had just a minor stumble. *All Things Must Pass* went off better, probably because it was the signal we were at half-time and only had the well-meaning words of colleagues to endure.

I attended the ceremony alone. Sam was called away by a phone call as we prepared to leave my townhouse for the funeral home. A security watchman at the Barlow growing facility in Jordan called to say that there was a problem with one of the greenhouses and Sam was needed. So I went to the funeral alone and sat with the family, hoping the Barlow family wasn't going to be in for another string of bad luck like that which had plagued them the previous year.

After several sincere and mercifully brief speeches, the service wrapped up me singing *Amazing Grace,* a common occurrence at Whittington services. Then the family began a stately departure, Matthew and Jon flanking their mother and Pauline as they walked up the aisle. Diane was pale and composed but Pauline was crying, her pretty face blotchy with tears. Diane smiled wanly at us and I was glad we managed a credible performance for her sake. The young men had such stiff shoulders they appeared like extras from the *Nutcracker* and both leveled glares at me that would have had me twitching on the ground if they could suit action to deed.

Betty Burke followed. She was an old family friend who had sat in the second row with the Second and Claire. They followed her as she left slowly leaning heavily on a cane and on the arm of her elderly 'gentleman friend,' a weathered black man with a natty suit and an appropriately solemn expression.

By the time I got outside most of the family was assembled on the wraparound porch, standing to the side of the wide front steps. John had been cremated, so the ash-flinging would take place later, probably on the shores of the lake at the family home. I hoped it would occur after Livvie's wedding and be private. She deserved a chance to have the spotlight.

I wended my way past people murmuring condolences to Diane, who was standing at the bottom of the steps in a receiving line sort of arrangement. I approached Charlie and Janelle to ask about the funeral lunch arrangements.

"Those songs were totally inappropriate."

I turned in surprise to find Matthew on the step below me. "I'm sorry," I said with as much sincerity as I could muster. "Your mother appeared comforted by them."

"Mother's in shock," he snarled. "She has no idea what is appropriate behavior or not. At least that man you're seeing made sure his ex-wife didn't show up and distress Mother further."

"I beg your pardon?" Matthew's angry countenance and disdainful words were hard to interpret. It sounded like he was praising Sam, but that didn't make any sense.

"It's the least you could do."

I shook my head slightly. Things did not compute in my foggy brain. "I'm sorry?"

"Your friend." He invested the word with enough venom to make it sound like a friend was a disgusting pervert. "He apparently diverted his ex-wife. She told me she was meeting him this morning."

Now I was thoroughly confused. Sam, meeting with Sheila? When did that happen?

Matthew didn't wait for me to parse his words but continued talking, standing so close to me I could feel the heat from his body, so properly dressed in his tailored suit. "I'm surprised you showed up, though. I thought I made it clear you weren't wanted here. You're not a member of the family."

Charlie moved to stand next to me and I was vaguely aware of Becky and the Second also drifting closer. "You did make it clear," I said quietly, conscious of the stares of other funeral-goers as they left the service. "But your mother asked me to attend so I did it for her."

"Why wouldn't Cassie attend?" Charlie asked, his gaze going from me to Matthew. "Is there a problem?"

"There's been a problem for years," Matthew snapped. "The favoritism you've received."

"Favoritism?" Charlie frowned and looked so honestly perplexed that Matthew stepped back, his face reflecting brief confusion.

I breathed a sigh of relief that the situation was defusing. Then Pauline joined us, her hanky in hand. She glared at me. "Grandfather always loved you and Uncle Charlie the most. It was so obvious. He always favored you."

The Second straightened in outraged surprise. "That's ridiculous."

"It's true." Pauline managed a choked sob before turning to Jon, who put an arm around her shoulders and murmured something consoling in her ear.

"She's upset," I said softly. "Let's go."

"I'm not so upset I don't know what your actions have done to our family." Pauline's voice was shrill and loud, cutting through the gentle murmur of sympathetic voices with the effect of a foghorn. She was on the brink of a hysterical outburst. The best thing I could do was put distance between us.

Becky had other ideas. "Oh, bullshit," she said briskly from my right. She shifted to one side to let people pass. "Father always tried to be fair to us but let's face it—it's hard not to favor Charlie. And Cassie...well, look at her."

I stepped back in surprise. "Me? What about me?"

Becky gestured expansively. "Look at her, she's so cute. She and Charlie were so cute together. Of course everybody loved them. Of course everybody wanted their marriage to succeed. We were all sorry when it didn't, but that didn't mean we would disinherit Cassie just because she and Charlie didn't work out." She shook her head in disgust. "That's got nothing to do with anything. Your father was an asshole, Pauline. That's why nobody loved him. It didn't have anything to do with anyone loving Charlie or Cassie more."

"That's unforgiveable," Matthew snarled. He made a grab for Becky's arm but I was in the way. As he reached for her, he managed to push me to one side. I stumbled, my foot slipping on the step. I flailed out, trying to catch my precarious balance but I was too tipsy. I started to fall into the flower bed that edged the big white steps.

Becky lunged for me, but missed. She began to totter, too, but her husband drew her back from the edge just in time.

Charlie jerked his nephew's arm, pulling Matthew around so Charlie could glare at him in the eyes. "Apologize."

Matthew stared at Charlie. "Never." He drew his arm back to take a swing.

I landed on my butt near the rose bushes and watched as, for the second time in the year, the Whittingtons were involved in a brawl on the steps of the Tedesco Funeral Home.

Chapter 11

"I don't understand why this family is incapable of civilized behavior when we all gather in public," the Second said three hours later. "You certainly weren't raised to behave in such a reprehensible fashion."

"It's not the whole family, it's just John's family," Carlton pointed out. "If you'll recall, last year it was John who took a swing at Cassie." He sat next to me in a padded folding chair on the porch at the family home in Minnetonka watching as Livvie and T.J. spoke to the Justice of the Peace who was conducting the wedding rehearsal. T.J.'s son, Paul Watson, stood next to his father and Becky stood near Livvie, all of them listening attentively.

"Actually, I took a swing first," I corrected.

"You should have decked him last year," Cory, Becky's nineteen-year-old son, said from the seat behind us.

"I tend to agree. You did have just cause to hit him." Carlton turned to look at his stepchildren, seated behind us. "But please keep your voice down."

We were on the first run-through of the wedding rehearsal. The Second had just escorted Livvie into the porch from the doors leading to the lawn. She had insisted on what she called 'ad hoc' seating, so there was no aisle, no 'bride's side' and no 'groom's side'. Everyone would sit in a hodgepodge with the first two rows of chairs reserved for family. Such egalitarian seating arrangements would undoubtedly prove interesting tomorrow when the hoi polloi of high society mingled with graduates of detox programs, waitresses, and T.J.'s biker friends.

After handing her over to T.J., who stood on the low raised platform at the south end of the porch, the Second took his seat with me, Charlie, Janelle, Carlton, and Claire in the first row of chairs. Becky's sons and her daughter sat behind us with some of T.J's friends from his restaurant and an enormous leather-clad man introduced as 'Spike, T.J's buddy from 'Nam.' Spike and Becky's boys were getting along like old school chums and I suspected some mischief was being plotted for bride and groom tomorrow. Behind them should have been John's family. Those seats were empty now, of course, and I doubted we would see any of them on the morrow for the wedding.

"At this point in the ceremony I'll have a short homily about marriage," the J.P. said, his deep voice carrying easily through the small space. He was a tall, thin man with a shock of white hair and a plain face, like an older Dennis Leary minus the sardonic smile.

"Who's the minister guy?" I whispered to Claire.

"Mark Felson. Jeanette Felson's husband." She said it as though I knew the Felson family. "I play bridge with her at the Club."

Trust Claire to come up with a Justice of the Peace who was also a family friend. I looked at my watch. Sam was late. I expected him at the funeral lunch, which had been a silent and awkward affair that I escaped as quickly as possible with Charlie and Janelle close behind me. I thought Sam would be waiting for us at the house, but when we arrived he wasn't there and he hadn't left word about what was keeping him.

I considered checking my Blackberry again but I had checked it before the rehearsal began. My attention was jerked to the front when Livvie turned and looked at me. "This is where I want you to sing," she said.

I nodded my understanding. "I haven't practiced yet, Livvie." I saw the panicked look on her face. "Don't worry. I'll be ready, not a problem. I know the song by heart already. Who's got the music?"

"We have a D.J. hired. He'll have a sound system set up here and at the restaurant for the reception. He promised he would have the right mix." She frowned and I knew this was another worry in an already long list for her. "I'll have him email it to you so you have it ahead of time."

"I can sing *a cappella* if I have to," I assured her. I couldn't, of course. The song required musical accompaniment because of its pacing, but she probably wasn't thinking about that. As long as the D.J. mixed the song right, I could sing it.

"What are you singing?" Cory asked, leaning forward to whisper loudly.

"*Beauty and the Beast*," I replied softly. "The Stevie Nicks one."

"Cool. What's Uncle Charlie singing?"

I looked past the Second to Charlie, sitting next to Janelle near the end of our row. "I don't know, he hasn't said."

"Can you come over here, Cassie? We'll pretend for now."

I bounded to my feet and walked to the platform that elevated the wedding principals from ground level. I went where Livvie pointed, taking a place in front of them to one side so I wouldn't obstruct the view for the audience.

The J.P. waved his arms slightly and hummed

Here Comes the Bride. "We have a song and when it finishes, Mrs. Whittington will resume her seat."

"Ms. Whittington," I corrected. It was a common misconception but one that rankled since Janelle was sitting right there and she would, presumably, become the next Mrs. Whittington very soon. But when I looked at her as I walked back to my chair I saw that she wasn't paying attention. She had withdrawn a cell phone from her purse and was listening to something, her face perplexed and worried.

"Next we'll have the exchange of vows," the J.P. said. "And the exchange of rings." He looked expectantly at Paul, a weathered-looking man in his late thirties with curly black hair and a tall, lean physique. Like his father, Paul had led a rough life as an addict before settling down as a pastry chef at a high end restaurant. His face, and sometimes his manners, reflected his rocky past.

Paul mimed handing T.J. something and Becky mimed handing Livvie something. They went through the motions of exchanging rings then T.J. looked at Charlie. "That's your cue," he called out. "Time for your song."

Charlie was standing, bending over to listen to something Janelle said. He looked at me, his green eyes wide with shock. "What is it?" I asked, a tight feeling of dread starting to unfurl in my gut.

"It's Sam."

I jumped to my feet and the Second stood, too, putting an arm around me and pulling me to a halt when I would have rushed to join Charlie. "What is it?" he asked, his hand gently squeezing my upper arm. "Is there a problem?"

"He had to go to Jordan to check on something at the greenhouse. Is he okay? Was there an accident?" The greenhouses were isolated, located in farm country on a narrow twisting two-lane county road. Since our car accident the previous year I was paranoid about driving on roads like that.

"The police have him. They're questioning him about a murder," Janelle said.

"Murder?" My knees sagged and I was glad to have the old man's arm holding me up. "What? John's murder?"

"No. Sheila's. He was found standing over his ex-wife's body. She was killed in one of his greenhouses."

****

"It's crazy," I repeated for the third time as we sat in the police station at Pickaway, the south metro suburb where I lived. It was the county seat where Jordan was situated and also had the only jail adequate enough to hold an accused murderer. "Sam wouldn't kill her. He hated her but he wouldn't kill her."

Charlie, Janelle, the Second, and I came to the police station, leaving Livvie and the others to carry on the rehearsal without us. I promised to send regular updates via phone or email then we rushed out. The Second drove my car, following Charlie and Janelle who led the way. I was glad my ex-father-in-law was behind the wheel. I was incapable of rational thought. Sheila, dead? Sam, accused? Holy crap, what was the world coming to? Wasn't it just a few days ago that Sam and I were driving to a police station and Charlie was accused of murder? And then a day later I was sitting in a police station? At this rate I would have an intimate knowledge of just about every suburban police station in the Twin Cities metro, a dubious achievement at best.

"This will be cleared up," the Second said, as always an island of calm in the chaos that surrounded us. "The police had to take him into custody because he found the body and because of their acrimonious past. But once all the facts are gathered, it will be obvious Sam had nothing to do with this."

I looked gratefully at him. This scene was scarily reminiscent of one the previous autumn, when he and I sat with Livvie as T.J. was interrogated during a murder investigation. The Second reacted then with the same assurance and aplomb that made me believe the whole thing was just an unfortunate misunderstanding that would be cleared up once reasonable people sat down and chatted about it. I was beginning to appreciate his imperturbable strength, which had been so in evidence during this tumultuous year. Grandy's death, my inheritance, my relationship with Sam, Livvie's falling in love with T.J. and T.J.'s brush with the law—through all of it the Second remained a reliable figure who was there when we needed him and who faded into the background when things started to right themselves.

I stood and paced the small waiting area once again, a regular occurrence in the hour since we arrived. I glanced at the newspaper, which someone had discarded. The headline on the sports page blared something about the Kentucky Derby. The words made no sense to me. How could anyone care about a horse race when the man I loved was in danger?

The thought made me stop so suddenly it probably looked like I was being jerked to a halt. *The man I loved.* This was what Charlie meant when he said that seeing Janelle in danger made him realize how much he cared for her. The thought of Sam in danger like this was incomprehensible. I had experienced fear the previous year when we had our accident and we weren't sure if he would fully recover from his injuries, but then I was so incapacitated with my own injuries that the fear for Sam just blended with my own pain. After he came through the surgery, I felt pity for him because of the intense pain during his physical therapy and recovery.

But I felt fear now—fear that I might not ever see him again without the confines of a cell around him. I had no illusions about the intelligence of law enforcement. Sam was an obvious suspect and depending on what the evidence showed, his innocence might be irrelevant.

"Cassie."

The Second's voice startled me out of my grim thoughts. I turned to find him standing nearby, looking down at me with his patrician face concerned. I saw wisdom, compassion, and understanding in his green eyes, so like Charlie's. "It will be all right," he said softly.

"Will it?" I could barely enunciate the words. "It just feels like there's been so much death, C.R. My father killing Gloria, Grandy dying, Mike Peavey, Aaron, Sheila." All the past deaths seemed to tumble together in my head, all the deaths associated with me in some way, shape, or form.

"You were never responsible for what your father did," he said immediately, putting a firm hand on my left shoulder. "Your mother fled from him to save herself as well as save you. It's not your fault that your father followed her to our home."

"I know." I *did* know it, but sometimes the guilt crept up on me, like now. "But what about Sam? Matthew was right. Because of me, Sam got tangled up with the family and that brought Sheila into the picture. If it wasn't for me, none of you would be involved with her. John might still be alive and—"

His hand tightened. "That's like saying because of me John was born in the first place so it's my fault he died. It's true that your relationship with Sam brought Sheila Peavey into our purview, but it's not the only reason why things happened the way they did. Don't let Matthew bother you. He's been distraught about his father and the business. He's saying things that don't make much sense." The old man hesitated then added, "John's children do not have an unbiased view of the family. I'm just starting to realize that. I have some reparations to make in that department, to Diane and the children."

We both turned as Charlie emerged from a doorway, Janelle close behind him. She came to us immediately while Charlie paused to talk to a tall policeman in a dark polo shirt and jeans who walked with them, a badge dangling from a lanyard around his neck.

"They don't have enough evidence to hold him," Janelle said. "He remains a person of interest but he's free to go. We may need to post bail at some point, though." She looked at the Second as she said it.

"Shall we make arrangements ahead of time in case it's needed?" he asked.

"It might not hurt. Detective Carlson said if you sign some forms then that would help the process." Janelle glanced at Charlie and the man talking with him.

"Of course." The Second squeezed my shoulder again, smiling down at me. "Don't worry, Cassie. We'll handle it." He nodded to Janelle then went to Charlie, shaking hands with the detective who turned to meet him.

"He didn't even ask how much." I regarded the two Whittington men, both of whom were so willing to help me, each in his own way. "What did I do to deserve people like that?"

Janelle smiled. "You're family, Cassie. That's how it is. Did you think Charlie's father would abandon you or Sam?"

"Abandon?" The thought had never occurred to

me. Before I could consider it further, the door opened again and Sam emerged, limping visibly. "Sam!" He still wore his funeral clothes—sports coat, Dockers, and white shirt but his necktie dangled out of his coat pocket instead of being neatly tied around his neck. He looked exhausted, angry, and upset— and he was sight for sore eyes.

I threw myself at him, hugging him so hard I think he gasped. His arms went around me and I buried my face in his neck, drinking in his sweaty-musky-Sam smell. "Gee, I guess I should go in jail more often," he murmured. "This is a great reception."

"Don't you dare." I snuffled against his cheek, feeling the rasp of his whiskers. "Was it awful? How did she die? What happened?"

He pulled away, flicking a glance first right then left. "I'd rather not talk about it here."

I glanced around, too, really seeing the place for the first time. It was about six years old, a brick building with bright white walls in the waiting room and cheerful red cushions on the chairs. As police stations went, it wasn't so bad. At least it looked clean, new, and fresh. Of course, I was becoming an aficionado of such things.

Sam stared past me. "I don't mind Janelle, but did he have to come, too?"

I followed his gaze. "Oh, for heaven's sake. Charlie's a lawyer."

"And he's your ex-husband and someone you still love."

"We're not having this discussion," I hissed as the others walked toward us.

"I'm sure you'd like to get out of here, Sam," the Second said as he tucked a Mont Blanc pen into his suit pocket. "Why don't we go to your home so we can discuss what happened? I'll ride with Janelle and Charlie. I have some things to discuss with them anyway."

The Second, in my home? He had never been there. "Sure," I said uncertainly. Sam looked exhausted and I was reminded that he only recently finished his last round of physical therapy. His leg probably hurt like crazy. "We'll order some pizza or something. Are you hungry?"

Sam smiled gratefully and put an arm around my waist. "Famished. Let's go."

I longed to pepper him with questions as we drove but I refrained, seeing how he leaned against the door, his face bleak. "Are you okay?" I asked quietly as we drove onto the quiet street of my townhouse development.

He looked at the tidy yards and tree-lined streets, so peaceful and serene. "Sheila's dead. It was bad, Cassie. She..." His voice trailed away then he said, "I don't know how I feel. It's weird."

I tried to imagine what he must be feeling. He and Sheila had a rocky relationship, but still she was a part of his past, a person who had once been important to him. How would I feel if my ex died?

As soon as the thought came I was horrified. Good God, Charlie was my ex! I'd be devastated if it was him. I squeezed Sam's hand. "Don't worry. We'll figure it out." I sped up as though getting home would solve all our problems.

When we arrived I left the garage door open so Charlie and the others could come in. Sam went immediately to the bedroom and I heard him talking quietly to Houdini, who followed him. I caught a word here and there. "...jail...dirt ...stupid..."

I put on a pot of coffee then tucked my Blackberry in its cradle to charge. By the time Charlie and the others came in, Sam was sitting at the kitchen table and I had already ordered the pizza. The Second looked around with interest at the kitchen, open family room, and small eat-in area.

The morning paper was still on the table. He nudged it with one finger. "I have ten on the number four horse in the Derby."

"Ten?" Sam asked.

"Ten thousand," I interpreted. Sam blinked in surprise. "Who's the horse?" I asked.

"Paul Parker's son is training him." The Second pulled out a faux oak chair and sat next to Janelle who was eyeing the cookie tray in the middle of the kitchen table.

Those six words summed up all the motivation the Second would need to risk ten grand on a horse race. I glanced at Sam. "Paul and Charlie went to school together," I murmured.

"Ah. The blessing of the son." Sam scowled at Charlie who paused as he handed Janelle a glass of water.

"Now what did I do?" Charlie asked.

I laughed. "Nothing." I was so relieved to have Sam there I felt buoyant. I got out mugs, plates, and spoons and soon we were all gathered around the table, coffee mugs in hand for those of us who weren't pregnant.

The Second was thoroughly examined by cats, who sniffed his Armani-suited ankles with great deliberation. He bore it with stoic amusement, bending down once to rub Houdini's golden ears. "Big cat," he commented.

"He's a husky boy," I said. "Or so the vet says."

The Second raised an eyebrow. "Husky. Indeed." He turned his attention to Sam. "Can you tell us what happened?"

Sam frowned, his dark brown eyes staring at the placemat with intense concentration. "I got a call around ten-thirty this morning, saying there was a problem at the number three greenhouse in Jordan."

"Tender annuals," I muttered.

The Second looked from me to Sam. "Is that

significant?"

"Not really. It's just that number three is set back from the other greenhouses." Sam took six napkins out of the holder in the lazy Susan in the center of the table, arranging them in a two-by-three grid. "Number three is the farthest away from the front entrance and in the back corner of the lot." He tapped the napkin designating the greenhouse. "We had some breakage there last year and I've been keeping an eye on it, thinking vandals might come back. That's why I had security out at the lot."

Charlie sipped his coffee, leaned back in his chair with his right arm resting on the back of Janelle's chair. She stared at the napkins in front of Sam, obviously visualizing the scene in her mind. "Did you recognize the man who called?" Charlie asked. "You're sure it was the watchman?"

Sam shook his head. "That's just it. I'm not sure now. He identified himself and said he was with Simmonds Security. They rotate people in and out, so I've never gotten to know any of them."

"Did you call Simmonds?" the Second asked. "Did you verify that the watchman was there?"

"The police did." Sam ran a hand through his thick white hair and I made a mental note to remind him to get a cut. He was starting to look shaggy. "They said that the watchman made his usual rounds and saw nothing amiss."

"That makes no sense." Janelle finally succumbed to temptation and took a cookie from the plate. "How did Sheila get in? How did someone manage to kill her and not be noticed?" She glanced at Sam. "How was she killed?"

His mouth tightened into a thin line. "I think she was strangled. Her face was...blue. And I don't think it was recent."

"What? Why not?"

"I've seen corpses when they've been left for a

day or more. They start to bloat."

I opened my mouth but no words came out. *I've seen corpses...* Good Lord, this was a side to Sam I knew nothing about. I started to ask him but caught a glimpse of the Second, who shook his head slightly.

"Marines, right?" he asked.

Sam nodded. "It was cool last night but we keep the greenhouses warmer than the outside for obvious reasons. And of course there are the bugs." He shrugged. "It's a greenhouse. Bound to be bugs."

"Bugs? Oh." Janelle pushed her cookie plate away and got to her feet. "Excuse me." She bolted for the door to the mudroom and the tiny powder room that opened off of it.

The doorbell rang and I got up to answer it. Charlie handed me some money and I grabbed it as I passed. I stopped in my tracks when the Second said, "I'd like to know why the hell someone is trying to frame Charlie and anyone associated with him."

I gaped at him, my eyes wide. "What?"

Neither Sam nor Charlie looked surprised. "It's obvious," Sam said with infuriating calmness. "I was called out to the greenhouse and about five minutes after I arrived, the cops arrived." He and Charlie exchanged assessing looks. "Charlie got a call from John, asking to meet him, but when he got there, John was dead and there were no witnesses to Charlie's arrival. And Cassie got a call from John, asking to meet, and a short time later, John was killed." He shot the Second a grudging look of admiration. "Somebody has your family in the cross-hairs."

The old man nodded, his face as hard as flint. For an instant the veneer of social correctness slipped and I saw the construction foreman glaring out. "Whoever it is has picked on the wrong man to fuck with." He tapped the table hard. "Nobody messes with my family."

Chapter 12

What if it's another member of the family? I thought. I saw the same idea in Charlie's eyes as I passed him. He looked so worried I ruffled his hair and got a faint smile in return. As I headed for the door I saw an assessing look in Sam's dark eyes that matched his frown.

I paid for the pizza and came back to the kitchen, plopping the two boxes on the lazy Susan after I shoved off the cookies and napkins. Sam got out some beer and plates, handing both around.

"Sorry," Janelle said as she re-entered the room. "I just remembered what the police said when they were interrogating Sam. They talked about the bugs and..." She looked at the pizza boxes on the table and sighed. "I think I'll pass for now."

"I'll save some for you for later," I promised, putting two slices of sausage-laden pizza on a paper plate and setting it to one side.

"Thanks. Do you have any ginger ale?"

I gestured toward the pantry, next to the fridge. "Help yourself," I mumbled around a bite of cheesy yumminess. "Ice in the freezer." I looked at Sam. "What else happened?"

He took a pinch of cheese and offered it to Truffles, who took it with a delicate nip of her sharp teeth. Sam was one of her favorite people, especially when food was involved. "When I got there, the Simmonds guard was at the front gate. I asked him if he was the one who called, and he said he didn't know what I was talking about."

I waited impatiently as Sam washed down his bite of pizza with beer. Janelle was sitting once again next to Charlie, looking pale in her navy blue-and-white linen dress with matching white jacket. She and Charlie looked like an advertisement for *Vanity Fair* with their crisp good looks and stylish clothing. I mentally compared them to me and to Sam. His clothing was from Target and he was decidedly wrinkled after his day with the police. My jacket had long ago been abandoned, I had a smudge of pizza sauce on my white-and-red top, and my polyester pants looked like I had slept in them. Sam's next words jerked my attention away from my concerns about haute couture.

"The guard and I split up and I went down the rows of greenhouses, checking—"

"Who suggested splitting up?" the Second asked. He was eating his pizza with a knife and fork, a maneuver I admired but didn't try to emulate.

"I did. About five minutes after I got there, I went into Number Three greenhouse." Sam once again lined up the napkins, this time two of them touching each other. He tapped to the left of center of the long rectangle they made. "She was in the middle, against the far wall."

I narrowed my eyes, visualizing the scene. I had only been in that greenhouse once or twice, but the Barlow greenhouses had the same floor plan. The consistency ensured a smooth transition when people shifted from working in the greenhouses at the retail center or at the growing facilities. All employees spent a stint in both areas, allowing them a chance to figure out the best fit for their talents.

If that greenhouse followed true to form, there would be about forty six-foot long potting benches in the greenhouse arranged in ten rows, four benches to a row, with aisles between them. "The chemicals are always stored on that side, aren't they?" I asked.

"Yep. She was lying near the chemical locker."

"Was it locked?"

"Locked tight. I was just bending over her when the police came in."

"Where was the security guard?" Charlie asked.

"He was in Number One. The police rounded him up, too."

A small comment someone made nudged at my memory. "Somebody said...I think it was Matthew...he said Sheila told him she was meeting you." I squinted my eyes, trying to dredge up the exact words. "It was at the funeral this morning." Good heavens, had it only been a few hours ago? Was it still Thursday? It felt as though an eternity had passed. "When we were out on the porch at the funeral home. He said that he had talked to Sheila and she was meeting you." I looked expectantly at Sam.

"I had no plans to meet her." He polished off the slice of pizza on his plate and reached for another. "I wonder where she got that idea. You said it was this morning?"

I nodded, darting a quick look at the Second, who regarded me with patient understanding. "Before the fight, correct?" he asked, wiping his hands fastidiously on a napkin. He looked down and saw Houdini peering up at him. The old man took another piece of pizza, sliced off a small triangle from the tip and offered it to my cat.

Sam almost choked on his pizza. "Fight?"

I gestured it away impatiently. "Just another tussle on the steps of the funeral home. That place brings out the worst in us."

The Second raised an eyebrow but didn't correct me. His gaze returned to Houdini, who was licking at pizza-coated fingers. The Second quirked a smile and cut another small wedge to share.

"I got a voice mail from Sheila yesterday," I said.

"You did? When?" Janelle pulled her Blackberry out of her purse. "You didn't mention that to me."

"I also talked to that detective from last year." Good heavens, I forgot all about that. I almost spit out pizza in my haste to fill them all in. "He called and said that John was the one who hired some guy to fiddle with our tires."

Surprised looks greeted this not only from the humans but from the cats, who had been deprived of their food-giving companions, both of whom paused to regard me. "Sorry," I mumbled. "I forgot to tell you."

"What else did you forget to mention?" Janelle asked.

Oops. I told them about my shopping excursion and the phone call from Detective Madison. "He said that some guy said that John hired him." I frowned. "He said that it was John and maybe John's son and a woman. I assumed he meant Diane but maybe..."

"Maybe it was Sheila." Charlie pulled out his Blackberry. "I think I'll give Billy Armstrong a call. He can ask for a copy of the files." He got up and walked away from the table, his phone pressed to his ear.

"After I talked to the detective, I finished shopping," I continued. "Then Sheila called me. She sounded mad." I eyed another slice of pizza but restrained myself. I knew that T.J. had an excellent wedding feast planned for the morrow and I wanted to save my calories for that.

"What do you mean 'she sounded mad?'" Sam asked. I noticed he was on his third slice of pizza. Of course, he didn't have to worry about his weight or waist.

"It sounded like she was yelling at somebody. She called earlier and said she needed to talk to me. Then she called again. She said she knew who killed John."

The Second dropped his silverware on his paper plate with a clatter. "And you didn't think to mention this to the police?"

I made a disparaging noise, a cross between a snort and *oh, pa-leeze*. "What could she know? And if she knew something, why would she call me? We aren't exactly best buds. Besides, if she knew anything about John's death, the police would be on her like a duck on a June bug."

Janelle winced. "Please. Don't mention bugs."

"Sorry. Sheila said something like, 'don't do that' or 'what do you mean' then she hung up. As soon as she did, I got another call from Diane. So I went over there and in the planning for the funeral I forgot all about Sheila and that detective."

"What time was this?" Janelle asked, thumbing furiously at her Blackberry.

"Three o'clock or so, yesterday afternoon. I went over to see Diane. Then Matthew called me last night and said he talked to Sheila. So she must have been alive then."

The Second got to his feet and went to my kitchen sink, washing off his hands and drying them on the bar towel hanging on my fridge handle. He looked at Charlie who stood near the family room, his phone pressed to his ear. The Second's face was unreadable, his eyebrows drawn together in a frown as he considered some thought only he was privy to. Then he looked at me, but I know he didn't see me. Those usually sharp green eyes looked sunken in his face, as though some weight pulled them and his thoughts inward. His mind was obviously a million miles away.

My mind was just confused. "How did Sheila get into the greenhouse? And why?" I asked the room at large.

Sam took a last bite of his pizza then tugged off the cheese into a little ball. Truffles put her velvety black paws on the side of his chair, waving her right front paw in the air. *Feed me,* she plainly said. *Feed me. Feed the little kitty, so tiny compared to the Big Guy. Feed me, the poor homeless orphan until I was found by the pretty lady. Feed me.* Sam heard her pleas and held out the squishy ball, which she took with a dainty click of her teeth.

"My guess is she met someone there during the day," he said, wiping his greasy fingers on a napkin. "The greenhouses were open yesterday because we were transporting stock to the retail center."

"I don't understand," Janelle said, setting her phone back on the table. "A person couldn't just walk in there, could they? That's why you have a security guard, right?" She looked from Sam to me.

"This is a busy time of year," I said before he could reply. "They can't keep guards on the houses all the time. That would be too cumbersome. Seasonal workers are carrying stock in and out, trucks are coming and going. I mean, people have ID badges, but sometimes they're not always visible."

"It would be easy." Sam leaned back in his chair. Truffles correctly interpreted that as a sign that no more food was coming and she sat down at his feet to bathe. "Cassie's right. This is our busiest time of year. We've got employees coming and going." He pursed his lips thoughtfully. "Sheila was wearing a Barlow T-shirt and jeans when I found her. Anybody seeing her would figure she was from one of the stores, coming to get something."

"Where did she get…?" I subsided before finishing the question. Barlow T-shirts were sold in both retail stores as well as given to employees. She might even have one still from when she was married to Sam. The design and colors changed now and again, but no one would remark on an older version.

"Who did she meet?" the Second asked, coming back to the table. He looked down at Houdini, who was stretched out on the Second's empty chair. The big cat looked back at him, yawned then settled his head on his paws. The Second looked at me as though to ask for help but I shrugged. The Second took Charlie's still empty chair next to Janelle.

"The police said they're gathering descriptions from the different people who were there yesterday, trying to figure out who was where. But it still doesn't make sense." Sam glared at his empty plate as though it was the cause of all our worries. "How could someone kill her and leave her there and no one find her until today?"

He was right. What would keep people out of a busy greenhouse during retail season? People were constantly coming and going in those greenhouses, transporting stock from there to the stores. I considered and discarded several ideas in the time it took to draw breath.

"Billy said he talked to Detective Madison over in Mound." Charlie came back to the table, glanced at Houdini then picked up the big cat and sat down with fifteen pounds of cat on his lap. Houdini blinked sleepily then settled into a pile of purring golden fur with a long sigh. "They got a statement from a man who said John paid him to loosen the valve on Cassie's tires. All it took was a few minutes of driving and the tire would go flat."

"Does that mean John didn't plan for an accident?" the Second asked. "Was it just a malicious prank that went terribly wrong?"

He sounded hopeful. I suppose he hated to think that one of his children was capable of planning a catastrophic accident like the one, which almost killed Sam and me. I reserved my opinion, a task made easier by Sam pressing his foot against mine under the table.

"That's irrelevant," Charlie snapped. "The consequences are what are important." He looked at me, his face tight and angry. "Cassie and Sam were almost killed."

The Second winced, his craggy face suddenly sagging. "Almost is the operative word." I tried to sound light-hearted about it, but inside I was seething. No one knew how much pain Sam underwent during surgery, recovery, and therapy. I didn't know where John was currently, but I hoped at least some of Sam's agony was visited on him.

"I wish I could make sense of this," the Second said. "Who is trying to harm our family and why?"

Sam rubbed his forehead. "I don't know, but it's giving me a headache."

Janelle pushed away from the table. "You've had a hard day." She glanced at me and raised one eyebrow and I nodded fractionally, blessing her for noticing his exhaustion. "We've all got a big day tomorrow, too. We'll let you get some rest."

The Second looked momentarily surprised then he stood, also. It took Charlie a bit longer since he had to dislodge my portly old cat, but eventually he, too, got up. Sam walked with the Second and Janelle to the door while Charlie and I followed behind.

"Someone framed Sam for this," Charlie said softly. "Father was right."

"None of it makes sense to me. Sheila was alive last night and she told Matthew she was going to meet with Sam. When will they have the autopsy results?"

Charlie hesitated. "It will take days. Sam's free but..." He looked ahead of us, where Sam stood near the front door, talking to Janelle. "Let's take it one step at a time."

My stomach knotted when I heard that. It wasn't like Charlie to be so gloomy. Of course, it wasn't like Charlie to be involved in two murder investigations, either. He brushed a kiss against my cheek. "Don't forget, you need to practice for Livvie." He stared down into my eyes. "We can't let her down."

I met his gaze, reading regret, loss, and uncertainty there. Or was I just projecting my own feelings? "What song are you singing?"

He smiled, dimples appearing at the sides of his full lips. "A secret."

Janelle laughed. "He won't even tell me, Cassie. See you tomorrow."

I felt a momentary stab of jealousy at the proprietary way she said that then she and the Second left, calling good-byes over their shoulders. Charlie followed after, saying something to his father that made the old man grin.

Sam closed the door behind them. "I thought they'd never leave." He swept me into his arms and before I knew what was happening, his lips fastened on mine and I was gasping for breath. A long, passionate moment later he released me. "God, Cassie. I was so scared." Sam's breath was warm on my neck. I shivered when he shuddered against me. "I was innocent and I was scared. Can you imagine what it must be like if you're guilty and the police have you?" He pulled back and looked at me.

"I was scared, too," I murmured, running my fingers over the stubble of his beard. "I was afraid I wouldn't see you again. I was afraid..." I pulled him to me and kissed him hard.

"You know what I'm afraid of now?" he asked when we finally broke apart.

"Hmm?" I had his shirt undone and was working on his belt.

"I'm afraid we might not make it to the bedroom." His hands slid over my silky top and he started working on the small buttons on the back. "Why the hell do they put so many fasteners on these things?" he muttered.

I reached behind me, undid the top two snaps then pulled it off over my head. "Just to frustrate men like you."

He laughed and grabbed me, kissing me and edging me backward until we landed on the living room couch. "Let's celebrate my thankfully short brush with the law."

I shivered and I'm not sure if it was from remembering my earlier thoughts or the chill in the air. It didn't matter. I pulled Sam to me. "How would you like to celebrate?" I asked as I stood to shed my dress pants.

He smiled up at me. "Lady's choice."

"Well, if you insist..." I pushed him back and started working at his belt in earnest.

****

We eventually made it to the shower then back to the kitchen for a warmed-up slice of pizza. I decided to broach the subject that was buzzing in my brain. "This whole crazy week has made me think a lot about, well, about us, I guess."

Sam sprawled on the family room loveseat in sweatpants and a T-shirt, Houdini next to him. I sat on the opposite love seat, my feet tucked into my bathrobe and a glass of wine nearby. Sam rubbed Houdini's ears and the big cat rumbled happily in response. "I know what you mean. When I was talking to those cops, I kept thinking, 'I can't believe Sheila's dead'." He leaned back, the light over the kitchen sink illuminating half of his face and leaving the other half in shadow, like a parody of Batman's nemesis, The Riddler. "I knew Sheila almost all of my life, just like you knew Charlie."

"I didn't know that," I said slowly. Some small fact percolated in my brain, something someone said to me months earlier. "She grew up in town?"

He nodded. "Her father sold my father the land where the landscape center sits. I remember going out to his place. It was a farm then. She was younger than me, but I remember her. She was so young and so pretty. When I got out of the Marines, I saw her again in college. I was starting school late but she was there and…" Sam shifted position, easing his right leg up so he could prop it on the coffee table. "The last few days have made me think—or maybe re-think—what I've been feeling." He finally looked me, the light on his glasses hiding his eyes. "Maybe re-think about what we should do."

The pizza in my stomach suddenly felt leaden. "I'm not sure what you mean," I said warily, picking up my wine glass.

"It was when I saw when Charlie and Janelle were going through." He stared past me, obviously sorting his words carefully. "They're facing life changing decisions. It's obvious that Charlie loves her and she loves him, but I don't think they're in love with each other."

I started to protest this description but he held up a hand. "That's not a bad thing. I think, once you get past a certain age, it's hard to fall *in* love. But it may be easier to love because we aren't distracted by all the hormones and the fluttery feelings and the emotions."

I thought about what he said then nodded slowly. "I think I see what you mean."

"When you were young, you and Charlie fell in love. And when I was younger, I fell in love with Sheila. Those relationships didn't last for whatever reason. You and Charlie stayed friends and you love each other. Sheila and I…" He shook his head regretfully. "We weren't so fortunate. Now Charlie is trying to put that love in perspective so he can make a life with Janelle."

"I think he's done that," I said, although I wasn't sure at all. "I know I have."

"Have you?" Sam looked directly at me, his brown eyes dark and mysterious.

"Yes."

He searched my face for a long moment then looked away. "I'm not sure I have. I'm not sure if I love you enough to marry you, Cassie."

I went hot then cold, as though dunked in ice water. Fragmented thoughts raced through my brain. "There's not much I can do about that," I finally said. "Like you said, I love you, but I'm not in love with you. I don't feel the same thing for you that I felt for Charlie, all those years ago. This is different. I think it's worth building a future on, but if you don't..." I stood, suddenly unwilling to put myself through any more emotional gymnastics. Sam wasn't the only one who had done a lot of thinking in the last few days. I felt like my head was stuffed full of emotions, memories, and regrets.

"I'm not sure," he admitted in a low voice.

Several retorts sprang to mind: *when you're sure, call me. There's no such thing as a sure thing. I'm sure even if you're not.* Instead I said, "I need to get some rest." I managed a smile. "It's Livvie's big day tomorrow and I won't let her down."

"I'm sorry, Cassie. I wish I could be more positive."

I hesitated at the kitchen doorway. "It doesn't really matter, Sam." He looked so surprised I smiled. "I'm way past the age my heart can be broken if a man doesn't love me."

"I didn't say I didn't love you," he said quickly.

"You're splitting hairs." I was tired and I didn't care that he saw it. "It's pretty straightforward to me, Sam. You love me or you don't. You want to be with me, or you don't. If you don't want to commit to the future now, that's fine. But someday we have to face it. Someday we need to decide if we're going to be together."

He nodded in understanding. "It's just all confused now."

I turned away, praying he wouldn't see the bitter anger on my face. Confused?

He had no idea.

Chapter 13

I awoke before Sam and slipped out of our warm bed in the grayness of pre-dawn. Houdini stirred sleepily from his spot pressed against Sam's legs, blinking at me before tucking his head under one arm. Truffles padded after me, an attentively silent shadow.

It was a chilly morning, typical for the first of May in Minnesota. A haze of light frost or heavy dew dusted the front lawn, making it shimmer in the early light. I made a pot of coffee and huddled on the window seat in the kitchen to stare at the outside world.

I was curiously detached from my emotions, as though my talk the night before with Sam had worn me down to a nubbin and all that remained was an outline. I had no idea what my future might hold. I was drifting and I was content to have it so. I didn't want to think. I had done too damn much thinking in the past week and I was content to stop for a while.

I pulled out a mixing bowl and made my favorite scone recipe, one that was simple and foolproof. Soon the kitchen smelled of cinnamon and coffee, comforting aromas that made me think of my mother, Grandy Theo, and baking days from my past. My childhood was a schizophrenic mix of beauty and tragedy, the bloody memories of murder mingling with an idyllic home life. My mother always said a good muffin could go a long way to solving the world's problems and I often followed that advice in my personal life.

I considered the day ahead. Livvie wanted the women of the family at the house by one in the afternoon to help her prep for the wedding ceremony. I thought a two-hour prep time was a bit excessive, but I wasn't going to deny Livvie the excitement of her day. She had been through hell with her first husband and a form of hell after his death when she escaped the psychological abuse he piled on her by climbing into a bottle. T.J. helped her climb out and I would do anything I could to make sure their Big Day went the way they wanted.

"That means I should practice," I told Truffles, who peered out the window with me at the birds gathering around St. Frank, pecking at the seeds Sam put out earlier. I ran through the lyrics in my head as poured a thermos of coffee and dabbed a generous dab of butter on a warm scone.

I went to my office and checked my email. Livvie had mailed me the music file from the D.J. so I downloaded it to my phone. I took a quick peek at my Facebook page, noting that Cory's status said, *Wedding day to attend and good things planned— pictures later!* I made a mental note to talk to Carlton and make sure the boys didn't blow anything up. I updated my status with a quick, *'Big wedding today! Shout out to Livvie and T.J. and best wishes to them.'* I had several pending friend requests but I decided to save those for another time.

Next I snuck into the bedroom and grabbed some sweatpants, a T-shirt, and some socks before sneaking back out. Neither Sam nor Houdini acknowledged my intrusion. I dressed in the bathroom and was out the door in five minutes, pulling on a dark green hoody to protect against the morning chill. I tucked the thermos under my arm as I polished off the scone before crossing the street in front of my townhouse. I wiggled through a waist-high hedge of red-twig dogwoods, just starting to leaf out. On the other side of the bushes was a small up-hill, which leveled off before dropping down steeply to a drainage pond. Beyond that was a major boulevard in town.

I walked downhill until the townhouses were lost to sight behind me and stopped at a big boulder in the middle of the scrub brush and grass. I occasionally came to this open field to practice my singing since there was no one to hear me and I could sing as loud as I liked. I fiddled with the phone so I could hear the music and I started to sing, trying out different types of pacing and intonation for parts of the song. I didn't have Stevie Nicks' breathy voice. Mine was a bit more powerful and I had more range, so I experimented with using it to best effect with the simplified music the D.J. had devised.

The lyrics were amazingly appropriate for Livvie and T.J. and as I suspected, they were also appropriate for me, for Charlie, and for Sam. As I sang, memories crowded around me like a silent audience in the meadow. Summers at the cabin in northern Minnesota, all of the Whittington kids and me playing at the lake or camping out with friends. School in the wintertime, my mother waiting for us after classes in the kitchen, waiting to hear what happened that day. High school and the cliques there, the girls who ignored me because my mother was a nanny and the others who tolerated me because I was Becky and Livvie's 'big sis.'

Saturdays spent with Grandy Theo at her house in Minnetonka, having 'tea parties' and discovering my singing voice. Lessons, a small career in singing then discovering how much I loved Charlie, discovering that he was the first love of my life.

Charlie...Charlie was a part of my life since I was ten years old. Now we were finally parting ways and I was bereft, as though a part of my soul was being severed. I could sense my memories fading and dissipating, like ghosts on the breeze. My past was escaping me and I longed to hold on to it, I longed to have that safety net there to catch me. Through everything in my life I had Charlie there to back me up, Charlie I could call when I needed a shoulder to cry on, Charlie I could talk to when I needed advice. It was all changing. It was all going away.

And Sam...in the year I had known him, he became an integral part of my life, almost as much as Charlie was. I relied on his opinion, I worried about his health, and I plotted and planned to create a future for him. We had danced around the idea of love and forever since we met, both of us convinced that to do so would jinx our relationship. My inheritance complicated matters, making Sam wary about what people would say when they found out I was rich. I knew exactly how he felt because for years I felt that way about Charlie and me.

And now...? I re-cued the music and sang the song again, but my voice clogged with tears and I couldn't continue. Now Sam wasn't sure how much he loved me and Charlie would be getting married and starting a life that excluded me. I felt like a spider dangling on a strand, twisting in the breeze. The next good wind might blow me somewhere completely new.

I sniffled and looked around me. The sun was fully up and the birds zoomed around me, snatching at bugs only they could see. "Well, if it blows me somewhere new, I hope it's interesting," I muttered. I turned and looked up the hill. I wanted Sam in my

life, but only if he wanted to be there. If he didn't...
"Life is all about how you handle Plan B," I said to a
swallow that darted past me.

It dipped a wing, cutting upward so fast I could
barely follow the flight. Then it twisted, turned, and
came down again just a foot or two from my face. I
laughed at the sight of something so graceful, so
purposeful, and so agile.

By the time I got back to my townhouse I knew
how I was going to sing the song. This was Livvie's
day and the song was all about her and T.J. My past
was behind me and an unknown future was in front
of me and that's just how it was. I was smiling when
I entered the kitchen, but I stopped when I saw Sam
sitting at the table, an open newspaper in front of
him next to a plate with a half-eaten scone. "Early
morning walk?" he asked.

I put my now-empty thermos on the kitchen
island and pulled a mug out of the cupboard.
"Practice," I said. "I want to get the song right for
Livvie."

"Hmm." He took a bite of scone and watched me
as I got some coffee then joined him at the table. "I
didn't mean to sound so harsh last night. That
experience with the cops really shook me. And
finding Sheila like that..." He drew in a long,
shuddering breath.

I took his hand and gave it a little shake. "It's
okay, Sam. Really. We'll figure out where we're
going before we get there." I picked up my coffee and
sipped it, regarding him over the rim of my Neil
Young *Rust Never Sleeps* tour mug.

He looked perplexed. "I guess I figured you'd be
a bit more..."

"Pissed off?" I supplied. "I'm not going to worry
about it today, Sam. This is Livvie's day and I'm
going to do everything I can to be upbeat, positive,
and make sure this is the best wedding she can

have. Everything else can just take a back seat—my feelings, your feelings, murder, blackmail...”

“Blackmail?”

I blinked in surprise. “Where did that come from?”

“Freudian slip? Something you heard?”

“I have no idea.” My phone chimed *Wasted Time*, my default ringtone. “Who’s calling this early?” I looked at the teapot-shaped clock over my kitchen entryway. It was just barely eight o’clock. I grabbed my Blackberry and stared down at the caller ID. “PPD1? Who’s that?” I put the phone to my ear. “Hello?”

“My name is Alex Sanders. I’m with the Pickaway Police Department. Is this Cassandra Whittington?”

Good Lord. Yet another cop. “This is she.”

“We’re partnering with the Jordan PD regarding the murder of Sheila Peavey.”

I looked at Sam. I wondered if the Pickaway PD knew I was sleeping with their prime suspect. If they did, I needed to watch what I said. And if they didn’t, maybe I could get some intel. Then I shook my head. Who was I kidding? I was totally inept in the intel department. “How can I help?”

“Phone records show that Mrs. Peavey contacted you yesterday afternoon. Do you mind telling me what was discussed?”

“We didn’t discuss anything. She left me a message.”

“On an answering machine?” His voice quickened.

“On my phone.

“Do you still have it?”

“The phone? Yes.”

Now he sounded aggravated. “The message.”

“Oh. Probably. I’m not very good with the ins and outs of this phone yet.”

168

"Can you stop by the station at your earliest convenience? We'd like to make a copy—"

My phone vibrated in my hand. Either someone was calling me or I was getting email, I couldn't remember what vibration indicated. "Sure. I'm a bit busy today but I'll drop by this morning."

He gave me directions how to get there and who to ask for then he hung up. I checked my phone screen. *One missed call.* "Guess what?" I told Sam as I accessed the voice mail menu. "The Pickaway PD want my help."

He snorted. "Did you decline to assist them?"

I held up a hand as Diane's distraught voice sounded in my ear. "Cassie, I need to talk to you. The estate is in disarray. John left everything to Sheila, but she died earlier than five days after his death so she can't inherit. It's some kind of law or something. So the estate reverts to the children, which is what John wanted before he met that bitch. But now it has to go to probate and that means we can't get any money until it clears probate. We're destitute, Cassie. I'm not sure what to do. John's creditors are calling me and the bank has said that the house isn't paid for. I thought it was. I've tried calling Charlie but he's not answering his phone. I don't know what else to do. Call me as soon as you can." There was a pause. "Please."

"Why the hell is she calling me?" I asked Truffles, who sat across from me at the table and peered over the edge, golden eyes glued to the scone on my plate.

"I meant to tell you," Sam said. "I talked to Joe Swenson yesterday. He wanted me to drop by today to go over some of the business papers at Min-Gen." His phone chimed. Sam fished it out of the holster on his belt. "What's up, T.J.?" I heard him ask.

I pressed the menu button on my phone, poised to call Diane back when my phone chimed *New Kid*

In Town, my ringtone for Janelle. "Good morning," I said when I answered.

"I'm glad you're up. Guess what?"

"Hmm?" I looked at Sam, who was reaching for a notepad and nodding as though T.J. could see him.

"You're a rich woman. The probate clerk just called. The judge handed down his ruling yesterday. We need to sign some papers and you'll be fifteen million dollars richer."

"Holy buckets." I grinned at Sam. "I'm rich."

He glanced at me. "I know. Where is it, T.J.? Do I need to bring some potting soil or—okay, good." He returned his attention to the notepad and the numbers he was jotting.

"He's not impressed," I told Janelle. "What kind of papers do I sign?"

"A bunch. Can you meet me in an hour?"

"Hey, Cassie." Sam looked at me from across the table. "I need your car. T.J. has some stuff he needs me to do and my car is still at the greenhouse out in Jordan."

"I heard that," Janelle said. "I can pick you up."

"Give me an hour," I said. "I haven't showered yet."

"Why don't you just bring along your wedding clothes? It's going to take us at least two hours at the courthouse then we can just go to the house to meet Livvie." Janelle sounded suddenly doubtful. "I mean, I guess I'm supposed to meet her. She told me to come over."

"Of course you are. You're a Whittington woman now." Sam looked up when I said this and shot me a puzzled look then started to speak. I made a shushing motion.

"Well, not yet, but...Charlie asked me to marry him again and I...I'm not sure, Cassie. I think he's sincere."

I turned away slightly, trying to use what little

privacy I could find. "I know he is, Janelle. Please consider it."

She chuckled. "Oh, I am. I'll see you in an hour."

I clicked Disconnect and dropped my phone on the table. Sam had ended his phone conversation and now stared at the notepad, frowning. "What's the problem?"

He added a column of figures. "The florist screwed up. They delivered Rave of the Waves petunias instead of Sugar and Spice."

I grimaced. "Whoa. That's a problem." 'Rave' was neon purple while 'Sugar' was a pastel yellow. I stood and stretched.

"No kidding. Luckily Livvie knows a guy in the landscape business." He waggled his eyebrows.

"Do you have Sugar and Spice at the store?" He shot me a disbelieving look. I raised a hand. "Sorry."

He looked slightly abashed. "She needs ten flats."

"Ten flats?" I made a quick mental calculation. There were ten four-plant packs per flat. "That's four hundred plants. What does she need all that for?"

"They're edging the patio and the porch with them in some kind of urn. I need to make some calls. I'm not sure I have that much stock." He peered down at his phone. "I can call Bobby over at Linder's. They'll have some. And I need to call Barb Bachman. She'll have the roses."

I paused as I left the room. "The roses? What's wrong with the roses? Livvie wanted those pale yellow roses all around the stage thing."

Sam glanced at me. "You don't want to know. Go shower. Janelle's picking you up?"

I nodded. "I'll just take my wedding duds and dress at the house. Why don't you meet me there this afternoon?"

"Will do." He looked at his watch. "I'll call Joe and see if I can meet with him tomorrow instead. I think this is going to keep me busy for the morning at least. Will that goof up any plans for the weekend?"

I shrugged. "We can go open the house on Sunday. It's just you and me going there, so it doesn't matter what time we leave or what time we get there."

"Good. I wanted to go over some orders with Polly, too, but that's not going to get done today. Let's plan on going north on Sunday then." Sam started dialing a new number on his phone, his thoughts obviously consumed by the problem of finding four hundred petunias on May first at nine o'clock on a Friday morning.

I was halfway through my shower when I remembered Diane and her woes. As I toweled off I thought through her dilemma. By the time I was dressed in jeans and my red 'Everything Goes Better with Ketchup' polo shirt, I knew what I wanted to do. I put some lotions and cosmetics into a tote bag with my marrying shoes then grabbed my marrying outfit, still in the J C Penney bag. I left my gear in the foyer and went back to the kitchen where the cats were in their usual spots on the window seat, eyeing the world outside. Sam had tidied up our plates and left a note in the middle of the table.

I love you and want to be with you. I just need some time to think.

I sighed. Time to think. We were short on that commodity lately. I felt as though we were all being herded along a path by some unknown dog nipping at our heels. I ran a hand through my hair, still damp from the shower. I was tired of being pushed. It was time for me to push back. Houdini looked over one massive golden shoulder at me and blinked slowly as though agreeing with my thoughts.

Janelle's dark green BMW pulled into the driveway. I grabbed my costume from the coat hook and went out the front door.

"Beautiful day for a wedding," she said after I hung my dress from the ceiling hook in the back seat of her car. Another dress bag hung there, too and another small tote bag sat on the back seat. Apparently Janelle would be changing out of her Lawyer's Uniform as soon as we finished our business.

I slipped into the passenger seat and buckled up. "Thank God. I had visions of a late season snowstorm." I looked appreciatively at the budding trees, bright sunshine, and tulips swaying as we left my townhome development. The air was chill with the heady aroma of cut grass wafting on the breeze. "Sam is busy finding four hundred petunias for wedding decorations."

"If anyone can do it, Sam can."

"I need to stop by the police station." I smiled at her skeptical look and explained about my early morning phone call in between giving her directions to the station.

"That's interesting," she said as we walked into the building. "I wonder what other phone calls Sheila made."

I was so surprised I stopped, almost getting hit by the door as it swung shut. "What do you mean?"

"I just wonder if she called anyone before or after you."

We didn't have time to discuss it. I reported in at the front desk and soon my phone and I were in a technician's office. The phone was plugged into a device while I accessed my voice mail, flubbing the password a couple of times in my nervousness. But finally I found the correct message. A copy was made and I was ushered out again just a few minutes later. I signed some papers then Janelle and I were on our way.

"So are you excited?" Janelle asked as she

steered us onto the freeway that ran into downtown Minneapolis where the county courthouse was situated.

"It's hard to believe, after all this time, I might actually inherit. Can we set up the trust fund and the charity like we planned?"

She nodded. "All the paperwork is ready. It just needs signatures and notarizing."

"I want to make one small change."

She hazarded a look at me before merging onto the freeway. "Okay," she said cautiously. "What kind of small change are we talking about?"

We discussed my idea for most of the thirty minute drive. By the time we pulled into the parking ramp at the Hennepin County Courthouse the details were ironed out. "Are you sure?" Janelle asked as we rode the elevator upstairs to the ninth floor. She nodded to a couple of men in power suits riding with us. Their gazes swept over me in my casual wear and I felt invisible. Of course, invisibility in a courthouse wasn't a bad feeling so I didn't mind.

"I'm sure," I said. "Let's face it, I'm inheriting fifteen million. I may as well put it to good use and help the family at the same time." I didn't lower my voice and the startled look on the faces of the suited ones was sweet reward.

She led the way out of the elevator when it stopped. "I think it has merit. And I think Grandy Theo would approve." She flashed me a quick smile then pulled open an imposing wooden door. "She just disliked John, but I don't think she had a beef with the kids. Although she told me once that Matthew gave her the willies."

I thought about that as Janelle gave our names to a secretary and we were ushered into a wood paneled boardroom. I always attributed my aversion to Matthew as part of my aversion to John and his brood, but Grandy Theo was right. Matthew was an odd child, prone to cold anger and a rigid, inflexible morality that made him a prig. He had matured into an equally inflexible adult who made everyone around him uncomfortable.

More power-suited men rose to their feet as we entered the room. I pushed my worrisome thoughts aside when I saw the stack of papers waiting us on the table. "It's about damn time," I muttered.

Two of the men blinked in surprise but the other two just hid smiles. They were lawyers with Janelle and had been involved in the litigation. "No kidding," Janelle said as she pulled out a chair. "Shall we?"

I sat down, picked up the heavy gold pen, and grinned. "Let's do it."

****

It was almost noon by the time we finished. My 'one small change' necessitated the reprinting of several hefty documents, which delayed us, then one of the lawyers for the charitable trust wanted to revise some of the wording in the contracts we were using.

But at noon Janelle and I walked out. I had half-a-million dollars available to me in a money market account and almost ten million invested in various places. I had ample funds available for investing in Min-Gen Botanical Research and Development but that had to be put on hold because of Sheila's death.

"I don't know how that will play out," Janelle said as we went to the parking garage. "It all depends on what kind of will Sheila had. Her part of the company may revert to Joe Swenson, making him sole owner. Or she may have left her holdings to an heir." She clicked the lock fob and her car chirped in response. "This means the property lawsuit she and Sam were tangled about is resolved, too. The land should come to him free and clear now." She hesitated as she opened the rear door of her car and stowed her briefcase inside. "At least, I think that's what will happen. Charlie mentioned last night that he was going to look into it."

"More papers to sign, I suppose," I grumbled, but I didn't really mind. I was thinking about the charitable trust we had just created. Five million dollars of my inheritance was invested in assorted areas to fund the Gloria Penningford Whittington Foundation to assist women to leave abusive relationships. Originally I wanted Matthew and Marcy, Becky's daughter, to serve on the board of directors and oversee setting up the foundation. But Diane's phone call changed my mind and I tapped her instead of Matthew to represent John's family. A reasonable salary would keep her head above water and a short-term loan of a million dollars would keep the wolf at bay, at least for now. It was what programmers called a 'kludge,' a temporary stopgap measure that would need to be fixed permanently later.

As we drove out of the garage my phone chimed *Wasted Time.* I put it to my ear but all I heard was static. "Hello?"

"...call earlier?"

I looked down at the display. "Oh, hey, Diane. Listen, can I call you back? The reception is bad here."

"...police talk to...and he's not here..."

"Diane, I can't understand you." I held my head nearer the car window in the foolish belief I could have better access to whatever random satellite was handling our call. All I got was more static and a voice fading in and out.

"...to do..."

We emerged from the parking garage onto the city streets and her voice was suddenly loud in my ear. "You don't understand. Matthew doesn't handle this kind of stress well. I'm afraid of what he'll say."

"I'm sorry, Diane, I didn't catch most of that. Janelle and I are in the car." I considered telling her about the plans I just put into place but decided to wait until I saw her. "We're going to the house now. Are you coming over?"

"Don't you understand?" Her voice was shrill and I winced. "The police are looking for Matthew. They think he killed his father."

Chapter 14

"Whoa, hold on, Diane." I looked at Janelle, who was shooting me puzzled glances. "The police are talking to everyone. There's nothing to worry about."

"You don't understand. Matthew gets…nervous sometimes. I'm afraid of what he'll say. That's why I want you to call Charlie and have him find Matthew."

I blew out an exasperated breath. "Have *you* called Charlie?"

"Didn't you get my earlier message?" Her voice was starting to sound shrill. "Charlie won't answer the phone for me."

She was probably right and I really couldn't blame him. But I couldn't say that. "Okay, listen. Janelle and I are on our way to the house to hang out with Livvie. Why don't you and Pauline come over soon? We'll talk about it when you get there."

"This is serious, Cassie. You need to call Charlie and—"

I waggled my phone out the window. "Bad signal, Diane," I said when I pulled it back in. "I'll talk to you later." I pressed Disconnect and leaned back. "I know I did the right thing to help Diane, but she's a bit much at time."

Janelle smiled. "The way the Foundation is set

up, you only have to meet with her directly once a month."

"Thanks to whoever thought of that little provision. She said the police were looking for Matthew, to question him about John's murder."

"They're talking to everyone," Janelle said dismissively, steering us onto Interstate 394, a major east-west freeway.

"I tried to explain that." I pressed the C on my phone, my speed dial indicator for Charlie. "I need Charlie to talk to her."

Janelle shook her head. "He won't like it. She's been bombarding him with questions since John died."

"Then a few more won't hurt." I shrugged when I saw her wry look. "Hey, Charlie," I said when he answered the phone. "I need some help."

"So does Livvie. Father hired a valet to handle the cars for the wedding at the house. Those people going to the reception afterward will have their cars driven to the restaurant. For the others, the valets are supposed to meet guests and take the cars to the Club for parking. But apparently the Club is worried they might need to open the auxiliary parking lot in order to accommodate the extra cars because they have another event there that's using the main parking lot, which is sure to fill up."

"And the problem?" I prompted when he didn't continue.

"The auxiliary parking lot is scheduled to get blacktopped today. I have to go to the Club and if the lot isn't available, I've got to find another parking lot for forty cars somewhere within a three-mile radius of our house. Do you know how hard that will be?"

Almost impossible, I thought but didn't say. "What about the church on the corner?"

There was a pause. "Maybe. What denomination is it?"

"How would I know? It's your family's neighborhood." I thought about it. "Methodist? Call Betty, she'll know."

"Damn. Why didn't I think of that? Betty knows everybody in the neighborhood. I'll do that. What's up with you?"

I quickly explained Diane's problems and what I had done. "You're too nice," he said when I finished. "I'll give her a call as soon as I sort out this car crap. Have you seen Janelle? Did she go back to the office?"

"She's driving. We're heading to the house. Livvie wanted us there early."

"I'll see you there, then. I wasn't sure if I was supposed to pick her up or not."

"Livvie wanted all the Whittington girls there to share the day." I waited to see what he would say to that.

Charlie laughed but it was forced. "Livvie is making sure I make it legal and soon."

I kept my face pointed straight ahead but I was aware of Janelle next to me, her attention supposedly on the road. I wondered if she could hear the conversation. "It's what you want, right? I mean, it's not just the right thing but it's...you know, the *right* thing. Right?"

He laughed again and this time it sounded normal. "Right. I know what you mean and that's sort of scary. I'll call Diane."

"Thanks." I pressed Disconnect and dropped the phone back into my purse. "Problems with the valet parking," I said to Janelle.

"Did Livvie delegate it to Charlie?" she asked, not taking her eyes from the road.

"You bet. There's some kind of foul-up at the Hunt Club." I hummed *Beauty and the Beast* under my breath, mentally rehearsing my pacing.

We drove in silence for several minutes then

Janelle asked, "Do you mind that Charlie and I will probably get married?"

I looked at her in surprise. She clutched the steering wheel tightly, far more so than the moderate traffic congestion required. "Mind?" I chose my words carefully. "I suppose I do, in a way. I've had Charlie to myself for decades. I mean, I've shared him with others, but this is the first time he's been really serious about someone. Just like this is the first time I've been serious about someone else. It's a shock for both of us, I think." I shifted in the seat, turning slightly so I could see her more clearly. "It's going to be an adjustment more than anything. But it's nothing like what you and Charlie are going to face. Twins. I can't believe it."

For an instant she looked frightened, her hands open and closing on the wheel and her shoulders stiffening in her black lawyer's jacket. Then she visibly relaxed. "I think as long as he's with me, I can handle it."

"I know you can handle it." I said it with more confidence than I really felt. Twins? Charlie? It boggled my mind. Diapers, crying, eventual tussles over dating, Internet use, the car...I couldn't imagine it.

"Why is Diane so upset about Matthew?" Janelle angled the car toward the upcoming exit. She looked thoughtful. "Now that I'm about to be a parent, I can suddenly understand why people are so protective of their kids, even when they're grown up. Is Matthew really that sensitive?"

I snorted. "Sensitive? No. Try 'jerk.' He's liable to say something that seems perfectly logical to him then is shocked when others think it's rude or insensitive or idiotic."

"But the police are trained to overlook that sort of behavior. Is it possible...?" She looked directly at me as we waited at a stop light. "Could Matthew have anything to do with it?" Her dark blue eyes were hidden by sunglasses but I could imagine the speculation there.

"Matthew?" I tried to inject disbelief in my voice but I think I failed. I hated to admit it, but the idea had merit. "I'm not sure if he could have done it. Pauline said she talked to him earlier that morning. He was at the office. Then he went to talk to John, but Sheila was with John so Matthew left then returned." I shook my head, trying to visualize the complicated timeline like the crisscrossing of footsteps on a snowy field. Some of them overlaid the other and some led to nowhere. "I'm not sure."

Janelle faced front again as the light changed. "Do you think he could have done it? Is he capable of it? Could he murder his father?"

I started to make a flippant comment like *Kill John? Hell, yes.* I curbed my tongue though and thought about it. We drove in silence for several minutes then I finally said, "You know, I'm not sure. If you had asked me that question a year ago, I would have said 'No way.' But in the past year I've seen two murders up-close. And people I know were suspected. I've seen how the law works and how it doesn't work sometimes. Wasn't it the Second who said anyone can incite murderous thoughts?"

Janelle nodded. "I was thinking the same thing. I don't know Matthew or his siblings well, but being raised by John has to put a strain on anyone's sense of morality."

I considered her comment as we drove through the neighborhood where I was raised as a child. John always assumed wealth was his right and I know he passed that idea on to his children. I, on the other hand, knew that I had no wealth but I lived where I did because of my mother and what she contributed to the family.

John's outrage at my inheritance had more to do

with his sense of justice than anything. To him, it was unjust that I, an outsider, should inherit when he, an insider, didn't. The fact that he never spent time with his grandmother and never helped her when she was ill didn't figure into it. I was bound to the family by love and devotion. He was bound by blood. He thought blood was worth more and I knew it wasn't.

"I used to think Charlie's father encouraged the idea that they were better than everyone else," I said. "But I saw how he treated T.J. during that mess last fall and I started to wonder. His investments in Sam's company totally threw me for a loop."

Janelle turned onto the maple-lined street that led to the Whittington house. I noted that the church parking lot on the corner looked busy, several young men rushing around the perimeters draping pale yellow crepe paper streamers on trees and shrubs. It looked like Charlie had figured it out. "I never thought that," Janelle said. "After all, how could Charlie be so sweet and unprejudiced if his father was an idiot?"

"My mother had something to do with it," I pointed out. "She was largely responsible for the upbringing of the kids."

"Even though he remarried so many times?" Janelle slowed to enter the driveway at the house. A handsome young man in black slacks and a white shirt bounded off the front steps and approached us.

"He didn't remarry until Livvie was in junior high and by then, my mother had us firmly under control. The Steps never had much to do with the kids. They were more involved in spending C.R.'s money." I smiled at the young man who leaned over, looking in Janelle's window. "Trust Livvie to hire the cute ones."

We got out of the car, another young man

approaching and helping us with our bags and dresses before whisking Janelle's car away. We went inside, pausing in the large round foyer. "Where is everybody?" I wondered aloud.

"Who's that?" a voice called from the top of the double-wide stairway.

"Cassie and Janelle!" I called back.

"Get up here! We're having too much fun!"

Janelle and I took our bags from the valet and headed up the stairs. I made a right turn at the top of oak and marble staircase.

"I've never been up here," Janelle said, looking at the portraits arranged on the dark brown walls, white wooden borders outlining each one like a frame.

"The boys had rooms here," and I nodded toward the two doors on the north side as we passed them. "C.R. and the Step had the rooms at the back of the house, facing the lake." I glanced behind us. "The girls were in the front of the house."

"Where did your mother…" Janelle looked at the two doorways in front of us.

"Mom and I had a suite on the third floor." I gestured with my shoe bag to the narrow doorway between the girls' rooms. "We had a sitting room and a couple of bedrooms." We used to have three small rooms under the eaves but the rooms were freshly painted every other year and attractively furnished.

I walked into Livvie's old bedroom, a spacious L-shaped room with the bed in the corner under the eaves. It was a guest room now but it still had pale yellow walls that contrasted so beautifully with the dark oak floors. When I was growing up I loved this room with its odd ceiling angles and pretty white ruffled coverlet and curtains.

Livvie was seated at her vanity table, her ash-blonde hair pulled away from her face with a scarf. She wore an old white bathrobe over a brilliantly pink T-shirt and fuzzy pink slippers. She peered at me in the mirror. "It's about time you guys got here."

Betty Burke, our old family friend, sat in a rocking chair to the left of the doorway like a small dark queen overseeing the proceedings. Her wizened black face reflected her advanced age but the snapping humor in her eyes was ageless. She wore a navy blue dress with a bright pink T-shirt strained on her ample bosom. I peered at her chest, trying to make out the lettering. "Here you go," she said, leaning forward and tugging the T-shirt tight so I could easily see it said *Virtual Mom*.

"I take it you called somebody and found Charlie a parking lot?" I asked.

Betty nodded. "Pastor Vickers at my church called Minister Baldwin at the Methodist Church on the corner. They were happy to help."

"It pays to know people who know people," Becky said. She and Marcy, her daughter, were sprawled on the bed in equally bright pink T-shirts and panties. Becky's T-shirt said *Matron of Honor* and Marcy's was *Flower Child*. A bottle of champagne and two glasses sat on the nightstand and a plate of crackers, caviar and pate sat on a white lacquered tray on the bed with them next to a photo album and scrapbook.

I took Janelle's dress with mine and hung them in the walk-in closet. As I came out, Livvie said, "Here's your costume." She tossed a pink bundle at me. I caught it and opened up a T-shirt that said *Honorary Sister*. "And here, Janelle."

Janelle caught the bundle tossed to her. She opened it and smiled shyly. "I hope so," she said then displayed it. *Future Sister-in-Law*.

I shot Livvie a frowning look but she just smiled and held up her champagne glass. "Fill up and join us," she said. "There's food over there..." and she gestured to the dresser on the far side of the room.

"And there…" She gestured to a card table in one corner, near the door that led to the bathroom she and Becky shared as girls.

"Where's Claire?" I asked as I shucked out of my ketchup polo shirt and into the pink T.

"Did you hear about the flowers?" Becky asked, dabbing caviar on a piece of toast. I nodded. "Claire volunteered to help Sam get that all straightened out."

"I think she was bored," Marcy said. She was a short, plump young woman in her twenties with straight dark hair and beautiful hazel eyes. "When we brought out those scrapbooks, she ran for the hills."

"I think it was the T-shirt," Betty said from her chair. She shot Livvie a chiding look.

"What?" Livvie leaned forward and stared at her makeup in the mirror. "It was appropriate."

Marcy snorted. "*Society Queen?*"

I laughed. "She probably thought it was a compliment."

"And it was," Livvie said. She caught my eye in the mirror and grinned. Her gaze shifted to Becky. "Are you sure those boys of yours don't have something nefarious planned?"

Becky sighed and smeared another cracker with pate. "Carlton promised me they won't blow anything up. I think that's the best we can hope for with my kids."

"I'd rather have your hellions than have John's boys," Betty said, rocking vigorously. "Those children could put the freeze on a summer heat wave."

"They do have standards," Marcy murmured. "You should have seen the email Jon sent me when I sent him my Facebook URL. The way he acted, I may as well have had pornography there or something." She sipped some champagne. "I got a Tweet from Cory. He said Sam found a dead body?"

How the hell did he find out? Knowing my ex-nephews-in-law, they probably had spies in the police station. I exchanged a look with Janelle then decided, *What the heck.* I filled them in on the events of the past day: Sam finding Sheila and being interrogated and me becoming fifteen million dollars richer. When I finished Marcy bounced to her feet and hugged me.

"Are you okay with working at the foundation?" I asked her. "I'm counting on you and Diane to manage things."

She nodded, dark hair slipping forward to bob around her chin. "It's what I've always been interested in doing. This is a great opportunity." She raised her glass. "Here's to Auntie C and the start of a long and happy business relationship."

"And here's to Sam," Livvie said. "A man who knows how to come to the rescue of women in distress." She arched an eyebrow at me and I grinned.

"I'd like to second that," a shrill voice said from the hallway. "I just wish Sam did kill her. If he did, I'd thank him."

Janelle approached the door cautiously and opened it. She stepped back in surprise. Diane stood framed in the door, swaying slightly. For an instant nobody moved then Livvie walked forward, holding out her arms. "Diane." Her voice was soft and sympathetic. "I'm so glad you came." She looked beyond her sister-in-law. "You and Pauline. Now all the family girls are here." She ushered the two women into the room.

Marcy and Becky made strangled noises from their spots on the bed. I glanced quickly at them, catching a glimpse of broad grins then they turned away to refill the plates from the buffet on the dresser.

I looked back at Pauline and Diane. They wore

similar dark blue dresses but Pauline's had a narrow band of red stitching around the square neckline. Diane's was high collared, framing her pale face and dark hair like a curtain around a stage. Both women appeared tentative and uncertain as they stared as us, all in similar pink shirts.

The shirts. *Oh, God. I hope Livvie has T-shirts*, I thought.

"Here you go," Livvie said. She rummaged behind her on the chair and emerged with two more pink T-shirts. *Sister-in-law* and *Godchild* were revealed. I forgot Livvie stood as godmother to Pauline.

Diane stared at it incomprehensibly. "I don't understand." She looked at us all and I saw tears in her eyes. She didn't mean the T-shirt. She didn't understand a damn thing that had happened to her in the past week.

I came forward and put an arm around her. "Have a seat." I steered her toward an overstuffed armchair and she sank down, staring at the T-shirt as though the words were written in a foreign tongue.

She looked up at me, her eyes red-rimmed and haunted. "Charlie told me what you did. What you did about the foundation. You didn't have to do that, Cassie."

I smiled. "I know. But I think you'll be good." She would be a lot better at charitable giving than Matthew, who probably didn't have a charitable bone in his body.

Pauline looked at the bed then at Marcy, who still stood near the dresser, her *Flower Child* T-shirt rumpled and twisted on her plump body. That familiar look of disdain flitted across Pauline's face then with a visible effort she smiled and pulled on her pink shirt over her blue dress. "Thanks, Aunt Livvie," she murmured.

Marcy held out a champagne glass and Pauline took it with a smile. That seemed to break the obvious tension in the room. Those with empty glasses refilled them and soon we were all pouring over the photo albums, jostling to show Janelle our favorite memories.

One champagne bottle later the hairdresser arrived and we all watched as Becky and Livvie were primped. Next it was time for the makeup woman, who plunked down a suitcase full of goodies that could have handled a major movie production.

Throughout it all Livvie and Betty kept up a chatter of conversation, including Diane and Pauline in everything, making sure they had food and making sure they were a part of the group. When Pauline's phone rang and she answered it, she was laughing but as soon as she saw the caller ID, she sobered, her face paling. I was sitting next to her on the bed and saw the words on the small phone screen. *Matthew.*

She got up and meandered to the far side of the room, near the doorway. I couldn't eavesdrop without being obvious so I went to sit with Diane, who watched as Janelle helped Livvie into her dress.

"It's beautiful," I said. The dress was Pure Livvie: pale yellow and twirly, a slender pale sheath covered by layers of gauzy fabric printed with darker flowers. Yellow high heels and a wide-brimmed white hat with yellow flowered bow completed the ensemble. "Only Livvie could wear something like that and get away with it."

Diane smiled tiredly. "John always said she didn't care about what was right or proper. Livvie would do what Livvie wanted and the devil could take the consequences."

I thought that was a bit harsh, but it was essentially true. Next it was Becky's turn to suit up in a pale green dress with flowers like those on

Livvie's. The color suited Becky's darker complexion and hazel eyes. That was the signal for everyone else to shed their T-shirts and head for the clothing hanging in the closet.

Pauline tucked her phone in her purse and came to join us. "They talked to Matt," she said in a low voice, leaning close to Diane. "But there's no way he could have been involved, in either of the..." She glanced at me. "The murders."

"That's a relief," I said when I saw the instant relaxation in Diane's shoulders. The two women still looked worried, though, and it was obvious they wanted to talk privately. I murmured an excuse and went to my bag, opening it and pulling out my phone. I had a vague thought about posting a Twitter update but got sidetracked by the Facebook icon, which had a big red star on it. I accessed it and saw updates from the boys with promises of *The plan is executed, now we just need the bride and groom* and *Hope the relatives are cool about what we have planned. They're pretty hip but this might strain their hipness...*

I glanced at Becky but she was talking to Livvie and I didn't want to disturb their fragile sibling harmony. I fumbled the little trackball onto an icon that said "Notifications." I clicked it and a list of names scrolled on the tiny screen. *Barb Torvald wants to be friends.* I smiled. Barb was a former classmate. I would have to contact her.

My smile faded when I saw the next notification. *Sheila Peavey wants to be friends.*

Chapter 15

"Holy crap," I muttered.

"What is it?"

I looked up. Diane was standing next to me, looking down at my phone.

"I forgot to charge it." I pressed the Disconnect button and the screen darkened. "Oops." I dropped the phone back in my purse and glanced at the bedside clock. "Wow. It's almost three. I'd better get dressed, too."

What the hell was Sheila doing, sending me a message? I didn't know enough about the software, much less the mobile version, to figure out when it was sent. It would just have to wait. I went to the walk-in closet where Janelle was pulling on an empire-waist dress of dark blue with a white linen jacket. Her baby bump was visible as the folds of the dress settled over her.

"Can you zip me up?" she asked, twisting up her long hair to reveal the zipper up the back of the dress. I did the honors, patting her on the shoulder when done. She surveyed herself in the full-length mirror. "I bought this dress before I knew I was pregnant. It's going to come in handy, I think."

I shed my clothes and pulled on the long shirt-dress I brought. "It's a good all-purpose dress," I agreed as my head popped free of the collar. I fluffed out my hair with my fingers then stepped into the red sandals I dug out of my bag.

Janelle laughed. "I wish I could get ready that fast." She brushed through her hair, twisting it up with a clip.

"That's one reason I got my hair cut," I said. "It used to be long but I got tired of fussing with it." I picked up my short red jacket and walked back into the bedroom. Pauline handed me my glass of champagne as I went to the dresser to fix myself a snack.

"You look happy, Aunt Cassie. I think Sam must be good for you."

I looked at her in surprise. "I suppose he is. After what we've been through, it's nice to finally have a chance to relax together."

"That was an awful accident." Her thin face took on a pinched look and I wondered if she knew that her father was accused of paying someone to cause it. "You're lucky to have him. I didn't think so at first, but he's so nice to everybody. He and Uncle Charlie are so much alike."

I almost choked on the caviar in my mouth. "They are?" I mumbled.

"Of course. They're both nice. They're..." Pauline looked at her mother then at Livvie. "T.J. is nice, too. All of them...I don't think it matters if you're rich or not. They wouldn't care. They just like people for who they are, not what they can do or how they can help." She frowned. "I'm not saying it's right, but you know what I mean, don't you?"

I nodded slowly. She was right. Sam and Charlie were decent, honest, hard-working, kind men who were willing to help and willing to believe in other people.

"My father was never like that," she said in a low voice. "He taught Jon and Matthew to feel the same way. They're both very opportunistic. They're always looking at people and trying to figure out what they can use them for." She sipped from the champagne flute in her hand. "I don't want to be like that." She sounded frightened, as though worried such a trait might sneak up on her when she least expected it.

"You don't have to be," I assured her. "Your mother has changed a lot in the past year. She used to be like that and look at her now. I'm asking her to run a charitable trust and I would never have considered her a year ago."

"You're right. She has changed so much." Pauline turned when Marcy joined us.

"Come look at the flowers outside." Marcy grinned at me. "Sam really came through for Livvie. The flowers are great." The two younger women left the room, laughing.

I started to follow them, but Pauline's word seemed to mire me to the spot. Charlie and Sam, alike? I was suddenly dazed, the champagne swirling in my brain. It felt as though a constricting veil had been removed and I was tantalizingly close to realizing a universal truth about the men I loved in my life.

A knock sounded on the door and Diane, getting ready to leave, opened it. Sam peeked in. "Guests are coming, Livvie." He looked around the room, smiling at the all the women. He wore his dark tweed suit coat with the black pants, the outfit that looked so good with his salt-and-pepper hair. "Quite the flower garden in here."

Betty laughed as Janelle helped her out of the chair. "Trust the nursery man to see the flowers among the weeds. Help me with this shirt, honey." She wiggled her arms and Becky tugged off the oversized T-shirt, folding it and setting it aside. "Do you mind if I go downstairs with you and Pauline?"

the old lady asked Diane.

"Of course not." Diane hesitated at the door, smiling at Sam, who stood to one side. "We'd love to have you sit with us."

"Come look at the flowers," Pauline called.

We all left the bedroom, Livvie and Becky coming behind us, talking, and laughing. We crowded around the window at the back of the house that overlooked the lawn leading to the lake. The patio below was edged in pots of pansies and petunias, the vibrant colors of the pansies a pretty contrast to the pale yellow of the petunias.

"You're the best, Sam," Livvie said. "Thank you. It looks beautiful."

"I couldn't get all the petunias you wanted, so I went with the mix. I think it came out okay." He looked modest and pleased with himself.

"It's beautiful," Livvie repeated.

"Not as beautiful as you. I got the roses you needed for the porch, too. You'd better get down there and marry that guy. He's so nervous he's about ready to faint."

She smiled and kissed him on the cheek. "He'd better not faint until I get him hitched."

I put a hand on Sam's arm. "Thanks. It's perfect."

He smiled, his brown eyes warm and loving. "Anything for the family. Ready to go?"

I hesitated. I had a song to sing in a few minutes and for the first time in a long time, I was nervous.

"Are you ready?" Livvie asked softly.

I looked into Sam's eyes. "Yes," I said. "I think I am."

Livvie kissed me on the cheek. "See you soon."

Janelle walked down the broad stairs ahead of us, her hand sliding along the oak railing. Charlie waited at the bottom, looking up like some movie hero from the golden age of Hollywood. He smiled when he saw Janelle then his gaze shifted to me. Our eyes met and I saw love and sadness in their green depths. Then he held out an arm and Janelle took it.

Sam tucked my arm firmly over his. "Are you okay?" he asked softly as we walked onto the porch and he led us to our seats in the first row.

I nodded. I was so busy mentally rehearsing the song that I barely noticed anything around me although I did see T.J. and Paul standing at the front, pale yellow roses in their lapels and roses in vases all around the low stge. Charlie and Janelle took seats near Claire at the other end of our row. Becky's family sat behind us and behind them were Diane, Jon, Pauline, and Betty, already seated. Matthew was absent and I wondered fleetingly where he was.

"Are you nervous?" Sam whispered.

"I am," I admitted. "I don't want to mess it up. It's Livvie's big day."

"It's your big day, too," Sam said.

I looked at him, startled. "What?"

"Your inheritance. You're a rich woman." His smile was sincere but I saw a shadow of uncertainty in his eyes.

"I've always been a rich woman, Sam. I have you." I kissed him on the cheek then stood as the Processional sounded from the speakers hidden behind the roses.

Livvie paced down the side of the porch, her father escorting her. Like all brides, she looked radiant, her gaze locked on T.J. who did look so nervous I thought he might pass out.

The Second paused at the platform and passed Livvie's hand to T.J. She leaned over and kissed him on the cheek then her father turned and joined Claire.

We all settled down with a great rustling of

fabric then the J.P. started speaking. I caught one word in three or four, such phrases as "...turn of fortune that brought them together..." and "...circumstances that strained but did not sunder..."

Then, suddenly, it was time. Livvie turned her head and smiled at me, nodding toward the side of the platform where I was to stand. I stood, twitching my jacket so it was comfortable. Sam caught my hand and kissed it. "I love you," he whispered.

I squeezed his hand. "I love you." I walked the four or five steps to the microphone and took a deep breath. My gaze swept over the gathered people. As I suspected, there was an eclectic mix of rough looking men in leathers, society matrons, young people in their obvious Sunday best, and other people who looked ill at ease. They were probably from the rehab center or the restaurant. I smiled and a few people smiled tentatively in return. I nodded to the young man seated in the back corner and the music began to play.

I initially kept my gaze fixed on Livvie and T.J. as I sang. I saw his face soften, the craggy lines of his face loosening when emotion making him gulp as the words unfolded. *My darling lives in a world...* I thought of all T.J. had been through in his life. Viet Nam and the loss of his arm; drug addiction; trouble with the law; getting straight and finding his new career only to almost lose it because of a murder. I thought of the odds of him and Livvie finding each other, and my voice strengthened. *Who is the beauty, who is the beast?*

Livvie gripped his left hand with both of hers, his right arm ending in a hook resting lightly on top of her hands. Her eyes were intent on him, love radiating out from her. I remembered all that had happened to her, starting with her near death at the hands of my father when she was just a baby. Her horrible marriage and our relief when her brutal husband died. Her alcohol addiction and recovery. She deserved every minute of happiness she could find.

When I got to the line about *Two children too blind to see* I glanced at Charlie and a tear trickled down my cheek. His green eyes were wide and glistened with unshed tears. He struggled to smile, but all he managed was a brief up-twist of his lips. As the words of the verse faded and music filled the pause, he nodded briefly. He knew what I was saying.

Music rolled over us as I waited for the next verse to start. I looked at Sam. No matter what happened, I wanted him to know. He *had* to know how I felt.

My love is a man who's not been tamed. He smiled suddenly, his eyes locked on mine. I looked back at T.J. and Livvie. *We come from different worlds...*

I never doubted your beauty...I've changed.

I stepped back from the microphone and faced the guests. Janelle looked stricken, her face contorted with grief. The Second smiled sadly as Claire dabbed at her eyes with a hanky. I took a wobbling step toward Sam but my knees wouldn't obey. He stood and walked to meet me, pulling my arm through his and letting me lean on him for support.

"Hell of a song, Cassie," he murmured.

I was so drained of feeling I couldn't speak. I sat down heavily and leaned against him, thankful for his warm strength. Livvie looked over her shoulder at me, her eyes bright with tears. Then she faced the J.P. again as they started to read the vows. I heard the words through a buzz in my brain, like muted highway noise through the trees. I stared at T.J. as he repeated the words, slipping a ring on Livvie's finger, her wrist balanced delicately on the hook on his right hand. Then Livvie held his hand and did the same, repeating the vows.

The room went still as Charlie stood, smiling down at Janelle. He crossed the room in front of us but before he got to the platform, he paused, turned then came to me. To my shock, he knelt in front of me on one knee. I was pinned by amazement, my eyes so wide I was afraid they'd pop. Next to me Sam drew in a sharp breath and went rigid.

Charlie looked up at me, his green eyes fringed by dark lashes. He gently took my hands in his, squeezing my fingers gently. "I love you, Cassie, and I always will. Thank you for sharing my youth. Thank you for teaching me what love is."

I nodded, unable to speak around the sudden constriction in my throat. Charlie was saying good-bye to me, saying good-bye to our childhood together. I leaned forward. "I love you, too, Charlie. Be happy." A tear wound down my cheek as he released my hands and stood.

He turned and took two steps to the platform, picking up the microphone I had set down. Music began to play and when I recognized the song, another tear joined the first one that tumbled off my chin. Sam took my hand and squeezed it as Charlie sang *Said I Loved You, But I Lied*. He sang softly, gently, focusing on Livvie and T.J. and glancing once at Janelle, smiling at her as he sang the words.

When he finished he set the microphone back on the stage and resumed his seat. I stole a glance around us and saw several teary faces. Even Betty, normally so pragmatic and stolid, was busily wiping her eyes. The J.P. said a few more words then he said, "I'd like to present to you, their family and friends, the new husband and wife: Olivia and Thomas Watson." Livvie clung to T.J's arm when they stepped down from the platform and hurried down the impromptu aisle to the thunderous applause of the assembled guests.

Sam took my arm as *All You Need Is Love* started to play on the speakers. Laughing, we led the guests out of the porch to the patio beyond where Livvie and T.J. were standing, waiting to greet their friends before going to the restaurant where the reception would be held. The champagne came out, toasts were drunk, and Charlie then the Second made small speeches.

Twenty minutes later I slipped back upstairs to grab my purse and Janelle's. We decided to leave our clothing at the house to pick up later that weekend. I paused in Livvie's bedroom and looked at the scrapbooks still sitting on the bed. One was open to a picture of the family at the house on Lake Vermillion. Charlie and I were teenagers, sitting on the dock with the younger children playing in the shallows and Livvie standing behind Charlie, her arms wrapped around his neck. We were all tanned, healthy and laughing, a frequent occurrence at the lake house.

"Cassie."

I turned. Charlie stood in the doorway. We stared at each other for a long minute then I dropped the purses and moved into his arms. We hugged silently and I leaned my head against his chest, hearing his solid heart strong under my face. He smelled so familiar, so unique. I looked up at him and he smiled down at me, dimples framing his mouth. "Thank you," he said. "For that song."

"Thank your sister," I said. "It was her idea."

He smoothed my hair back from my face, his thumb tracing a line down to cup my chin. "You'll always be special to me. But I'm looking forward to the future with Janelle. It's so right for me to be with her. She's..." He stopped, looking for words. "I love her, Cassie. I love her so much. I can't imagine living without her."

I nodded my understanding. "I'm looking forward to watching you be a father, Charlie. You'll be a good one."

He laughed shakily then dipped his head to brush a kiss on my forehead before releasing me. "I hope so. What about you?"

I leaned over to pick up the purses, avoiding his gaze. "I'm an heiress now," I said lightly. "I've got to figure out what I'm going to do."

"Are you going to be with Sam?"

I straightened. "I'm not sure."

"Oh, I think you can count on that," Sam said from the doorway. He was leaning against the doorjamb, his hands jammed into his pants pockets. His eyes went to the scrapbooks on the bed then he met Charlie's gaze. "I never understood why Cassie still loved you. I figured everybody who got divorced had to be bitter or angry, like me. But then…"

His face relaxed and his gaze turned inward. I knew he was seeing something in his memory, something hard to remember. "Then Sheila died. I've seen death before. I was a Marine and I saw combat. But seeing somebody you once loved dead like that made me realize what kinds of mistakes I've been making. When I divorced Sheila I divorced that part of my life. Cassie was right. I loved botany. I loved botanical research. I refused to admit that because I divorced that part of me."

He pushed away from the door and came into the room, putting an arm around my shoulders. "Cassie taught me to love that part of my life again. She taught me to put Sheila and that part of my past behind me. If I couldn't embrace it, the way she had, I had to let go of it. Cassie taught me how to do that."

I tilted my chin and kissed him on the cheek. "I'm glad you learned," I said softly. "You'll be a great researcher. I expect a tree named after me someday."

Charlie grinned. "What kind of tree would that be?" he asked, starting toward the door. "Short with dark gray leaves?" He ruffled my hair.

Sam laughed. "I was thinking more of a willow, something that bends but doesn't break." His arm tightened on my shoulders. "Something that gets better as it ages." We emerged into the hallway and peered over the edge of the staircase. Livvie and T.J. were standing in the middle of the stairs, photographers taking pictures of them. Becky and Paul stood behind them.

"Livvie looks great, doesn't she?" Charlie said, smiling down at his baby sister.

She looked up. "Hey, come on down. We need family pictures. Come on, Sam. You too, Cassie. Everybody in the picture!"

Charlie hurried down the steps in front of us. "I meant it," Sam said softly. "You've taught me a lot."

"It's mutual." I dropped the handbags on the steps and leaned into Livvie's embrace. "You look beautiful."

"So do you," she murmured against my ear. "Thank you for the beautiful song."

I leaned back to look down into her eyes. "Thank you."

"You just needed a nudge." She leaned against T.J. "Right?"

He looked down at her and smiled. "Whatever you say, honey."

We all laughed. "She's got you trained already," Carlton said as he snapped a picture with his cell phone.

Dozens of pictures later we all moved to the front of the house. Cory and Nathan pulled open the big double doors and bowed low, gesturing toward the white limousine sitting at the curb. Livvie walked forward cautiously. "What did you boys do?"

she demanded.

Cory put a hand over his heart. "You cut me to the quick," he said with mock solemnity. "Would we do anything foolish to our favorite auntie?"

"Hey, I thought I was your favorite auntie?" I said, slapping Nathan on the back.

"You're our favorite singing auntie," he said with a grin. He disappeared back into the house as Cory held open the limo door.

"Come on now, get inside. We can't start dinner without you." He ushered T.J. into the back seat of the car then held Livvie's bouquet as she got in, handing the bouquet to her before closing the door behind her.

Cory slapped the roof of the limo. "Let's get this party started!" he shouted.

The limo pulled away from the curb in a clatter of sound. All manner of kitchen gear was tied to the rear bumper. Spoons, whisks, egg beaters, and sieves all bounced merrily behind the car as *Who Let The Dogs Out* blared from speakers.

The Second glared at Becky who just laughed. "At least nothing blew up," she said.

That's when the first cherry bomb exploded in the shrubbery behind us.

Chapter 16

It was, indeed, a feast for a queen.

T.J. pulled out all the stops for his wedding
dinner. Their restaurant, *La Suzette,* was decorated
with pale yellow streamers and each of the ten
round guest tables had a centerpiece of petunias and
roses. The cake, created by Paul for his father and
stepmother, stood in pride of place on a separate
table to one side. The amazing concoction had four
tiers, each a different shape: circle, oval, square, and
pentagon, each tilting impossibly as though it might
tumble. Around each tier was a small highway with
tiny motorcycles, cars, and trucks driving. Edible
flowers, ribbons made from icing, and hand-painted
scenes of Lake Minnetonka, the restaurant, and
people in the restaurant decorated the sides of the
tiers. At the top of this creation were two
mascarpone figures that looked remarkably like
Livvie and T.J. on a motorcycle. The perimeter of the
cake was edged with small pansies in adorable little
white vases.

"The pansies are your handiwork?" I asked Sam
as we took a seat at a round table near the long head
table that stretched the width of the restaurant.

He pulled out a chair for me. "I have friends in
the business." Our name cards placed us nearest the

head table where Livvie sat with T.J., her father, Claire, Becky, Carlton, Paul and Paul's date, a woman introduced as 'Cindy, a sous-chef at *Philippe's*'. Livvie whispered in an aside that Paul and Cindy were dating and "Thank God she's normal, not like that bitch he used to date." I raised a glass of champagne to that sentiment since I well remembered the woman Paul used to date.

Janelle's name card was next to mine with Charlie next to her. I pointed to it. "This might have been an interesting dinner if things had worked out differently."

Sam grinned. "Livvie knows you better than you know yourself."

Betty and Albert, her date, sat next to Charlie. Cory, Nathan, and Marcy filled the rest of the seats at our table. Diane and her kids sat at another nearby table, equally close to the head table. Matthew was there, which surprised me because he had missed the wedding. "Did the cops let him go?" Sam asked softly, leaning over to speak in my ear as the waiters put a small plate of appetizers in front of each guest.

I shivered at the close contact. "Pauline said he was cleared. Apparently he has an alibi for John's death." I remembered what she said. "And Sheila's, I guess." I sorted through the information in my brain. "I talked to him about Sheila on...Wednesday night, I think. The night everybody came to the house to figure out the funeral songs. He said then he had just talked to Sheila. So I guess that tells us she was still alive then."

Sam sat back, touching the heavy silverware on the creamy linen counterpane. "Whoever killed Sheila was pissed off. I think it was spontaneous."

I swallowed hard, the feathery bite of truffle-infused cheese suddenly clogging my throat. Sheila was strangled. What would it be like to be in a struggle with someone, to have your breath restricted? What would it be like to look in someone's eyes and know that they were going to kill you? What would it be like to have your vision fade...?

"Can't they get thumbprints or something from the throat?" Cory asked, his voice loud in a sudden lull of conversation.

I closed my eyes. Trust a teenager to think of something like that and mention it at a wedding reception. Before I could remonstrate with him, Betty reached over Albert and rapped the teenager sharply on the knuckles with her fork.

"You behave," she snapped. "You're at your auntie's wedding and you've caused enough excitement for one night."

Nathan grinned. "At least we're alive. Not like our cousins." He nodded toward Diane's table where the children all sat in stony silence. Diane looked as though one wrong move would shatter her fragile self-control. She hadn't touched the food on her plate but stared into the distance as though the world didn't exist.

"Poor woman," Betty murmured as she picked up her champagne glass. "She looks lost. No matter what anyone can say about John, I hate to see a woman suffer so."

"She looks stunned," Albert said. He was a frequent visitor to my home because he and Sam shared a passion for Civil War battle discussions. Albert was approaching eighty years old but he and Betty had an active social life and traveled often. We frequently received postcards from faraway lands. "I remember my Aunt Phillipia looked like that when Uncle Horace passed on. It wasn't until I was grown that I discovered Uncle Horace had a passion for his wife's underthings and she was trying to decide whether or not to bury him in her black silk drawers or keep 'em for herself."

I covered my mouth with my napkin, restraining the guffaw that threatened to burst free. "Somehow I can't visualize John in silk," Sam said, laughter in his voice.

"She's probably relieved," Marcy said in a low voice. "From what Pauline told me, her mother and father seemed to fight all the time."

"Jon hated his dad," Cory said, eyeing the waiter who hovered near our table, waiting to refill wine glasses. "Grandpa said I could have some wine."

"Some," Marcy said. "You've had one glass."

"So? Nathan's had one glass and he's only seventeen. I'm nineteen."

I smiled. As though two years really mattered. I nudged my glass toward him. "Don't gulp it," I advised. "And hold out for the port with dessert. It's really worth it."

Cory grinned, looking so like his Uncle Charlie at that moment I had a momentary sense of déjà vu. "Thanks, Auntie C. You rock."

I leaned back so the waiter could take my plate. Funny. I never noticed that before. Matthew and Jon never called me "aunt." It was an honorary title at best. I was divorced from Charlie years before they were born, but Becky's kids always called me "Aunt."

"Why do you say Jon hated his father?" Sam asked, looking with interest at the next plate being whisked in front of us. "What's this?"

I peered at the colorful concoction then picked up the menu from the centerpiece. "*Terrine des legumes.*"

Sam stared at me blankly.

"Veggie loaf," Nathan translated. "Jon told us he hated his dad. He was pissed off that Uncle John was having it off with that lady."

Betty blew out an exasperated breath. "Your mother raised you better than that, young man. You lower your voice and watch your language."

Nathan flushed. "Sorry. All I meant was that Jon and Matt knew about their dad having an affair long before their mother did. They were pi...mad about it and told their dad he had to stop or they'd tell their mom." He jammed a bit of vegetable terrine in his mouth. "Their dad just laughed at them and told them to go ahead and tell."

"Man, that's cold," Sam said, taking an experimental bite of his hors d'ouevres. "Not bad. What's in it?"

"Probably truffles, baby veggies, some kind of congealed broth and mushrooms." Whatever was in the dish, it was excellent. I caught T.J's eye and gave him a thumbs up. He raised his wine glass and grinned at me.

The next dish arrived, this one mini-*quiche au samon et poireaux.* "Salmon and leak quiche," I translated for Sam. "Egg pie, really."

"Real men don't eat quiche," he said as he polished off the last crumb from his plate. "How long did Matt and his brother know about John and Sheila?" he asked the nephews.

"A few months," Nathan said. His gaze shifted to me. "He's going to be really mad that you aren't having him run the foundation."

I set my wine glass down. "Does he know that?"

"I suppose. After all, I read it on Marcy's Facebook page."

I looked across the table at Marcy, who went pink with embarrassment. "I was so excited, Aunt Cassie. It's the job of my dreams."

Janelle and I exchanged bemused looks. "I wish I could be that young again," she murmured. "I wish I could get that excited about a job."

"I am," Sam said as another plate was set in front of him. He sniffed it cautiously then wrinkled his nose.

"When do you start?" Charlie asked. He saw Sam's perplexed look. "Warm goat cheese on arugula salad. Smelly, but good."

"That was part of the all the paperwork today," I said. "Now that Sheila's…" I hastily re-thought what I wanted to say, "…gone there isn't an impediment to the purchase. Janelle contacted Joe, who inherited the shares in the company. Not only that, the patent lawsuit can be dropped now, too. Sam can finally get the profits from that azalea." Sheila's death solved a lot of problems for us. I considered sending a silent *thank you* to whoever did it, but I suspect whoever killed her didn't care a fig about my thanks.

"It's not just the profits from the current plant that's exciting. It's what's in store for the future." Sam leaned forward, talking around Janelle and I. "Joe said some pharmaceutical companies were interested in the research Mike Peavey and I did while we were in college. Joe wants me to go back and look at it and see if there's some potential there."

"That sounds intriguing." Charlie sipped his wine and regarded Sam thoughtfully. "I wonder if Min-Gen would like some more investors."

Sam smiled slowly. "It's something to consider. I'll talk to Joe about it when I go in on Tuesday. Cassie and I are going to the lake house on Sunday to open it so Tuesday will be my first day on the job." He grinned at Charlie. "I can't wait to get started."

I glanced at Matthew, who was seated several feet away, in profile to me. "I suppose I should talk to him about asking his mother to do the foundation job instead of him."

"I heard him talk to Grandpa about it," Cory said, polishing off his salad. "Matt said something about needing a new job because of the shit, um, stuff, his dad did to the company." Cory glanced furtively at Betty, who shot him a warning look. "The embezzlement stuff."

"Good heavens. Does everyone in the family know everything that's going on?"

The two teenagers and their sister all nodded. "Sure. Between Facebook, Twitter, and MySpace, we're pretty much in the loop."

"I don't like Twitter that much," Nathan said dismissively. "Too many old people." He glanced at me. "No offense."

"None taken." I suddenly remembered the Facebook request sitting on my phone. When did Sheila send that request? And why? She and I certainly weren't friends by any stretch of the imagination.

"So what's the main dish?" Sam asked, looking at the menu.

I peered over his arm. "Looks like several different ones. I suppose we'll have a choice."

"Nope," Betty said. "Livvie told me T.J. was having them prepare everything for everybody. Whatever you want, you get."

"Wow. That could get pricy." I examined the entrees. Filet mignon in pepper sauce, salmon in champagne and shallots, garlic and rosemary lamb.

"She's got the money and he's got the talent," Marcy said. "It's a match made in heaven." She grinned at me and Sam. "Kind of like you two. Auntie C has the money and you can go out and create new plants and stuff."

Sam and I exchanged a startled look. "How did you know?" I shook my head. "Don't tell me. Facebook?"

The kids all laughed.

By the time dessert arrived I was stuffed with good food and wine. But I did save room for wedding cake, aged port, a smidgen of chocolate mousse, and some selections from the fruit and cheese plate. As I relaxed with a cup of coffee I watched the Second circulate around the room, wine glass in hand as he chatted with friends and colleagues.

T.J. and Livvie were also moving around. "Let's head out to the patio," T.J. said, gesturing expansively to the enclosed porch and patio beyond. "We need to give my people a chance to clear the floor for dancing."

People started drifting toward the porch overlooking a patio and beyond that, Lake Minnetonka. Betty, Albert, Sam and I took our time, chatting with friends and pausing for pictures from the many amateur photographers present. The Real Pictures had already been done before dinner and the hired photographers would be snapping pictures all night.

As we emerged onto the stone patio outside the porch I saw the Second and Matthew at the far edge of the property, staring out at the lake. A waist-high decorative wrought-iron fence kept onlookers safely away from the drop-off to the rocky beach below. Something in the way the two men stood told me they were talking privately, but the press of people behind me separated me from Sam and propelled me forward toward them. I started to turn away but the Second turned and smiled at me. "The flowers were beautiful, Cassie. Sam has my undying gratitude."

Matthew's smile was brief and perfunctory. "Yes, it was useful to know someone in the floral business." He looked down his nose at me, his tone so condescending it sounded like nails on a blackboard.

I longed to wipe the smirk from his face and started to snap a reply but restrained myself. He was right. "Yes, indeed. It does pay to know the right people."

His face shifted, hardening into harsh planes and angles. I saw a small vein pulse at his throat as he glowered at me. "Just what is that supposed to mean?" He took a step toward me, his hands clenched.

I instinctively stepped back. "It's just a saying."

The Second shot Matthew a quelling look. "Matthew and I were just discussing how useful it can be to have the family name behind you. It can go a long way to making a bank more willing to consider short and long term loans."

I sipped my wine. "I'm sure it does." I looked up at Matthew, but he stared past me, looking at the crowd of people spilling out of the restaurant. "I wanted to apologize if you're disappointed about the foundation job. I never had the impression you were interested in it and I think your mother needs something right now to focus on."

"I suppose she does." He sounded completely disinterested in Diane's emotional state. "My father's death has been challenging for us all."

Challenging? I looked at the Second, my eyes wide with surprise. That was an odd word to use for the murder of a parent. The old man stared at Matthew, his mouth thinned to a narrow line. For a second I thought he might slap the younger man then he turned, his body visibly relaxing as Charlie joined us and they went to the fence to look out at the lake in the distance.

The sunset framed the three men. The resemblance was eerie, like seeing a time-lapse picture of one person. There was the Second, white-haired and tall, his shoulders still broad but looking frail around his face and hands. Next was Charlie, a man so handsome it took your breath away. The touches of white at his temples and the fine lines on his face only added character and depth to his chiseled features.

Then Matthew turned and I saw Charlie as a young man, athletic and strong with thick dark hair and perfect features that made you feel you were looking at an advertisement come to life. How could three such handsome, perfect men be so different? Three different generations, three different personalities. The Second, autocratic and tough. Charlie, sweet and kind. And Matthew…What was Matthew? He seemed to change as I watched, smiling at his mother, eyeing Sam with dislike, looking disdainfully at his younger cousins. Who was Matthew?

The breeze off the lake brought with it a scent of seaweed and sand. I sniffed eagerly, remembering those smells from my past. When a child grows up in Minnesota, there's always a beach somewhere in your life. I turned to Charlie to comment about it but stopped when I saw the considering looking in Matthew's icy blue eyes. I shivered.

"It's chilly tonight," the Second said.

"It's only May first." Charlie leaned against the fence and watched Livvie talking with Becky's teenagers. "The boys really gave her a send-off, didn't they? You missed it, Matthew. It was a nice wedding." Janelle walked up to us and Charlie put an arm around her, pulling her close against him. "I take it everything went well with the police?"

"Well?" Matthew hunched his shoulders in his dark suit as though shaking off a memory. "I suppose you could say that. I told them what I was doing when my father was killed and they appeared satisfied with my explanation."

"What were you doing?" Charlie asked quietly.

I gaped at him in amazement but he didn't notice. His entire attention was on Matthew. I glanced at the Second and caught a glimpse of bewildered confusion in his green eyes. Then the old man cleared his throat and tilted his head forward attentively. Janelle, too, was watching Matthew and I suddenly realized that she and Charlie were evaluating him: lawyers watching as a client talked.

Matthew regarded his uncle with icy calmness. "Pauline called me at the office on Monday morning to tell me she overheard my father and mother arguing. I thought my father was coming to the office but—"

"The office in town or the one at the construction site?" Charlie interrupted.

What does it matter? I wanted to ask, but I saw Janelle nod. It must have been a lawyerly kind of question.

"The office in town." Matthew pushed his hands into his slacks pockets and jiggled the coins there. "Father didn't come to the office. I tried calling him but couldn't reach him. I checked the accounts, of course, once Pauline told me what was going on. I realized there were problems. I spent most of the morning trying to find out the details."

"My secretary said you called." The Second put a hand on Matthew's shoulder, squeezing it gently then releasing him. "I'm sorry I wasn't available to take your call. It must have been terrible for you."

Matthew's lips twitched in what might have been a smile. "No one was available. I called several people. I wasn't sure what to do. I finally got through to Father. He said he was meeting Aunt Cassie to discuss the lawsuit. He was going to ask for a settlement."

"We met that afternoon," I said. "I was surprised when he started talking about Sheila Peavey. I didn't know they knew each other."

Matthew's eyes flickered from me to the crowd behind me. I know he was looking for Sam. "No one knew, did they? Apparently she and my father kept their affair quite secret. But that's irrelevant now, isn't it?"

Secret? If the nephews were right, it wasn't much of a secret at all. And irrelevant? It was probably amazingly relevant, at least to the police. I started to point that out but Matthew was already speaking again. "I finally met with my father in mid-afternoon at the construction site. He was contrite. He told me he made a terrible mistake. He was going to end his affair and not divorce my mother."

My jaw sagged open. Holy shit. I saw the same shock reflected on the Second's face. Neither Janelle nor Charlie looked surprised. They either anticipated that comment or they hid their shock well.

"We talked and he told me he was meeting Mrs. Peavey, to end the affair. He asked me to leave and come back later. He told me we would work together to set it all right. Of course, nothing could set it right again." Matthew smiled sadly. "But he said he wanted to try. He went to check on the progress at the construction site. Mrs. Peavey was to meet him there." His mouth twisted with distaste. "I believe it was one of their…assignation sites."

My jaw sagged again. John and Sheila, having it off in a half-finished house? Would wonders never cease? Matthew took a long breath and once again the change jingled in his pockets as his hands moved. "I saw her car pull in. I was so angry about what she did to our family." His eyes narrowed and I thought I could see Sheila reflected in them, her smug face and taunting eyes mocking him.

"I can imagine," the Second murmured.

"What did you do?" Charlie prompted.

"I left." Matthew crossed his arms on his chest and sighed. I think it was supposed to sound long-suffering but it reminded me of a child who didn't get his way. Perhaps I was filtering my impressions through my dislike. He was too cold, too calm. If it was me, I would be so mad I couldn't think straight. Imagine it. Your father has embezzled hoards of cash, your company is facing bankruptcy, you and your father are facing prison, and your father is having it off with a floozy. Good God, I would have...

I gulped at the thought. *I would have killed him.* I stared at Charlie and Janelle and saw the same knowledge there. *They think he did it. They think he killed John.*

"Where did you go?" Janelle asked, her voice light and curious. "You must not have gone far. You and Sheila Peavey showed up together later."

He regarded her with flat, cold eyes. "I went out for coffee. I needed to think and I needed to give him time to handle her. When I came back, she was at the office. I demanded to know why she was still there. She told me she was waiting for my father. She said they hadn't talked. She was lying, of course." He didn't pause for our comments but hurried on. "We saw Uncle Charlie's car drive in. I guessed that Father had called him, to ask for legal advice. I stalled her to give them a chance to talk. But then we saw Cassie pull in with Sam Barlow. It enraged her. She hated Barlow with a passion. She insisted we go see what they were doing. So I drove her to the house and..." He shrugged. "You know the rest."

"So you and Sheila were separated before Charlie came in?" the Second asked.

Matthew nodded. "The police didn't say, but, well, it appears to me she had ample opportunity to follow my father and kill him."

"But why would she come back and wait for you to show up?" I blurted.

"She didn't know I was coming back," he replied imperturbably. "Perhaps she was distraught. Or perhaps she left something in the office and came back to pick it up." He shrugged. "I'm sure the police will figure it out."

"Time for photographs!"

I looked back over my shoulder. Livvie waved to

us from the porch. I fell into step with the Second and Matthew as they headed back toward the others.

"You're opening the lake house this weekend, aren't you, Cassie?" the old man asked.

"Of course." I wanted to assure them that my inheritance wouldn't interfere with family tradition. "We've always opened it on the first weekend in May in time for the Grand Opening on Mother's Day. Grandy would expect me to follow in her footsteps and I won't let her down."

"It was always so much fun to go the lake house. Remember those camping trips we took? Matt was always the best navigator in the woods."

Matthew hesitated, staring at his grandfather. For an instant the two men were distorted mirror images of each other, hard, immobile faces staring into such similar eyes. Then Matthew smiled. "Yes, it was fun. Thanks for reminding me of that, Grandfather. Father liked it so much."

John *hated* camping and I well remembered it, but I didn't correct Matthew's happy memory. We resumed walking toward the crowd of people waiting for us.

"You're going on Sunday?" the Second asked.

I nodded. "Sam needs to meet with some people on Saturday. We'll go up early on Sunday morning."

The Second sipped his wine. "Well, it doesn't matter if the house is opened on Saturday or Sunday, as long as it's ready for the family on Mother's Day." His shoulders were tense and his smile was tight, more like a grimace.

"It will be," I assured him. I smiled at Matthew but it faded when I saw he wasn't really listening to us. He stared into the distance, his eyes thoughtful. "We'll keep up the old traditions."

"Good." The Second looked at Matthew then beyond him to Livvie, Cory, Nathan, and the others.

"Keep the family traditions safe."

Janelle put a hand on my arm, pulling me to a stop. "What did you think about his story?" She nodded toward Matthew.

"Story? You mean about that day?" I shrugged. "I don't know. It makes sense to me."

She nodded. "It does make sense. But...you realize it's his word against Sheila's?" Janelle pulled her jacket tighter as though warding against a chill. "And Sheila's dead."

Chapter 17

I didn't have time to question Janelle or Charlie. We were caught up in the festivities, dancing, eating, drinking, and laughing until almost midnight. I put suspicion, fear, and enmity behind me and pretended everything was fine. To be honest, I couldn't believe that Matthew was a killer. I still thought of him as a slightly spoiled child, a boy I watched grow into a man. Could someone I know be a killer?

As Sam drove us home, I told him what was discussed but my retelling was probably a bit incoherent because I had consumed quite a quantity of alcohol. "The cops are good at their jobs," he said when we pulled into the garage. "I think they'll figure it out."

"It still doesn't answer who killed Sheila." I tipped out of Bilbo and managed a credible walk to the door. I dropped my purse and party shoes inside the door and collapsed on the nearby couch. A solid thump from the bedroom told me Houdini was on his way to join us.

"If Matthew killed his father then it's a good bet he killed Sheila, don't you think?" Sam came in and tossed his suit coat over a kitchen chair. "You want a glass of wine or a beer?"

I waved a hand. "Not for me. Help yourself, Mr. Designated Driver."

"Don't mind if I do." He poured a tall beer then joined me on the couch, nudging Houdini over so to make room.

I snuggled against him, my head spinning slightly and my brain sluggishly reviewing the night's events. I finally gave up. "I watched Matthew grow up. He can't be a murderer."

Sam sighed and I moved with the movement. "Anyone could be a murderer, Cassie. Hell, there were times when I could have killed Sheila."

Could I kill someone? I tried to visualize a reason why I would kill someone and failed. Unless...I twisted to peer up at Sam. "If someone tried to hurt you, I could probably kill them. But I couldn't do it otherwise."

He kissed me lightly, his breath smelling of beer. "Good to know." He stared into my eyes, his own brown eyes like dark pools. "You know I love you, right?"

I nodded.

"I'm thinking the marriage thing is a good idea."

I frowned. "You're just feeling that way because Livvie had such a great wedding."

He smiled. "Probably. But I still think it's a good idea."

"Hmm." I slid my arms around him and he set down his glass, dislodging Houdini in the process. The big cat made a 'hmprfh' of protest then sagged to the floor in exhaustion. "Betty always told me to test drive a man before I made it permanent."

"She did, hmm?" He lay back and pulled me on top of him. "Well, test away."

****

I awoke to the sound of someone talking. I opened one eye, peered around the still dark bedroom, and considered going back to sleep. Then

Truffles jumped up on my pillow, nudging me with her black nose.

Sleep was gone. I got out of bed and stumbled into the bathroom, peering at the bedside clock as I passed. Seven o'clock. A.M. I yawned. Despite the amount of alcohol consumed the night before, I felt surprisingly good. I regarded myself in the mirror and decided I looked passable for a woman who had just a few hours of sleep. My gray hair was standing up in spikes, but it actually looked pretty good that way. Maybe I'd found a new style.

I dragged on my bathrobe against the early morning coolness and wandered into the kitchen, pausing at the window to look out on the day. St. Frank was in morning shadow but the sky above him was clear, with just the first outlines of clouds showing. It promised to be a beautiful spring day. Sam sat the table, drinking a mug of coffee, his phone to his ear. He smiled at me as I pulled a mug out of the cupboard and joined him.

"Okay, Joe. That sounds great. It works out better that way." Sam sipped his coffee and nudged the plate of scones toward me. I pounced on them and smeared one with butter from the dish on the lazy Susan. "Okay. We'll plan on that. I'm sure it'll be fine with Cassie. I'll call you if the plans change."

"I'll agree with what?" I mumbled around a bite of scone as he set the phone down.

"Joe wants me to meet with some people on Monday, so he's put together some papers for me to review while we're up north. You don't mind, do you? We can drive up today, open the house then drive back tomorrow."

"That's fine with me. What kind of people?"

Sam's smile broadened. "The pharmaceutical people. There might be one hell of a contract in it if that research I worked on years ago pans out."

"Then by all means, let's make sure it works

out." I held up my mug and he clinked his against mine. "Here's to new ventures."

"Are you sure it's okay to go up to the house early?"

"Not a problem. We just need to swing by the house and get some stuff."

He paused, mug raised. "What kind of stuff?"

"You know—sheets, blankets, guns."

He blinked at me. "Guns?"

"There's a gun locker that we keep at the house. Just a rifle and a shotgun and a pistol. It's more for protection against bears and raccoons than anything. We store the gear at the Whittington house for the winter then schlep it up to the lake house in the spring." I thought over the items given to me when I inherited Grandy's estate. "John never included the homes in the lawsuit so I've got keys." I looked at the clock. "I'll call Claire after I shower. The gear is all packed in boxes and ready to go, so it's just a matter of us stopping by and getting it."

****

Two hours later we were on the road north. When Minnesotans talk about 'up North' it can mean any spot north of the Twin Cities, but in my case it meant Lake Vermillion, one of the larger lakes near the Canadian border. We took the 'fast' route, using the Interstate and arriving at the lake house three hours later.

The six-bedroom home was on the north shore of the lake, accessible via a narrow county road and an equally narrow half-mile driveway. You could also reach it by boat, of course, and that was really the simplest way to get there from the nearest town. It had been in the Whittington family for generations, coming to them through Grandy Theo, whose husband's father built the house in the previous century. Over the years additions had been added so now it easily slept two dozen or more people in its

221

various wings and outbuildings. Towering pines surrounded it on all side with the west side facing the lake.

We parked in the drive and spent a busy hour opening windows, dragging cushions out of storage onto the screened porch for airing, and unloading Tupperware cartons from Bilbo. At one o'clock we took a break and sat on the porch to eat the sandwiches we brought with us. The house sat on a promontory overlooking the lake with the porch like the prow of a ship, jutting out almost over the drop-off. To the right was a steep hill with a path winding down to a beach and swimming area. To the left was a slope leading to a cove where we loaded and unloaded supplies brought in by boat. Between the two docks sat the house on four acres of wooded Minnesota headland.

"What's left?" Sam asked.

"We just need to check the well and the septic system then we can run to town for some groceries," I said around a bite of my ham and Swiss sandwich. "We'll just get some canned goods, paper products and some booze. When the family comes up on Mother's Day for the fishing opener, they'll bring the perishables."

"Are we coming on Mother's Day, too?" Sam asked, washing down a sandwich bite with a sip of coffee.

"Sure, if you want to. There's plenty of room. We usually make the kids sleep out on the porch and the grown-up take the bedrooms, but we've been known to do some camping, too." I remembered Matthew's comment from the previous evening. "John always hated to camp out but I thought it was fun. There's a camp site just a few yards up the hill." I gestured behind us. "It overlooks the lake. It's beautiful."

"The whole thing is beautiful," Sam said. "The house, the lake, the beach. Let's get a couple of steaks in town and have a cookout on the beach tonight." He nodded toward the stone fire pit, barely seen through the trees far below us on the small beach.

"Sounds good to me." I stood up and dusted crumbs off my jeans. "Let's get it done. I want to get into town and back before dark."

An hour later I met up with Sam in the living room. He was looking at the wall niche where the gun locker fit. "It's an impressive collection."

"I remember once Grandy Theo killed a coon that was acting strange. She got him dead on with the rifle. The Forest Ranger said it was rabies. Did you check them all?" I had put him in charge of the firepower while I made sure the well was functioning smoothly.

"Yep. All double-checked. Unloaded and locked. Where's the ammo go?"

I showed him the ammo locker in the kitchen, a metal safe behind a faux oak door in a bottom cupboard. The liquor cabinet occupied the top cupboard, locked as well and only left unlocked when the family was in residence. I pocketed the keys then we headed out the kitchen door down the steps leading to the loading dock. "Let's take the boat. It's faster and that way you can see the house from the lake."

He eyed me cautiously. "Don't tell me. You know how to pilot a boat, too."

I laughed. "Of course." I led the way to the dock where two boats were tied. We stored the boats at the boatyard in town with a standing arrangement to have them in the water on May first as long as the ice was out on the lake.

I jumped into the cabin cruiser, a twenty-foot classic Chris-Craft kept in pristine condition. I fished the key out of my pocket and turned it. The motor purred to life. Sam cast off our mooring and I angled the boat into the bay, steering us past the shallows and into the open lake. "I take it you've done this a few times," Sam said.

"It's one of those things," I said. "The Second made sure we knew how to shoot a gun, steer a boat and evaluate a good wine."

"An eclectic upbringing. That explains why you're so well-rounded." He blew me a kiss and I laughed.

We rode mostly in silence, with me pointing out an occasional landmark here and there. Half an hour later we pulled up to the docks in town and Sam jumped out, tying off the boat to the pilings. I showed Sam around town—two blocks of businesses, a cluster of houses, and a post office. I renewed my acquaintances with some of the store owners, getting updates on the people and events. We bought a case of beer, a couple of bottles of wine and two bags of groceries then we were back in the boat and on our way in an hour.

The day was turning overcast. I checked my watch. Four o'clock. At this time of year the sun would be down by eight, but the lake would start to get dark at six because it was surrounded on all sides by trees and hills. Dark clouds were scudding in the distance and at this time of year, this far north, that could mean rain or snow. I hoped it meant rain. The house had a rudimentary heating system, relying mainly on the fireplaces for warmth.

My phone chimed *The Boys of Summer* just as we left the docks. I put the boat into idle. "Hey, Charlie," I said, one hand on the steering wheel and the other pressing the phone to my ear. "We're in the boat, can I call you back?"

"What do you mean the boat?" he demanded.

"We're at the lake house."

"You said you weren't going until tomorrow." I heard him say, 'They're at the lake' to someone else.

"Sam has to get back to town for a business meeting on Monday so we came up today. We'll go back tomorrow. What's up?" I tried to wedge the phone between my shoulder and ear but the boat jerked in my hands. "Hold on, I'm handing you off to Sam."

"Wait a minute. Something's happened."

My stomach twisted. "Is Janelle okay? Livvie? Are they okay?"

"They're fine. It's Matthew."

For an instant the words made no sense. "What about Matthew?"

"He might be coming to the lake house."

"So? There's plenty of room."

"No, I didn't mean that. He might...wait a minute."

There was a long pause. Then a new voice came on the line. "Cassandra? It's C.R."

"What's wrong?" I couldn't quite put my finger on it, but the old man sounded grim or sad. "Did something happen to Matthew?"

"There's a warrant out for his arrest. The police think he killed John and Mrs. Peavey."

"Holy..." The wake from another boat made us wobble. "C.R., I'm in the boat. Can you talk to Sam? Give him the details. We're on our way back to the house from town. We'll be there in twenty minutes." I handed Sam the phone. "It's hitting the fan."

Sam raised an eyebrow. "Now what?" I caught snippets of conversation as I piloted us out of the harbor. "Didn't see him." "We just went to town." "We got here about noon." "That doesn't help us a lot, does it, Charlie?" He sounded pissed off. "Okay. We will." He stuffed the phone in his windbreaker pocket. "You weren't kidding. It hit the fan."

"Tell me." I drove as fast as I dared on the lake, which was getting choppy from the wind kicking up. Once I turned west it was almost a straight shot to our dock, but there was still a lot of open lake to cross.

Sam hunkered down in the seat next to me, keeping his head low and out of the wind. "The old man thinks Matthew is here."

"Here?" I looked around the lake. A few other craft were out and I saw lights in the few cabins on the shore. "Where? Why do they—?"

"Matthew thought we were coming on Sunday. He disappeared last night. The police tracked him to Duluth today where he purchased some camping gear. He couldn't get everything he needed. The police are looking for him and he knows it."

"Camping gear?" I steered on auto-pilot, my brain occupied with considering and discarding ideas. "He's going to Canada." I looked north. Ten miles away via boat was the border. People crossed over the national boundary all the time, going back and forth on one of the many lakes that dotted the border. "He can get lost for weeks in the BWCA." The Boundary Waters Canoe Area Wilderness and the Quetico Wilderness in Canada occupied almost two million acres of forest, canoe trails and lakes. A camper could go for weeks at a time and never see another human.

"Yeah. How about that?" Sam turned in his seat so he was looking forward, staring into the wind. His cheeks reddened almost immediately as the chilly air from the lake washed over him. "Charlie called from the road. He and his father are on their way." He smiled briefly. "Good thing we bought a couple of steaks."

I barely heard him. "It doesn't make sense," I said, speaking out loud. "Matthew wouldn't come here. He knows the lake house hasn't been opened yet. The only things we have that he could use are some sleeping bags and other camping gear. He probably has his own or he could buy them." Sam started to speak but I cut him off. "Of course, if he leaves from here he has an advantage. He knows the lake and the terrain around here. But it's been years since he's done any serious hiking or camping. Things change."

"He's desperate," Sam said. His voice was low, the wind catching the words so I barely heard him.

"Why? Hell, he can hire the best lawyers around. They'll make sure he gets off."

"Will they?" Sam turned to face me. "Think about it, Cassie. He killed his father and his father's lover in cold blood. Both of them."

"How do we know it was cold blood? Maybe he and John argued."

Sam shook his head. "Think about the story he told you. He said John was going to leave Sheila and go back to Diane. Do you believe that?"

I shot him a disbelieving look. "No."

"What else did Matthew lie about?"

I saw where he was going with that line of reasoning. If everything Matthew said was a lie, then... "He followed John and killed him. Then he left, came back, and confronted Sheila. How did he kill her?"

Sam's mouth twisted angrily. "She wore a Barlow's T-shirt. All he had to do was call her and tell her to meet me at the greenhouse. If he had a Barlow's T-shirt..."

"That takes guts." People would be coming and going from the greenhouses, moving stock to the retail centers. "How did he keep people out of the greenhouse? What would keep people from going into a greenhouse in the middle of growing season?"

"Fumigation."

I jerked the wheel, almost swamping the boat. "Damn. You're right." If someone put the fumigation notice outside the greenhouse door, everyone would avoid it like the plague. The houses were fumigated on a regular basis and often the schedule was shortened in the growing season because the doors were opening and closing so much. "We need to tell the police."

"I'll bet they're getting it all figured out."

I glanced at him but we were nearing the loading dock and I needed to keep my attention on the landing. The cove was shallow and I could see rocks under the clear water. The boys used to trap muskrat back here and once John caught a mink. I cried so much they never showed me their trophies again.

The boys, I thought as I carefully steered us closer to the wooden dock. Charlie was fifty-three and going to be a father and John...John was dead and his son was being chased as a murderer. It was a sobering thought.

"He won't come here," I said as Sam jumped out onto the wooden dock and hooked our mooring lines. "There's nothing he needs here."

"Then Charlie and his dad made the trip for nothing." Sam gestured toward the groceries. "Hand me the sacks and the beer."

I laughed. "The important stuff, right?" I handed out the gear then clambered out of the boat. "Here, take the keys." I handed him the key ring. "Put the beer and wine in the liquor cabinet and leave a six-pack in the fridge. I'll check the grill and make sure we've got firewood. There should be some charcoal in the storage locker down there, too. We'll get the fire started."

Sam settled a grocery sack on top of the beer and strode up the steps leading to the kitchen. I watched him for a minute, making sure he was able to keep his balance. He looked fine, though, and I breathed a sigh of relief. The staircase was steep and wobbly in spots. If Sam's leg was hurting him, I didn't see any sign of it.

Maybe the worst is behind us, I thought as I walked along the water's edge, around the base of the overlook where the house was perched so I could check the grill on the beach. A narrow path worn by many feet and paws cut through the scrub brushes, weaving in and out of boulders that fringed the shoreline. The water was deep here, dropping away just feet beyond the edge to twenty or thirty feet deep. We never swam here because of the weeds and the rocks under the surface.

I kept my right hand on either the rocks or the trees that served as an impromptu rail along the steep the path. This part of the promontory—the east side—was in shadow but out on the water the setting sun was blinding, reflections rippling off the waves and bouncing around crazily. It was like being inside a kaleidoscope, as though the prisms of light were exploding everywhere I looked.

The light off the water and my own concern about keeping my balance kept me focused on the path and not on the world around me. I suppose that's why I didn't see the men at first. I had to edge my way around a large boulder, taking care not to slip off the path that was just a foot or two from the water. I focused on my footwork and it wasn't until I emerged onto the beach that I saw them.

Matthew was facing my way, a shotgun in his hands pointed at Charlie and his father.

Chapter 18

Matthew's head turned slightly then his attention went back to his family. "Glad you could join us, Cassie."

"Cassie?" Charlie turned. "What the hell are you doing here? I thought you were in town. What are you doing here?"

I stopped, balancing at the top of the path. Six more steps and I would be on the beach with them. Two steps to the left and I would be in the lake. I put a hand on the rock wall to my right. The cold sank into my hand, making me shiver. My jacket was no protection against fear and a north wind.

"What are *you* doing here?" I asked. My voice came out as a croak, which didn't surprise me. My throat was suddenly dry and my stomach was doing flip flops. *God, don't let me puke,* I thought chaotically. "You were on the road."

The Second looked over his shoulder at me. Like Charlie he wore jeans, heavy boots, and a flannel shirt over a T-shirt. His face was sharply drawn and he looked like he'd aged a decade in the day since I saw him. "We came directly to the house." The black-and-white plaid shirt made his face look even paler as did the two sharp spots of color on his cheekbones. *He looks old,* I thought. *For the first time since I've known him, he looks old.*

"Come down here." Matthew crooked his right hand, a little 'come here' gesture. The gun balanced on his left arm, nestled against his left shoulder, didn't waver. His right hand returned to the trigger.

I stepped carefully down the path, trying not to jump when I crossed behind Charlie and into the trajectory of the gun Matthew held. I stopped a foot to the left of Charlie, the lake edge just a few steps away. "Why are you here, Matthew? Did you need something? What?"

He raised the gun slightly. "I needed a gun."

"The guns were locked up," I said. "How did—"

"I have a spare set of keys," the Second said in a low voice. "He stole them."

"Borrowed." Matthew corrected his grandfather with a quick, sharp word. "I knew where the keys were stored at the house. It was easy to get them last night once everyone left for the wedding reception."

"How long have you been planning this?" Charlie asked. He didn't have his hands in the air, but he was hunched, his shoulders rigidly tensed as though he could protect himself from a shot coming at any time.

"Since I killed John."

"John?" The Second's voice was strangled. I took a hesitant step forward, peering around Charlie to see the old man. He looked like any depiction I've ever seen of the wrath of God. His silver hair was waving in the wind, his eyes were like hard stones, and his mouth was a harsh line of inflexibility. If looks could kill, Matthew would have been eviscerated at our feet. "He was your father. How could you do that?"

"How could he do that?" Matthew shouted. The sound echoed up the slope behind us and seemed to evaporate into the trees above. It was the first sign of emotion from him and it made me wince. There was a raw, ugly undertone that sounded as though it was ripped from his heart.

Sam. Would he hear? Dear God, don't let him come down the path. Don't let him walk into this. Let him hear and call the police. Don't let him be hurt. Don't let anyone be hurt. Please.

"He ruined our family. There was no money left—none! He took everything and loaded it into an off-shore account."

"That's no reason to kill him." The Second took a step forward and for a minute I thought he might lunge at Matthew.

Charlie put a hand on his father's arm. "Did you argue? Was that it?"

"It happened exactly the way I said it did. I went there to see him, we argued. He went to meet his lover and I followed him. I killed him then I left. When I came back, she was there, waiting to talk to him. She and I argued then we saw Charlie come in." He recited his movements as though they were memorized, like plays on a board game. *I went three steps forward. I killed him. I waited then I went four steps back.*

"And you killed Sheila?" the Second asked, his voice hoarse.

I shifted position again. This end of the beach was bathed in sunlight, the sharp glow showing the tears on the old man's face. "Are you sorry you killed them?" I blurted.

Matthew's attention shifted briefly to me. "Of course not." Any emotion was damped down, banked again. There was no remorse, no concern. "My father was a hypocritical bastard. He demanded that his children conform to the highest standards then he broke every rule he told us was inviolate. He hated my mother, he tolerated my brother and sister, and he hated me."

"That's not true." The Second shook his head, bewildered. "John had his flaws but he was a good person. He would never—"

"He was a hateful, vindictive bastard." Matthew's condemnation was quick and so cold I shivered.

"He was my child," the old man whispered. "One of my children."

I swallowed hard at the stark grief in his voice. That was something I forgot during all of this. While we may have disliked John, he was still a member of the family. He was still someone's child.

"Why did you come here?" Charlie had moved. He no longer was parallel with me and the Second. Somehow he was slightly ahead of us, boxing us in.

Protecting us. It was an eerie recreation of that scene, forty years ago. Charlie moved to protect his father, the way he had moved long ago to protect his mother. Matthew stood just a few feet away, the gun raised. We were on a beach—the family beach. A madman faced us. A madman who held a gun and who hated us.

I stood near the shoreline, too far away to help.

There was movement above me, in the tree line. I stood the farthest away from the mass of land so I was the only one who glimpsed Sam, moving silently down the pebbled path from the house. It would bring him behind Matthew but the last ten yards were in the open. There was nowhere to hide. There was no way he could sneak up on the younger man.

Matthew smiled at Charlie. "I came here to kill you and him." He angled his head toward his grandfather then he glanced at me. "Killing her is a bonus."

I took a step back, almost tumbling into the lake. The cold, simple way he stated it drove home to me what I was avoiding: Matthew was crazy. Somehow, somewhere, some*when*, he was crazy.

"You won't get away with it," I said.

"I don't care. I won't go to prison, so if I get caught, I'll make sure someone kills me. It's all gone. The life I wanted to live is gone. If I can't have that life, I don't want life." He tilted his head, his cheek resting briefly against the barrel of the shotgun before he straightened again. "I'm bored anyway."

If I can't have that truck, I don't want any truck. I remember him using that argument once as a child when he and Jon fought over toys. *Bored? Bored with life? Good God. Have a brush with death and tell me...* I looked at his eyes. There was nothing there. There was no flicker of humanity, no glimpse of personality. Matthew was gone.

"You don't know what you're saying." The Second stepped forward but Charlie immediately moved ahead, too, putting himself between the old man and the unwavering gun.

Sam moved into view. "Matthew. Put it down." He held a pistol in a two-handed grip, the barrel pointed at Matthew's head. He looked deadly, calm, and ready to kill.

I was too surprised to move. Sam? Then I remembered. The Marines. Disjointed pieces of conversation drifted through my memory, when Sam talked about his twenty-year stint in the Service and his combat experience. I had pushed it to one side. It was like talking about Sam in his life with Sheila. It had no bearing on my life now.

Except it did.

Matthew moved slightly so he could see the path and Sam standing there. "No."

"Put it down." The Second's voice was soft and commanding.

Matthew frowned at him. "You don't tell me what to do any more. You don't tell any of us what to do."

Charlie's foot moved fractionally to the right,

putting more of his body in front of his father. I took a step closer and Matthew's attention flickered to me.

"Cassie." Sam's voice was calm. "Move out of the range of his gun."

I swallowed hard, struggling to remember what the range was on a twenty-gauge.

"If you move I'll kill Charlie." Matthew's eyes darted toward me then back to Charlie and his father, standing like statues rooted in the rough sand.

Remembered fear consumed me. My father stood in front of me, his face twisted into a mask of rage. My mother confronted him, pleading. Gloria Whittington, Charlie's mother, was dead on the ground, baby Livvie sprawled next to her, crying. Charlie was lying in the shallows of the lake, his face bloodied, his eyes closed. He had pushed me out of the way of the first blast of the gun and my father kicked him, the blow knocking Charlie out and pushing him into the lake. I went after him, struggling to hold his head out of the water.

"Not again," I whispered. "Not again."

The Second looked over his shoulder at me and our eyes met. I saw the same memories in his face, the same fear and anger. He looked back at his son and his grandson. Uncertainty, grief, and anger twisted his mouth.

I took a step forward. "Give it up, Matthew. It's over." I took a deep breath, bracing myself in the hard sand.

"Cassie, don't!" The Second and Charlie both shouted at the same time. Charlie twisted, reaching for me as I lunged toward Matthew, diving low and aiming for his waist.

The gunshots, one after another, were deafening. Acrid smoke blew out in a haze around us, surrounding the beach like fog. I choked on it, the cordite coating my tongue and making me gasp. Then pain flared into my legs and I realized I was lying on the ground. I turned my head to peer around me. Matthew was sprawled three feet away, the shotgun nearby, still oozing a faint residue of smoke. He didn't move. The Second knelt next to him, his hand cupping his grandson's chin. I could tell by the anguish on the old man's face that Matthew was dead.

Sam raced down the slope but Charlie was already holding me. "You're an idiot," he said, bending over me. "Shit, look at it."

"What is it?" I tried to look up but my body was heavy, weighted down.

Charlie tore off his blue-and-white flannel shirt as I struggled to sit up. He pulled a phone out of a holster on his belt just when Sam reached us. Charlie handed him the shirt then turned aside, his phone to his ear.

Sam tossed the pistol on the ground and knelt next to me, wrapping the jacket somewhere I couldn't see. "Damn," he breathed.

"What happened?" I asked. My voice was thick and slow. I must have swallowed some sand. My mouth felt gritty.

Sam pushed my shoulders back when I tried to sit up. "You took some pellets in your leg," he said, his hands firm on my shoulders. "You shouldn't have moved."

"Did you shoot him?" I asked.

"Sit back." Sam held me down with one hand.

"He was going to kill Charlie." I turned my head, the sand rasping my face. It was cool and smelled of fish and lake and sunlight. It smelled like childhood. "He tried to kill Charlie and I saved Charlie's life. I had to save his life again. Otherwise the first time wouldn't matter. And it did matter. Because Charlie's going to be a father." I was babbling nonsense but somehow it all made sense to me.

I blinked up at the setting sun. It was warm on my face. I blinked again. The sun was lower. How did that happen? There was no sensation of sleeping or lack of consciousness. Somehow time just...passed.

"...self-defense but there still has to be..."

Feet were walking near me. I peered groggily at them. Who wore black boots? Charlie and the Second had brown boots and Sam wore sneakers. "...in the neck. He bled out so fast there was nothing to do...chest but the neck was faster and..."

Sam shot Matthew in the neck? Good Lord. How could he do that? I closed my eyes and dozed off.

Someone talking loudly nearby woke me. "...boat or plane. What's fastest?"

Well, plane, I thought. *That's a stupid question.* Pontoon planes landed all the time on the lake. I wondered if they were trying to figure out how to transport me. It didn't really matter. I wasn't feeling anything. Just warm. The sand was warm and a bit damp but it was really comfortable. Nothing hurt except my back and my leg, which itched like crazy.

"Hey, stay with me."

I struggled to open my eyes. Sam stared down at me, his dark brown eyes narrowed and intense. "I'm here," I said. "Is Matthew dead?"

"Yeah."

I heard stark grief in the word. I tried to say, *You had no choice. If you didn't do it, he would have killed us.* Somehow the words wouldn't come. I made a few 'gugg gugg' noises.

"Stay quiet." Sam smoothed my face, brushing the sand away.

It seemed like reasonable advice. I let my head fall to the side. A confusing collection of feet walked around me. Then I heard a thum-thum noise nearby. I realized my face was cold. I managed to push my tongue out of my cracked and dry lips.

"Raining?" I whispered.

Charlie leaned over me. "Yeah. The plane is here."

"Oh. That's good."

"We're taking you directly to Duluth and the hospital there."

That makes sense, I thought. Suddenly I was cold all over. I started to shiver and that's when I realized I was being lifted. Cold air rushed over me.

"She's going into shock," someone said.

I'm cold. That's all.

Then it was dark.

****

I was trapped in a Facebook page. Somehow I was in the page, stuck up in the update bar. I had to type in my status or I would fall off the page.

I laboriously spelled out…what? I couldn't see it because I was on the status line, words evaporating behind me like vapor trail from a plane. A red star winked at me. I struggled to focus. It was at the bottom of the page, winking. That's when I realized my eyes were closed. They were crusty and stuck shut. But I still saw the red star.

I wiggled my eyes, prying them open. And I still saw the red blinking thing. It was a machine near my face. "What?" I mumbled.

"You're in the hospital."

I managed to move my eyes. Becky sat next to my bed, a pile of crocheting in her lap.

"Don't tell me," I slurred. "I had a car accident."

"Nope. This time you were shot." She set the sewing to one side and stood to lean over me. I saw grief and anger in her hazel eyes. "Matthew shot you."

"Is Sam okay?" I asked, grabbing her wrist.

"He's fine." She covered my hand with her, squeezing it gently.

"I don't understand." I closed my eyes, struggling to find words. "Matthew acted so weird. Why did he do it?"

Becky's hand tightened on mine. "He was taking medication but this past week he went off his meds."

Off his meds. I had heard that expression before with friends who stopped hormone therapy or halted the use of some benign drug. It never had the effect of making someone murder another person. "What was it?"

"Some mood thing. Schizophrenia. Bipolar." She shook her head. "Remember when he was sent away to school? That's when he was diagnosed. No one knew, of course. John tried to hide it. Poor Matthew."

I gasped. "Poor Matthew? He murdered—"

"Hush. I know. I just can't help but remember him when he was a baby. You know how John must have treated him. John wouldn't tolerate any weakness in a child of his." She sniffled then straightened. "I need to get the doctor. They wanted to see you when you woke." She moved to the door but stopped before opening it. "Cassie?"

I blinked at her. "What?"

"Matthew wanted to die. Make sure Sam knows that. He needed someone to kill him and Sam happened to be there. Make sure he knows that."

I nodded dumbly, not sure what to say.

Medical people came into the room, poking and examining me. My left leg was swaddled in bandages but there was little pain except a dull throbbing. They explained how a dozen or more shotgun pellets were extracted from my body, and how a few chipped some bones, causing fever and a persistent itch. "You'll be released tomorrow," one cheerful youth in a white coat said. "A month or two of physical therapy and you'll be right back where you want to be."

Where I want to be? I want to be thirty years old, healthy, and innocent, I thought but didn't say. As soon as they finished, Sam entered, the Second behind him. I held out my arms and Sam gently held me while I cried, relief mingled with anger mingled with fear.

"Is Charlie okay?" I asked when I finally leaned back on my pillow.

Sam's hand tightened on mine. "He's fine. He and Janelle are working with the police to wrap up what happened."

"Wrap up?" The Second took the seat Becky had used. The window behind him looked out on a gray and dreary day, steady rain splashing against the glass. "It's not that simple."

Sam looked briefly irritated then said quietly, "Maybe I should have said they're trying to figure out what happened."

The old man sighed, his tense shoulders relaxing. He still wore the black-and-white flannel shirt, which told me I hadn't been in the hospital long. C.R. Whittington the Second never went a day without a change of clothing. "We know what happened. I don't know if we'll ever understand it, though." He smiled at me, his green eyes sad and confused. "Matthew tried to kill you and Sam last year, he tried to kill Janelle, and he wanted to kill Charlie. And me," he added after a pause.

His pained recitation left me breathless. "Why?" I managed.

"John made sure his children knew that Charlie and you were favored. That Charlie and you were special. Matthew took that knowledge and twisted it. His doctors..." The Second cleared his throat.

Sam's hand tightened on mine. "His doctors said that Matthew was fixated on Charlie. His father hated Charlie so much. When his father proved to be...human, Matthew snapped."

I tried to absorb it all but it didn't make sense. None of it did. How could someone hate me and Charlie so much?

"Matthew was ill." The Second stood and to my surprise, he leaned over and brushed a kiss against my forehead. "It's not your fault." He straightened and looked at Sam. "Neither of you are to blame for what happened." He sighed raggedly. "I should have seen it. Perhaps I did and I didn't want to face it. John was so difficult to handle and I thought it was just snobbishness, just foolishness. I never knew what kind of poison he was feeding his children." He frowned and I saw the old C.R. Whittington the Second start to reanimate the man in front of me. "I need to talk to John's other children and to Diane and mitigate what I can."

"It's not your responsibility," I protested but my voice was fading. I was so tired. Knowledge, pain, and guilt all seemed to weigh me down.

"Of course it is. I gave him the idea to go to the lake house."

He was right. When we all talked at the reception, the Second talked about camping and Matthew and... I looked up at him, wanting to say something cutting but I saw that he had already done that to himself. He closed his eyes briefly and when he opened them again, they were bright with tears. "I suspected him. I didn't want to lose him, too. I already lost John. I didn't know, though, that Matthew was already lost. John told me he was ill, but he didn't tell me how bad it was." He walked to the door and paused before leaving, looking back at me. "You did what Gloria tried to do. You tried to save my child. Thank you." He left, pulling the door shut behind him.

"I was so afraid," I whispered. "I was afraid he'd turn and shoot you."

Sam sat carefully on the side of the bed, my

hand still in his. "That makes two of us." He kissed my hand, pressing it to his lips then holding it against the stubbly beard of his cheek. "Let's try to go for a few months with no more hospital stays, okay?"

"Sounds like a plan," I murmured. My eyes were closing and I had no power to stop them.

Right before I fell asleep again, I heard him say, "I love you."

I love you, too, I whispered, but it was only in my mind.

Afterword

I didn't go to the lake house that year for Opening Day. I was just out of the hospital, weak from an infection that settled into my bone after the shotgun pellets were removed from my left leg. I would walk again, but I was going to have several weeks of physical therapy and would always be able to predict the weather. As Sam pointed out, between us both we now had two good legs. We should sign up for professional sack-racing.

Janelle came over to visit on the Monday after they got back from Opening Day. "It was sad," she said. We sat on lawn chairs near St. Frank in the side yard, basking in late afternoon sunlight and sipping iced tea. "We took out both boats and had the ash tossing in the bay. First John, then Matthew. Poor Diane. She was a mess."

"I can only imagine. Her husband and her son." I shook my head but stopped when the dizziness began again. The medication I was taking made me woozy and I avoided most sudden moves.

"Charlie said a few words for John then—it was terrible. Somebody had to say something for Matthew but nobody knew what to say. Charlie's dad looked terrible. I think he blamed himself for what happened. There was an awful silence, where we all just stared at each other. Then Cory stepped up and started talking." Janelle smiled but her eyes were sad with remembered pain. "He and Nathan told some cousin stories then Marcy said a few words. They did a good job. I think it comforted Diane and her kids."

I made a mental note to send Becky's kids a shout-out and 'thank you' on Facebook.

"How's Sam doing?"

I glanced at her. She was regarding me with a shrewd, assessing look. "You've been gossiping with Betty again."

She nodded. "She said that he was having a rough time of it."

"Albert came over and they talked. He's doing better now." I sighed, fighting back the tears. "Sam didn't want to shoot. He just didn't have a choice." The inquest and investigation cleared him completely. 'Death in defense of self and property' was the legal term for it. That didn't help Sam cope with the guilt, but Albert's talk had gone a long to settling him down. It would take time, but both Sam and I would heal.

"Listen...I have a favor to ask."

I tapped my leg, still in a cast. "As long as it doesn't involve dancing, I can do it."

"Will you and Sam be our witnesses at our marriage ceremony?"

I almost fell out of the chair. "Seriously?"

She nodded, smiling so broadly I thought her face might break.

"You know that Claire is planning a wedding, right?"

She nodded again.

I started laughing.

****

Janelle and Charlie were married a week later in a civil ceremony at the courthouse downtown. I had the pleasure of telling Claire all about it after the fact. The Second laughed and even Claire managed a small smile when she realized her plans for the Wedding of the Season were dashed.

Four-and-a-half months later Janelle gave birth to twins. Charles Richard (C.R.) Whittington the Fourth and Janelle Cassandra (J.C.) Whittington were healthy, noisy, and happy babies with a wide circle of godparents and several willing babysitters.

The Second, Livvie, Becky, Charlie and I combined our resources and paid the debt John owed, thus allowing the family to avoid bankruptcy. Diane and Pauline joined the charitable foundation I established, working with Becky's daughter Marcy to oversee the funds. Jon Whittington, Diane's youngest son, finished college and moved out of state, eventually ending up in Seattle and working as a lawyer there.

My first meeting with Diane was strained and businesslike. She didn't want to talk about what happened and neither did I. We discussed the foundation, Marcy there as a mitigating presence, asking pertinent questions and deferring to her aunt on several points. At the end of the meeting, Diane turned to me. "My family will never be the same because of you. Only time will tell if that's a good thing or a bad thing." She left the room, leaving me gaping at her in surprise.

Sam and I danced around the idea of marriage and finally decided it just wasn't necessary. Late in the summer we bought a rambling old farm in the country and installed St. Frank in the back yard near the window where Truffles and Houdini could sit to watch the birds. Sam started working on developing a plant to name after me and I spent time relaxing and getting my strength back. It was October when I finally got around to updating my Facebook page. That's when I re-discovered the friend request from Sheila.

Janelle had just brought the twins for a visit, the tiny babies content to doze while Janelle and I chatted. She and Charlie were building a home in Victoria, a small town about ten miles away. We spent a happy hour or two looking at paint swatches, carpet samples, and cabinet catalogs before she left to join Charlie at a furniture showroom to pick out baby furniture.

It was weird to read something written by a dead woman. I was sitting in a gazebo surrounded by autumn flowers, the smell of grass and the sounds of bees cocooning me in happy sensation. My mini-notebook was propped on my lap and a glass of iced tea was near at hand. And there, on the screen in front of me, was Sheila.

Her profile picture looked like a glamour shot. She gazed back over her shoulder, her tousled hair, seductive look, and smirky 'come hither' smile showing that she had one thing in mind and it started with S-E-X. Her page showed that I was her only friend. *Where's the irony in that?* I thought. *Sheila and I were enemies all our lives and I'm her only Facebook friend.* I examined her page and the information she had shared. 'Relationship status: It's Complicated.' I snorted. *No shit.*

I clicked the "Photo" tab but there was only one there, a picture of the hybrid azalea Sam had developed with her husband, Mike. I glared at it then I smiled. Now that she was dead with no heirs, the patent rights could revert to Sam and he would finally get what he deserved.

I never really explored other peoples' pages. It was all I could do to stay current with people commenting on my status, leaving notes on my wall, or browsing pictures someone uploaded. Why would Sheila friend me? I examined her page again. It looked different than mine. I compared the two and noticed she had a tab at the top called "notes". I clicked it and my eyes almost popped out of my head.

"Holy crap," I breathed. "It's a blog."

Matthew Whittington killed his father. I'm certain of it. I went to the construction site that day to see John. I went to the construction office. I saw Matthew leaving the subdivision, driving away from the house where John was later found. Matthew lied to me about where he was when he came back to the office.

I looked around at the flowers bending gently in the breeze. "Why tell me?"

I mailed information to Sam. Will he tell you about it?

I got to my feet. What kind of information did she mail to Sam? Why didn't he tell me about it? I was halfway up the walkway to the house before I realized I was there.

My steps slowed. If she mailed him something, he would take it to the police. The police might think he had something to do with her death. She would try to make trouble with him—and with me.

I stood in the sunlight, trying to sort through my disordered thoughts. Then I returned to the gazebo and stared down at the computer screen. Did she mail something or was she trying to make me distrust Sam?

I picked up my glass of iced tea. That was something she would do. I could imagine her smiling as she wrote it. *I'll tell her I shared information with Sam. Then when he doesn't tell her, she'll get pissed off. They'll argue.*

"Hey, Cassie!"

I looked at the house. Sam had come out on the deck, Houdini strolling next to him. The portly cat jumped up on the wide rail and peered down at me, Sam leaning next to him. His eyeglasses glinted in the sun and his white hair, thick but baby-fine, stirred in the breeze. I waved to him.

"Let's grill tonight, okay? I stopped and got some salmon."

"Sounds good," I called back. "I'll be there in a minute."

"I'll fire up the grill." He scooped up Houdi and turned toward the side of the deck where the grill was stored.

I looked down at my computer screen. What kind of information could she have? We knew Matthew killed his father. What could she add to it? Should I show this to the police? If I showed it to them, they would need to question Sam. We were just starting to put it all behind us.

I looked up at the deck. Sam was talking to my cat as he fiddled with the controls on the barbeque grill. Sam's healthy tan had returned and he limped very little any more. He loved his job at the research company. He checked in at Barlow's Nursery and Landscaping daily, but his main focus now was on botanical research. An extract he was working on showed promise for pain relief. He woke up excited every day, anxious to go to work. Life was getting back to normal.

I closed the computer and went to join Sam on the deck.

Thank you for purchasing
this Wild Rose Press publication.
For other wonderful stories of romance,
please visit our on-line bookstore at
www.thewildrosepress.com

For questions or more information,
contact us at
info@thewildrosepress.com

The Wild Rose Press
www.TheWildRosePress.com

To visit with authors of The Wild Rose Press
join our yahoo loop at
http://groups.yahoo.com/group/thewildrosepress/